Murder
at the
FBI

MARGARET TRUMAN

Murder at the FBI

A NOVEL

C.5

ARBOR HOUSE / NEW YORK

Manufactured in the United States of America
10 9 8 7 6 5 4 3 2 1

Design by Richard Oriolo

Library of Congress Cataloging in Publication Data
Truman, Margaret, 1924-
Murder at the FBI.

I. Title.
PS357O.R82M75   1985   813'.54   85-7345
ISBN: 0-87795-680-4 (alk. paper)

*For the thousands of dedicated special agents of the FBI,
men and women, about whom this book was not written*

Murder
at the
FBI

1

HARRY JONES, WHO wore flowered Bermuda shorts, brown shoes, black ankle socks, and a white T-shirt that read *Akron Volunteer Fire Department–Ladder Champs '82*, said to his wife, Maureen, "I never been so hot in my whole life."

They stood in a long line outside the E Street entrance to the J. Edgar Hoover Building on Pennsylvania Avenue in Washington, D.C., home of the Federal Bureau of Investigation since the fall of 1975. Before then, it had been housed in the Department of Justice Building across the street.

The new building had been described by various critics as a prime example of Washington's New Brutalism wave of architecture, a hunk of exposed concrete aggregate dominating the capital's "Main Street"; an obscenely expensive tribute in buff to the man for whom it was named. It looked like a huge toaster with two slices of bread on top, standing as an imposing permanent monument to the name that was synonymous with the FBI, J. Edgar Hoover, shaper of America's federal police force.

It was August 10, a Thursday. It had been hot and humid all summer, typical for Washington, but three days ago a high-pressure front had stalled directly above the nation's capital and boosted what had been merely uncomfortable temperatures and humidity to intolerable levels.

"Jesus," Harry said as he wiped his face with a handkerchief. The strap of his camera bag dug into his beefy shoulder. His feet hurt and he shifted from one to the other. They'd been sightseeing since early morning, Harry and Maureen and their two children, Becky, twelve, and Walter, nine. It was now four o'clock in the afternoon. "Jesus," he said again.

"The line's moving," said Maureen.

A few minutes later they were blasted with blessed air conditioning inside the Hoover Building. A pert young woman wearing a blue blazer, gray slacks, and a white blouse invited Harry, Maureen, Becky, Walter, and 196 other tourists to take seats in a holding area. "Your tour guide will be with you in a moment," the young woman said into a microphone. "We ask that you not take photographs during the tour or use recording devices. We're pleased to see all of you here today and trust that your tour of the Federal Bureau of Investigation will be instructive and interesting. Please stay in your seats until your tour guide invites you to join her."

"I'm hungry," Walter whined.

"Shut up," his sister said.

"Don't talk to your brother like that," Maureen Jones said.

"Eat the Crackerjacks," Harry Jones said.

"I don't want 'em," Walter said.

"He's a nerd," said Becky Jones.

"Shut up," her father said to her. "Just shut up and sit still." He slipped out of his shoes and sighed.

Ten minutes later another young woman wearing a blazer and slacks stepped to the microphone and welcomed the final tour of the day.

Harry groaned as he wedged his heels into his shoes, stood, and fell in line with the rest of the group. They walked for an hour, from one exhibit area to another, the guide giving an enthusiastic explanation of what they were seeing. They learned many things—besides meaning Federal Bureau of Investigation, the initials stood for Fidelity, Bravery, and Integrity; authentic shields carried by special agents (*all* agents were called *special* agents) were the size of a half-dollar and had a raised seal covering an eighth of an inch of the agent's photo; there were almost 9,000 special agents, nearly 600 of them female; 176 million fingerprints were on file, and 25,000 were processed each day; blood type could be determined through the examination of a minute trace of saliva, and the lab could tell whether the saliva came from a human being or from a dog or cat; the firearm rooms contained 4,000 types of weapons, including 2,600 handguns and 11,000 different types of bullets; there were 10,000 types of paints used on automobiles, and the lab could differentiate between every one of them. . . .

An hour later they reached the highlight of the tour, the firing-range demonstration. This was what the half million visitors a year, especially the kids, seemed to remember. Walter, who'd complained every step of the way, was now alert and wide-eyed as they filed into a dimly lit, tiered and carpeted room and took seats. In front of them was a wall of bulletproof glass covered by heavy beige drapes. The curtains opened at the press of a switch, revealing the firing range, a long, brightly illuminated room. There was a table at the end nearest the glass wall. On it was an assortment of weapons. An overhead trolley ran from the table to the far end of the range; targets used during training could be electronically brought closer or moved farther away from the firing position.

A door inside the range opened and a tall, slender, handsome black man wearing a blue blazer, gray slacks, white shirt, and muted red-and-blue tie came through it. Harry Jones slipped his camera from the bag. One of four young women in blue blazers quickly came to him and whispered, "No picture taking allowed, sir."

Harry grinned sheepishly and put the camera away. His wife looked sternly at him. So did his daughter. "I just figured . . ."

The black special agent in the range said into a hand-held microphone, "Good afternoon, ladies and gentlemen. I'm special agent Harrison and I'll be demonstrating various weapons used by the bureau. We're issued three standard weapons—the .357 magnum revolver with a three-inch barrel, the Model 870 Remington pump-action twelve-gauge shotgun, and the M–16 automatic rifle, which has recently replaced the Thompson submachine gun. I'll be demonstrating the M–16 and the .357 magnum today."

He picked up the revolver and looked down the length of the range. Forty feet away was a large sheet of opaque white paper hanging from the overhead trolley. Drawn on it with thick black lines was the crude form of a person's head and torso. The target's "heart" was represented by a small circle outlined in black.

Harrison suddenly raised the revolver with both hands and squeezed off a quick succession of shots. He turned, placed the spent revolver on the table, picked up the microphone, and said, "I'll fire the M–16 on single-shot, then semiautomatic, then full automatic." He traded the microphone for the M–16, faced the target, and within seconds had discharged in all three modes of the weapon, ending with a machine gun–like burst.

Walter Jones giggled and grabbed his father's hand.

Special agent Harrison turned off all lights in the range except for a single lamp behind the paper target. The holes in the target were now visible. Every shot he'd fired from both weapons was neatly contained within the paper heart.

The crowd gasped, as it always did. There was applause.

"Jesus," Walter Jones said out loud.

Special agent Harrison entered the spectator room. He said slowly and quietly, "I'll be happy to answer any questions."

They came from all over the room, questions about how special agents are selected, what training they go through, how the bureau worked with local police organizations, questions about famous cases and whether television shows were representative of how the bureau really worked. Harrison answered each question thoughtfully and pleasantly, smiling at times, appearing somber at others. Maureen Jones noted how erect he was and how perfectly his clothing fit him. Walter Jones told his father he wanted to ask something.

4

"Go ahead," his father said.

The boy raised his hand and waved it at Harrison, who spotted it and said, "The young man over there. Go ahead, son."

"How many—how many of you been shot dead by . . ."

Special agent Harrison smiled. "By the bad guys? There have been twenty-six special agents killed in the line of duty. Thank you for coming today. I hope you found the tour interesting. Your guides will show you out."

The Jones family was staying at Maureen's sister's house in Rockville, Maryland, during their visit to Washington. They'd seen many things that day—the Smithsonian's Air and Space Museum, the Washington and Lincoln memorials, the Capitol, and the White House, but the FBI tour dominated their dinner-table conversation that night.

"Jesus," Harry said over coffee, "that agent was some cool customer. He—"

"*Special* agent," his wife corrected.

"Yeah, whatever. This guy put every shot right in the heart. And people criticize things like the FBI. Jesus, it's a good thing we got 'em on our side." His son held up an imaginary automatic rifle and mowed down everyone at the table.

"We've never even been there," Maureen's sister, Helen, said.

"You never . . . ?" Harry laughed. "You live right here."

"I know," his brother-in-law said. "That's always the way it is." He looked at his wife. "How about tomorrow? I'm off till Saturday." His kids were all for it.

"Just don't try to take pictures," Harry said. "I think they got cameras all over the place. Jesus, no wonder they're the best in the world. I always had respect for Hoover and the FBI but now—every shot right on the money. You got more coffee, Helen?"

5

2

HARRY JONES'S SISTER-IN-LAW, her husband, and their three children were in the first tour group to be admitted to the Hoover Building on Friday morning. The youngest boy carried with him a rifle-shaped water gun and was told pleasantly by a young woman in a blue blazer to leave it at the desk.

At precisely nine o'clock the tour guide invited everyone to follow her.

Special agent Paul Harrison looked at his watch. Nine o'clock. "Damn," he muttered. A car had broken down on the Key Bridge and traffic was at a standstill. He didn't want to be late; the first tour group would arrive at the firing range a little before ten, and he liked to have a few minutes to relax over coffee before demonstrating firearms to the tourists. He enjoyed the assignment, knew he was given it because he was one of the best. He'd excelled in the use of weapons at the FBI academy at Quantico twelve years ago, and had always placed in the top 5 percent in the bureau's semiannual firing-range exercises. His wife had told him he'd soon be bored with it, but it hadn't happened—yet. There was a pleasant satisfaction in the response of the tourists when he back-lit the target and all the holes were in the heart. He especially enjoyed the kids' expressions. "Face it," he told himself, "you're a ham."

He finally squeezed past the disabled vehicle and stepped on the gas. His car had been having radiator problems and in this heat ... He looked at his watch again. He'd make it, but there'd be no time for coffee this morning.

Special agents Christine Saksis and Ross Lizenby sat in the outdoor café portion of Au Pied De Cochon, on Wisconsin Avenue, N.W., in Georgetown. They'd had freshly baked croissants and coffee. Lizenby put money on the check, sat back, and smiled. "What's on the agenda today?" he asked.

Chris Saksis made a face. "Meetings, all day, at the Bureau of Indian Affairs. If only they'd talk less and do more." She was one of a half dozen FBI agents assigned to a unit investigating crimes on federal Indian reservations—which came under bureau jurisdiction—and she often attended conferences at other agencies pertaining to Indian affairs. Her father had been a full-blooded Maine Passamaquoddy. Her mother had been a Christian Scientist from Vermont. That Chris was half American Indian surprised no one. Her hair, which she usually wore pulled back into a loose chignon, was so black it seemed blue. Her cheekbones were high and prominent, her coloring a simmering copper that took on a burnished sheen in the summer. She was five feet, eight inches tall—and lean, although her bosom was surprisingly full for an athlete. She'd been a nationally classed half-miler and would have made the Olympic team if an injury hadn't sidelined her during the trials.

Whenever Chris Saksis and Ross Lizenby went out as a couple, which had only been happening the past few months, heads turned. He was as handsome as she was beautiful. They'd had little time to explore areas of mutual interest—except for sports. Lizenby had no peer in martial arts during his FBI training at Quantico. He was an avid tennis player and jogger, and a powerful swimmer. He usually beat Saksis at tennis, but just barely. They were a good match.

They walked to the street where their cars were parked. "Will I see you tonight?" she asked.

He shook his head. "Sorry. Pritchard's got the whole SPO-VAC team in high gear for the next couple of days. Nights, too. Maybe Monday, Tuesday."

"Okay." They kissed, a gentle touching of the lips, then a little harder, careful to keep their bodies apart for the sake of onlookers.

"I'll call you," he said.

The first tour of the morning was ushered into the tiered theater for the firing-range demonstration. The curtains were drawn over the bulletproof glass. The 200 tourists spoke in hushed tones; the room created that aura. There was something sacrosanct about it. Too, there was the anticipation of what they would see. Almost everyone had heard from someone else who'd taken the tour about the deadly proficiency they would witness. Would he miss this morning? Most hoped he wouldn't so that they could tell *their* friends of the marksmanship they'd seen on their tour of the FBI. A few hoped he *would* miss, but those were the ones who always hoped for failure in others.

Special agent Paul Harrison entered the range through its interior door. He knew he was upset at having to rush and told himself to calm down. Good shooting depended on relaxed muscles and a slow heartbeat.

He looked down the range. A fresh paper target was in place. The weapons were on the table. He quickly checked them. They were loaded.

He drew a series of deep breaths, then flicked the switch. The curtains opened with a "whooooosh." Staring at him from behind the glass wall were 200 eager faces. He picked up the microphone, turned it on, and welcomed the crowd. He told them what weapons he'd be using, weighed the .357 magnum in his long, slender hand, raised it, and discharged its rounds. He took the M–16, saw that it was on single-shot, and fired a few rounds, then changed to semiautomatic and then full automatic. As he fired he detected a slight tremor in his left hand and hoped it hadn't interfered with another perfect performance. It if had, the gasps would not be as loud, the applause more polite than enthusiastic. It had happened only once before in his four months as firing-range demonstrator. One bullet had strayed an inch from the paper heart. The tour guides had kidded him about it, and although he'd laughed along with them, he hadn't appreciated it.

He killed the lights in the range and turned on the single lamp behind the target. It took him a few seconds to realize that the light wasn't shining through the holes. "What the—?" Then, the reason became shockingly apparent. The body of a man in a blue suit hung on a hook from the overhead trolley behind the target. It pitched forward, tearing through the paper and landing face-first on the concrete floor.

Special agent Paul Harrison started toward the body, then remembered the 200 people behind him, most of whom were standing to get a better look. He quickly closed the drapes, picked up a telephone, and punched in a single digit. A member of the internal security force answered.

"This is Paul Harrison on the range."

"Yeah, Paul, how are you?"

"Not too good. Get somebody's ass down here right away. We've got a big problem."

"Did he kill him?" Harry Jones's niece asked her father.

"I think so. I think he did."

His wife's eyes rolled to the top of her head and she fainted.

3

TEN MINUTES LATER the dead man in the blue suit rested on a steel table in the FBI's forensic laboratory. Identification had been made the moment Harrison and others from building security looked down at the body on the firing-range floor. His name was George L. Pritchard; he'd been a special agent for seventeen years. He'd worked in field offices for most of his career, but a year ago had been brought into headquarters to establish a new tactical division known as SPOVAC—Special Office of Violent Activities (Criminal). Its focus was on "serial killers" and mass murderers.

A dozen men in white medical coats surrounded the steel table. Each was a forensic specialist, most were medical examiners from cities around the country who happened to be in the lab that morning as part of an FBI training seminar on new techniques of using lividity to determine the time of death in murder victims. The FBI did little actual forensic work, functioning more as a statistical and research center, but it was fully equipped and staffed for autopsies. Two other steel tables against the wall held corpses the visiting physicians had been working on when Pritchard was rushed into the lab.

"Boy, oh, boy," one of the doctors muttered, referring to the gaping hole in Pritchard's chest, created by the series of bullet wounds in a circle three inches in diameter. "Some shot."

"Look here," another doctor said, pointing to a single bullet hole slightly higher than the rest. It had been made by a small-caliber weapon. "A .22," the doctor speculated.

By now, the doorway and hall were jammed with people who'd heard about what had happened. Ross Lizenby, Pritchard's assistant on the SPOVAC team, pushed through the crowd. "Let me through, come on, move," he said as he gained access to the lab. He couldn't see past the wall of white coats. "Is it George Pritchard?" he asked.

Lizenby wedged himself between white coats. "It is," he said to himself. He looked around. "I'm special agent Lizenby," he announced in a loud voice. "Director Shelton is awaiting my report. I want everyone to vacate this room with the exception of the lab chief and any agent who happened to be here when the deceased was delivered." When no one moved, he shouted, "Now, damn it!"

Soon, Lizenby stood next to the steel table with the head of the forensic lab and a young agent who'd been there observing the seminar out of curiosity. Lizenby picked up a phone and dialed the office of the director of the FBI, R. Bruce Shelton. He identified himself to a secretary and was immediately put through. "The deceased *is* special agent George Pritchard, sir. Death appears to have been caused by multiple gunshot wounds to the chest." He listened for a moment, said, "Yes, sir," and hung up. He said to the lab chief, "Seal this room off, and that means to everyone. Get a staff together for an autopsy, but wait until I get back to you. I'm meeting with the director now." He started to leave and then glanced back at the young agent. "You were here?" he asked.

"Yes, sir."

"Come on."

They went to the seventh floor and entered the reception area of the director's office suite. A middle-aged woman behind a desk immediately said, "He's in the dining room, Mr. Lizenby. He said for you to go there."

They walked thirty feet to the executive dining room and

knocked. "Come in." They opened the door. Seated at an oval dining table having his hair trimmed by the kitchen's head chef was R. Bruce Shelton, director of the FBI since his appointment by the president four years ago. It was a ten-year appointment, but rumors had been thick lately that he intended to resign within the year.

"Good morning, sir," Lizenby said.

"Good morning," Shelton answered. He pulled off the cloth that kept hair from falling on his white shirt and said to the chef-barber, "That's fine, thanks, Joe." When Joe was gone, Shelton asked of Lizenby, "Who's this?" nodding at the young agent.

"He's, uh—"

"Special agent Jankowski, sir."

"Agent Jankowski was in the lab when the body arrived," Lizenby said.

"And?" Shelton said to Jankowski.

"Well, sir, I was just there for a few minutes. I was on my way to my office and stopped in because I was curious. They're having a seminar on forensic medicine and—"

"Please, get to the point," Shelton said.

"Yes, sir. Two gentlemen from building security, accompanied by a special agent, brought the deceased in and placed him on the only empty table. He appeared to have been shot numerous times in the chest."

"And?"

"And . . . that's all I know, sir. I intended to leave but—"

"Who were the security men and the agent who accompanied the body?"

"Names? I don't—" He looked to Lizenby.

"We're getting those, sir," Lizenby said.

Shelton swiveled in his chair and brushed away loose hair from the back of his neck. "It happened on the firing range? On our own goddamn firing range? Who did it?"

"We don't know that yet, sir," Lizenby said.

"It *was* an accident," Shelton said, standing and walking to a large window.

12

"We presume that, sir, but at this stage it's impossible to know what did exactly happen."

"Witnesses?" Shelton asked, his back to them.

Lizenby took a few steps toward the director and said, "Sir, I think we need a little more time to come up with the answers. It just happened. I suggest I get back downstairs and—"

Shelton slowly turned. He fixed Lizenby with steel-cold gray eyes and said, "I want this entire matter resolved before the day is out. I want nothing said to anyone about this except for those who must know. There is to be a total blackout about this. Does anyone outside this building know what's happened?"

Lizenby hesitated before saying, "Sir, there were two hundred tourists at the range as part of the tour."

"Two hundred—where are they?"

"I believe they were allowed to leave the building."

Shelton slammed his fist against the wall. "I hope that's not true, Mr. Lizenby. If it is, I hold you personally responsible."

"Sir, I wasn't even—"

"Get me answers. Good ones, and fast."

"Yes, sir."

Shelton said to the young agent, "Mr. Jan—what was your name?"

"Jankowski, sir."

"What office are you in?"

"A temporary assignment to administration, sir."

"Go to your office and stay there. Talk to no one. Understand?"

"Yes, sir."

Ross Lizenby went directly to the firing range. He took the back stairs instead of the elevator, thinking with each step that he wished he hadn't been where he was, and when, at the time Pritchard's body was discovered. He'd just walked into his office at SPOVAC when his phone had rung. It had been Wayne Gormley, one of three assistant directors named by Shelton shortly after his appointment as director. Gormley's division was investigation. SPOVAC came under it. The other two directors managed the administration and law enforcement areas of the bureau. Gormley's message to Lizenby had been short and to the point. There had been a shooting death on the firing range. The deceased appeared to be a special agent. "Check it out and report to the director and me immediately."

Lizenby was tired. He'd been in the building until two that morning working on a SPOVAC report that was due on Gormley's desk that afternoon. He'd planned to spend the night with Chris Saksis, but when he called her at two she vetoed the idea. Breakfast would have to suffice. He was tired, edgy, and irritable. And he didn't like R. Bruce Shelton, hadn't from the day he arrived as director. He hadn't particularly liked George Pritchard, either, but that didn't matter anymore.

He opened the door to a closet-size office just off the firing range where Paul Harrison was cleaning a revolver. "Hello, Paul," Lizenby said.

Harrison slowly shook his head. "I don't believe it," he said.

"You might as well. Pritchard's dead. What in hell happened?"

Harrison shrugged. "I was giving the demo and— Hey, Ross, are you here on official business?"

"Official?"

"You taking statements?"

Lizenby nodded. "The director has me on this."

Harrison raised his eyebrows and smiled. "I never saw him," he said. "I fired and wondered why the back light wasn't coming through the holes. Then, he falls off the track, right through the target."

"You never saw him?"

"Right."

"He didn't move?"

"No."

"He was hanging there knowing he was going to get a gut full of bullets and he never said anything?"

"Nothing. I never saw him. Look, Ross, I was late, didn't

have much of a chance to look around. I ran in, the folks were out there in their seats and I did my thing."

Lizenby looked down at the magnum Harrison had been cleaning. "Did you fire that?"

Harrison laughed. "Hell, no. The weapons I used are on the table in the range. Come on, Ross, give me credit for some smarts."

"What about the tourists who saw it?"

Another shrug. "They left."

"Shelton will hang whoever let them leave."

"It wasn't me. I called security, that's all. They arrived and I checked the body with them. It was George. I couldn't believe it. They canceled all tours for the rest of the day."

Lizenby nodded. "Hang around, Paul. Shelton might want to talk to you."

"I'm not going anywhere. I really can't believe it. Can you?"

"Shelton isn't interested in what we believe. He wants answers, and for Chrissake, don't talk to anybody about it unless you hear from me."

"You're heading this?"

"I hope not. Right now I'm on the griddle because I was in the wrong place at the wrong time. Check you later."

Special agent Charles Nostrand, who, as director of the Office of Congressional and Public Affairs for the bureau, was responsible for handling the press, called the office of Director R. Bruce Shelton.

"Sir, we're being swamped with press about the incident this morning. There's a couple of dozen reporters waiting outside, and the phones are ringing nonstop."

"It was an accident, an unfortunate accident," Shelton said softly.

"Yes, sir, but they want details."

"They'll get details when we have them."

"I know sir, but—"

"Prepare a short release and get it up to me right away. An accident on the firing range resulted in the unfortunate death

15

of a dedicated and exemplary special agent of the FBI. Couch it. It's the first time anything like this has happened. It was *purely* an accident. Special agent Pritchard was—"

"Sir, I'm getting all this, but my instincts tell me that to admit that one of our special agents was gunned down by another of our special agents on our own firing range might—well, it might open us up to ridicule."

There was silence on Director Shelton's end. Finally, he said, "Yes, you're right. Issue nothing until I talk to you again. I appreciate your candor and professional thinking. Tell the press they will be fully informed in short order. Thank you."

Ross Lizenby returned to his office and made three phone calls. The first was to Wayne Gormley, to whom he recounted what he knew to date. The second was to Director Shelton. The third was to special agent Christine Saksis. She was on her way out to her meeting.

"You heard?" Lizenby asked.

"Just fragments. It was George?"

"Yeah. Shelton's had me running."

"Why?"

"I was there. I'd like to see you tonight."

"You said—"

"Forget what I said. Dinner?"

"What time?"

"Eight."

"All right. You'll come by?"

"Meet me. At La Colline."

"All right. Ross, what *did* happen?"

"Pritchard got himself killed. That's all I know."

4

BY TWO O'CLOCK, it was evident to Director Shelton that the death of special agent George L. Pritchard could not be considered simply an internal problem. He called a meeting of his three assistant directors, who in turn held their own departmental meetings. Naturally, any agency investigation of Pritchard's death came under Assistant Director Wayne Gormley's jurisdiction. Gormley, in turn, charged Ross Lizenby with quickly establishing a special unit, whose only reponsibility was the Pritchard case.

Lizenby managed to arrange a second meeting with Gormley at four. At the first meeting, he hadn't expressed his feelings about running the special unit. Now, as the afternoon progressed, he decided to make them known. He said to Gormley, "Sir, I don't want this."

Gormley, whose round face and red cheeks testified to his fondness for vodka, stared at Lizenby with small blue eyes that were in constant motion. "Why?" he asked in a voice that indicated he really didn't care.

"Because I'm up to my ass in SPOVAC, that's why. Besides, I was supposed to be taken off SPOVAC and sent back out in the field."

Gormley popped a hard candy in his mouth. "That's right, I forgot. Ross Lizenby, the floater, the hired gun, one assignment to another, keep moving so they can't catch up with you."

"You can view it that way, sir, but—"

"I'm not interested in your personal view. I *am* interested in finding out who killed Pritchard. It happened right here, on our own firing range with two hundred goddamn tourists taking it in. The director is damn near hysterical, and you know that's not his style."

R. Bruce Shelton had been a federal judge. He came from old money in Philadelphia, was most at home at intimate dinner parties with Washington's arts and socialite crowd, and was known as a man who never raised his voice or lost his cool.

"I understand," Lizenby said, but—"

"No buts. You worked closely with Pritchard, which should be an advantage. You've spent your career with the bureau as an investigator. You do it. Inform me every step of the way. Keep it as internal as possible, use what staff you need, and get it over with."

"No choice?"

"No choice." Gormley sat back in his leather chair, rubbed his eyes, and sighed deeply. He looked across the desk at Lizenby and asked in a soft voice, "Remember the first rule—the *only* rule they hammered into you at Quantico?"

Lizenby smiled. "Sure. Don't embarrass the bureau."

Never embarrass the bureau. This thing is one goddamn and unfortunate embarrassment for everybody around here, and that's why the director's so upset. Don't screw up."

Lizenby knew it was futile to argue. He started for the door. Gormley stopped him. "Ross, get back to me at six. I'll have some ideas on staffing the unit by then."

"Staffing? You told *me* to staff it."

"Personnel is providing a list for me in an hour. We'll go over it."

"Whatever you say."

The autopsy was conclusive. Special agent George L. Prit-

18

chard had been killed by a single .22 caliber bullet fired at close range. All the other wounds had been caused by Paul Harrison's weapons during the demonstration, and had been inflicted about ten hours after the initial, fatal wound. Time of death was established between nine P.M. and two A.M. the previous night. Pritchard had died instantly. The .22 caliber bullet, although slightly higher than the cluster of holes from Harrison's weapons, had still struck the heart.

Special agent Charles Nostrand, who'd been fielding press inquiries all day, met with Director Shelton at five.

"What's the situation?" Shelton asked. He'd showered and changed clothes in a bathroom off his massive office. He and Mrs. Shelton were to attend a cocktail party and benefit dinner that night for the Opera Society of Washington. Funds raised would be used to replace the old wooden seats in the opera house, an ungodly red structure whose massive Austrian chandelier was considered its most redeeming feature, architecturally and, too often, even musically. The seat backs reached the floor, making it impossible for spectators to stretch their legs. It was Shelton himself who suggested a fund raiser after having spent a painful evening watching a touring company perform a spirited but agonizingly long version of *Wozzeck*.

"The press has been interviewing tourists who saw it, at least the aftermath of it. The word *murder* is being used in all reports."

Shelton, who'd made the best-dressed list every year since arriving in Washington, fingered the knot in his burgundy silk tie and gently ran his fingers down its length, as though checking for lumps. He was sitting behind his desk and had carefully crossed his legs. The crease in the trousers of his granite-gray British suit, custom-tailored for him by P. A. Crowe of London, was featheredged—looked like it could cut beef. He smiled at Nostrand. "It's been quite a day, hasn't it?"

Nostrand, who hadn't smiled all day, joined the director. It felt good. "Yes, it has, sir," he said.

"They're calling it murder?"

"Yes, sir."

"We're calling it an unfortunate accident, aren't we?"

"That's what we've been saying, pending, of course, a fuller investigation."

"It will continue to be an accident until further notice."

"Yes, sir." Nostrand had heard scuttlebutt about the autopsy result. Should he ask? He decided not to.

Shelton stood and offered his hand to Nostrand. "You've done a good job. Keep it up."

Nostrand stood and eagerly accepted the director's handshake. "Thank you, sir."

"Nothing changes. Simply tell them that it *was* an accident."

"All right. But I should mention that the press doesn't seem to be buying it, sir."

Another smile as Shelton came around the desk and slapped Nostrand on the back. "The hell with the press, Mr. Nostrand. The press wants to embarrass the bureau, and we won't let that happen. Will we?"

"Absolutely not, sir."

Shelton walked him to the door. He said as he poised to open it, "Interesting, isn't it, that we stand here in a building named for J. Edgar Hoover, a man who certainly was controversial but who built something more lasting and solid than anything any member of the press ever dared dream about. What we have to preserve, Mr. Nostrand, is infinitely more valuable to America than the sale of newspapers."

"I couldn't agree more, Mr. Shelton."

"Mrs. Shelton and I will be out. Mr. Gormley will be here throughout the night. Please confer with him in the event you have any questions."

"Yes, sir. I planned to be here, too."

"Fine, fine. Let's bury this thing and get on with more important business."

Ross Lizenby checked with the forensics lab before meeting with Wayne Gormley at six. Pritchard's body had been stored in a body-bin freezer. The autopsy, which had been performed in isolation by the lab director, had been sealed. Lizenby asked a question about it and was told it was for Director Shelton and Assistant Director Gormley's eyes only.

"I've been put in charge of this investigation," Lizenby said, not trying to disguise the pique in his voice.

"That may be true, Ross, but I know what I've been told. Straighten it out with Gormley."

Lizenby brought it up the minute he entered Gormley's office.

"Relax," Gormley said. "It's better to keep it tight. I'll fill you in on everything you need to know."

"Look, *sir*, I want to make my point again about not wanting this assignment. I didn't like Pritchard. I enjoyed SPO-VAC, but even that got old. I want out of headquarters, and I was promised that."

Gormley waved pudgy hands in the air. "I'm tired, Ross, and I didn't need this, having an agent murdered in this building. I was going on vacation next week. That's out. The wife's mad, I lost a deposit on the cruise we were taking, and my stomach is raising hell. Frankly, as Clark Gable said, I don't give a damn about what you want. Here." He slid a list of names across the desk.

Lizenby picked it up and read it. One name jumped up at him—Christine Saksis.

"That's your team," Gormley said. "Run with it."

"I don't want some of these people."

Gormley shook his head and mumbled, "Shit." He ran his hand over stubble on his chin and yawned. "Who don't you want?" he seemed to ask the ceiling.

Lizenby shrugged. "Saksis, for one."

"The Apache?"

"She's not—it doesn't matter. Why her?"

"Because she's free and because she's good. There's nothing earth-shattering going on on the reservations these days, some drunks, petty crime, that's about it. Who else don't you like?"

"Well, all right. Let me think about this overnight."

"Yeah, do that. But don't consider changing anything. It's a team—bodies—use them and let's get on with it."

Chris Saksis had escalope de veau tante Marie at La Colline. Lizenby had minute steak with béarnaise sauce. He told her of her assignment to the Pritchard case.

"I'm uncomfortable with it," she said as they finished what was left of a bottle of Pinot Noir.

"So am I. I told Gormley that."

"And?"

"He told me not to make changes."

"I can ask to be relieved."

"Maybe you should."

"I will, first thing in the morning."

"What reason will you give him?"

She shrugged and sat back. Light from a candle on the table played off her thick black hair. Lizenby stared at her across the table. He'd been with lots of women since his divorce ten years ago, maybe hundreds of them. The marriage had lasted less than a year. He'd been a struggling attorney then, trying to establish a private practice because he hated the thought of joining a law firm and having his individuality stifled. It hadn't worked; he hadn't given it much time. The moment the marriage failed he applied to the FBI and was accepted for special agent training.

Yes, he'd been with lots of women during those ten years, but none had approached Chris Saksis's beauty. She was exotic. He liked something different in women. So many of the others had simply been attractive, but there was such sameness.

He reached and took her hand. "Maybe it won't be so bad working together. Frankly, I think this will all blow over sooner than we think."

She frowned. "How can the murder of one of our agents 'blow over,' Ross? Somebody killed him."

Lizenby smiled. "What's the old line?" he said. "The suspect list includes everybody he ever met?"

"It doesn't matter that Pritchard wasn't very popular with a lot of people," she said. "An FBI agent murdered another agent. That doesn't blow away very easily."

"Why assume it was an agent? Could have been a lot of people."

"In the Hoover Building?"

"Sure. The place is crawling with outsiders. You know that. Maybe it was a secretary or a lab technician. He was known to play around a little."

"How many secretaries walk around with .22 revolvers in their purses? Besides, you said he was hanging from a hook on the target trolley. Pritchard wasn't a lightweight. Somebody had to put him up there."

Lizenby sighed. There had been enough talk all day and into the evening about George Pritchard's death. What he wanted was to go home, with Chris, and lie naked with her.

"Your place or mine?" he asked.

She looked as though a painful thought had crossed her mind. "What's the matter?" he asked.

She managed a smile. "I guess I'm more uncomfortable than I realized about what's happening between us, especially now that we'll be working so closely."

He came around the table and pulled out her chair. "Let's not worry about it. Let's take it a night at a time."

When she awakened the next morning, he was staring intently at her. She blinked, propped herself up on her elbows, and said, "Something wrong?"

He grinned. "Of course not. You're so beautiful, that's all. I'm admiring."

"You embarrass me."

"I don't mean to." He flopped his head back on the pillow and put his hands beneath his head. Now, it was her turn to scrutinize him. Handsome—no doubt about that, more handsome than most men. His Slavic-looking face was composed of chiseled planes, a strong chin, perfect teeth, a hairline that promised to remain in place throughout his life. His hair was brown and fine, closely cropped; his eyes pale blue.

She laid her hand on his chest and absently played with the hair there. He kept in superb shape, not an ounce of fat, muscular upper arms and shoulders, a flat, hard belly and long, tapered legs. Even his feet were nice to look at.

"Are you happy?" he asked.

"Yes, of course."

"Last night? Did I make you happy?"

"Oh, Ross, of course you did. Why do you ask?"

He smiled. "Because I want you to be happy."

"I am. I must say, though, that you were—well, you were almost savage."

He laughed. "That's a strange term for *you* to use."

"Oh, stop it. You know what I mean."

"You weren't exactly comatose yourself."

"Ross?"

"What?"

"We'd better be up and out of here in an hour. I have a feeling this day isn't about to be run-of-the-mill for either of us."

5

THE UNIT ASSEMBLED to investigate George L. Pritchard's murder was designated "Ranger." An empty suite of offices in a corner of the second floor was given over to it, and the team—Ross Lizenby; Christine Saksis; a Japanese-American pathology expert from Forensics named Raymond Okawa; a short, chunky blond computer whiz named Barbara Twain; Dr. Perry Prince, a psychologist borrowed from a statistical profile unit; two young special agents, Joe Perone and Jacob Stein; two secretaries; two clerks; and a tour guide named Melissa Edwards, who was working toward her master's degree in decision science and had applied for acceptance as a special agent—gathered together for the first time at ten o'clock that morning. The suite wasn't large enough to comfortably accommodate all of them, but Lizenby assured them it wouldn't be for long. "I just left Assistant Director Gormley," he said once everyone had dragged chairs in from adjoining offices. "He wants this investigation wrapped up as quickly as possible. I'm sure no one here would argue with that."

They started to ask questions, but he cut them off. "Look, this investigation obviously is unique. We have the entire FBI to draw upon, but we also have to keep in mind that this *is* the

FBI. There are going to be certain restrictions that we'll all have to live with. Here's the first: agent Pritchard's death will continue to be referred to as an accident. I'm sure you've all heard through the grapevine that he might have been murdered, but until I tell you otherwise, we stick with the accident story. There's to be no talk about this with anyone outside this special unit, and that means *anybody*, family, friends, other agents, bureau employees. A total blackout on information. Understood?"

There were nods and affirmations.

"Administration promises furniture and equipment by this afternoon. Tech Services will have us on-line with the computers by noon. We'll have two terminals up here." He glanced at Chris Saksis before saying, "I've been put in charge of Ranger. Special agent Saksis will be my assistant." He checked her reaction. She started to respond, but cut herself off, looked down, said nothing. Her only thought was that they seemed to be settling in for a longer investigation than Shelton had called for.

Lizenby gave out assignments that could be pursued elsewhere in the building. "We'll all meet up here again at four," he said, smiling as he added, "when we have something permanent to sit on."

He walked Saksis to her office in the Indian Affairs section of Investigation. She closed her door and said, "I'm getting off the Pritchard thing."

"Did you talk to Gormley?"

"Not yet, but I will. I'm trying to get an appointment now."

"I told him you wanted out."

"What did he say?"

"He'd been up most of the night and wasn't in the best of moods. He said he wasn't interested in what any individual agent wanted."

"What did you say?"

"Do you mean did I argue your side? No. I don't think it'll matter. Let's just keep our personal lives nice and quiet and ride this through."

"I'm still going to talk to him," she said.

"Sure. In the meantime, let's get started. Gormley gave me the lists of everyone who was logged into the building last night. It's broken down into two categories—bureau personnel and nonbureau personnel. He wants us to start with the non-bureau types. He's hoping it falls that way, that somebody not connected did Pritchard in."

"Don't embarrass the bureau."

"Right. Look, take the list and get together with the computer gal—what's-her-face?"

"Twain. Barbara Twain."

"Right. Let's break it down into groups—male, female, other agencies, foreign, domestic—as fine as you can."

He started to leave.

"Ross," she said.

He turned. "Yeah?"

"I don't like this."

"So talk to Gormley."

"I don't mean us working together. I mean the fact that an agent was murdered by one of our own. It's just begun to hit me."

"It was an accident. Remember? And if it wasn't, it was somebody outside the bureau."

"Sure."

"I'll see you later."

By five, the Ranger team was together in its cramped suite. Two computer terminals had been installed, desks, chairs, and telephones were in place, and it suddenly looked like a working office. Budget had assigned an expense number: Range-XP-6215873. Two separate phone lines came directly into the suite and a security system had been installed on the door leading to the hallway. Fireproof file cabinets were bolted to the floor. A large color TV, VCR recorder, reel-to-reel and cassette decks, and a multiband radio occupied one wall of the reception area. Lizenby had requested that one office within the suite be set up as a bedroom. Two yellow sleeper couches had been delivered, along with a small refrigerator, hot plate, and toaster oven. It meant losing a working office, but he felt

27

having a place inside in which to stay over would pay off down the road.

Chris Saksis and Barbara Twain worked out the coding for the list of non-FBI personnel who'd been in the building the night of Pritchard's murder. It was long—almost 300 names—visitors from other agencies, outside contractors, support personnel with varying levels of clearance, a few friendly journalists being briefed. "I'll need help," Twain said. Saksis promised to get someone from Tech Services.

Lizenby tuned in the six o'clock news on the television set. The lead story dealt with the Middle East. Right after it came coverage of an FBI press conference held in a media room off the public affairs office at four that afternoon. Assistant Director Wayne Gormley conducted it, with Charles Nostrand at his side. Lizenby noticed that the bags beneath Gormley's eyes seemed to have doubled in size. He looked as though he'd been drinking, but you could never be sure with Gormley. He often looked that way under pressure.

"This is the statement we have for you at this time," Gormley said, adjusting half-glasses and looking down at notes on a lectern. "As you all know, a special agent of the Federal Bureau of Investigation has died in the J. Edgar Hoover Building. Because of the unusual circumstances surrounding his death, a full investigation has been launched internally, utilizing every resource—manpower and technical—available to us.

"However, as of this moment, the cause of death has *not* been established. From what we've ascertained so far, special agent George L. Pritchard, a veteran of seventeen years of faithful and distinguished service to the bureau, was the victim of an unusual and unfortunate accident."

"Accident?" It was a chorus from the press.

Gormley held up his hands. "If you'll allow me to finish, Mr. Nostrand will be happy to accept a limited number of questions." He waited until the noise had subsided, then completed his statement: "Special agent Pritchard is the twenty-seventh special agent of the FBI to have died in the line of duty. The director, all who knew and served with special agent Pritchard, and I wish to extend our deepest sympathies

28

to his family, and to insure the American public that it will know every detail of his death at the appropriate time. Thank you. You may now ask your questions of Mr. Nostrand."

"I'd like to ask *you* a question, Mr. Gormley," a reporter from *Washington Weekly* shouted.

"Sorry, but I have another commitment. Thank you again."

Most of the questioners demanded to know why the word *accident* was being used when, in fact, 200 tourists had seen Pritchard "gunned down" on the firing range.

Nostrand's answer: "We are under the impression at this early stage of the investigation that agent Pritchard died of causes other than the firing-range shots. The tourists you refer to witnessed the unfortunate event from a distance and were not in a good position to see what transpired."

The questioning continued along the same lines, and Nostrand's answers never varied. The final question he took was from a radio reporter who wanted to know the name of the special agent in charge of the Pritchard investigation.

"I'm not at liberty to divulge that," said Nostrand. "I can say that he's one of the bureau's best, a skilled investigator. Thank you. We've prepared a release, which is available to each of you as you leave. You'll find in it background information on the deceased."

The Ranger team worked into the night. Food was ordered in. A second computer operator arrived and joined Barbara Twain in entering the names from the nonbureau list. Simultaneously, whatever background information was in the main computer on each of the names was retrieved and printed out in the bureau's hard-copy room a floor below.

Lizenby met with Saksis, and with special agents Joe Perone and Jake Stein, in the "bedroom."

Perone was a tall, muscular forty-year-old with heavy, sleepy eyes, a beak of a nose, and thick, black curly hair. He'd been an accountant before joining the bureau. Stein was considerably shorter and thinner. He'd been a lawyer before applying to the FBI. His brown hair was thin; most of it was gone from the front and top of his head. He wore round, tortoise-shell glasses; he'd barely met the bureau's requirements for corrected vision when he'd joined seven years ago, and he was constantly worried that one day his eyesight would deteriorate below the minimums of 20/200 corrected to 20/20 in one eye, and 20/40 in the other. Unlike Perone, who had a reputation as a tough field investigator, Stein was better known for his keen analytic abilities, and for being perpetually bemused at the bureaucracy in which he functioned.

"First of all," Lizenby said, "we've got to put together an immediate suspect list."

Stein laughed and looked at Saksis. "How many names were on that outsider list?" he asked.

"About three hundred."

"Not bad for openers."

"Gormley wants a viable list by noon tomorrow."

"That's ridiculous," said Perone.

"Tell *him*," Lizenby said. "Look, that list of three hundred has to have on it a core of people whose dealings with Pritchard can be turned into a motive."

Stein removed his glasses, blew on them, and carefully polished the lenses with his handkerchief. He said, "Everybody who ever worked with George Pritchard can be said to have had a motive to kill him. Right?"

"Well, he didn't top the good-guy list, but you don't go around murdering an FBI agent because he rubs you the wrong way," Perone said.

"You do if you're crazy," Stein said, replacing his glasses on his nose. "Who on that list doesn't play with a full deck?"

"Perry Prince is evaluating the names on it," Lizenby said, "on the off chance there's an obvious whacko. But that's unlikely. Let's split up the names and see if anybody jumps off the page based on what we know, or have heard."

Stein said, "What could we know about them, Ross? They're not FBI. Who are they?"

"We know some of them," Chris Saksis said. "They've been around a while—the ones in training here, regular contacts who were in the building."

"What about the other list?" Perone asked.

"FBI personnel?"

"Yeah."

"Forget it," Lizenby said. "Right now Gormley wants suspects who aren't bureau people. Let's not complicate this more than we have to."

Stein leaned back and did an isometric exercise with his hands. "I assume we're cross-checking names with .22 pistol permits."

Lizenby looked at Saksis. "We'll get to that as soon as we have the names and backgrounds coded," she said. "There's also a list of people on the sign-in sheets who came here that day to see George. That's probably the best place to start building a list for Gormley."

"What about his family?" Stein asked. "He was married, wasn't he?"

"Yeah," said Lizenby. "Her name's Helen. She lives out in Arlington with their daughter."

"Who's talked to her?" Perone asked.

"I don't know. Gormley said a team had been sent out as soon as we knew it was George, but I haven't had any feedback. I thought you might go see her, Chris."

"All right."

Lizenby stood and stretched. "Dr. Okawa's working with Forensics on further studies of the body. Again, let me stress that no one is to discuss this with anyone outside this special unit. No excuses, no reasons for breaking the blackout. Let's meet here at eight Monday morning."

Saksis followed Lizenby into the reception area, where the TV was now alive with a sit-com. Lizenby snapped it off.

"You going home?" she asked.

"Yeah."

"I'll go see Helen Pritchard first thing Monday."

"Good. I'd tell you what I know about his personal life, but I'd rather you start clean. Fill me in when you get back."

"Sure. Ross, I talked to Gormley about getting off this."

"What'd he say?"

"He said what you said he'd say, that he's not interested in my personal needs."

Lizenby smiled. He stepped close and placed his hands on

31

her shoulders. "Don't sweat it. It'll all work—be over before we know it." He felt a sudden rush of desire. "Want to come over?" he asked.

"No, not tonight. I'm beat, have all sorts of things to do, starting with paying my bills."

"I'll see you Monday then."

Ross Lizenby checked in with the Office of Congressional and Public Affairs on his way out of the building. "Any new guidelines from Assistant Director Gormley?" he asked the special agent on duty.

"Nope. All press inquiries are on hold until further notice."

"They don't buy the accident story, do they?"

"Would you?"

"Sure. It's the Federal Bureau of Investigation talking. Take it easy."

He drove his car, a new silver-blue Toyota Supra, to a telephone booth on a corner in Georgetown. A woman answered. "This is Mr. Adler," he said. "I'd like to make an appointment."

"When?"

"I'm not far away. I can be there in fifteen minutes."

"All right."

He parked in a fashionable area of Georgetown and climbed a set of steps to an ornate door. A buzzer and a speaker talk-box was set to one side. After buzzing, a woman's voice crackled through the box.

"Mr. Adler," Lizenby said. "I made an appointment."

There was a loud buzz, which unlocked the door. He pushed it open and stepped into a hallway. The floor was covered with expensive red Oriental rugs. The walls were stark white; prints of naked women from another era engaged in exotic sexual situations were handsomely framed.

He walked to the end of the hall and turned right into a parlor decorated and furnished out of the Victorian period. Three girls in revealing negligees, none older than sixteen, sat on a red velvet couch. A heavy mulatto woman dressed in a flowing

32

royal blue caftan said, "Ah, Mr. Adler, how nice to see you again. The choice is yours." She indicated the three young women with a sweep of her hand.

"I'd like a drink," Lizenby said.

"Of course. Do I remember right? Scotch—a splash of soda?"

"Yeah, you remember right," he said, sitting in a Belter chair upholstered in a heavy flowered purple fabric. "And no more than a splash."

6

CHRIS SAKSIS CALLED Helen Pritchard at eight o'clock Monday morning and was met with the widow's icy-cold voice: "Why bother asking if you can see me? You've already made me a prisoner here."

Saksis arrived at the Pritchard condominium in Arlington, Virginia, at nine. A few press people were hanging around the front of the building. She rode the elevator to the penthouse and knocked. Another female special agent, who'd been assigned to stay over at the condo, opened the door. Her name was Pat Busch; she'd graduated from the FBI academy at Quantico with Saksis.

They exchanged greetings and went inside. The penthouse was big; the living room was easily twenty by forty feet. Glass doors led to a terrace that overlooked the Potomac. The furniture was modern and expensive, with lots of chrome, steel, and leather; the carpeting was thick. Saksis wasn't an art expert, but the large oils and pastels on the walls looked very valuable to her.

A miniature gray poodle with a big red bow around its neck trotted into the room, yapped at Saksis, sniffed around her feet, and sat up. Saksis bent over to pet the dog and heard Helen Pritchard's voice: "Her name's Billie. Don't get too friendly. She'll pee all over you."

Saksis straightened up and smiled. She approached Helen Pritchard and extended her hand. "I'm Christine Saksis. I called."

"I know you did. Now there are two of you. There was an army yesterday." She walked past Saksis to a table where a silver coffee service was set up. "Coffee?" she asked.

"No, thank you."

Helen Pritchard poured herself a cup and sat in a leather-and-chrome director's chair near the sliding glass doors. She wore a bright yellow dressing gown trimmed with white lace, and sandals. Blond hair hung loose around a thin but pretty face. She looked to Saksis like a woman who was fanatic about her appearance, constantly dieting and exercising, but not living a particularly healthy life. That was confirmed when she lit a cigarette. It wouldn't have surprised Saksis if there were brandy in the coffee. Helen Pritchard talked in a whiskey-nicotine voice.

Saksis sat in a matching chair across the table. "This must be very difficult for you, Mrs. Pritchard," she said.

"Not any more difficult than when he was alive. What I can't stand is having bureau people here day and night. It's a joke." Her laugh was forced. "What are you afraid of, that I'll say something nasty about your precious FBI?"

"I'm not afraid of anything, Mrs. Pritchard. I'm here because I'm part of a special investigatory unit dealing with your husband's death." She looked over at Pat Busch, who'd chosen a chair in a far corner. "Pat, could I have a few minutes alone with Mrs. Pritchard?"

"Sure. Is the kitchen okay or—"

"The kitchen's fine. Thanks." She wasn't comfortable dismissing another special agent, but she remembered Lizenby's order that no one outside of Ranger was to know anything.

"Well, Mrs. Pritchard, I might as well start big and go from there. Any idea who might have killed your husband?"

35

Helen Pritchard laughed, then coughed. "I was hoping you'd ask who might have *wanted* to kill him. Then my line would have been, 'Everybody, including me.' "

"I see. But let's deal with my question."

"No idea. Besides, it was an accident. I watch TV."

"It probably was."

Another laugh. "That's bureau PR, my dear. You know, my deceased husband mentioned you once. He talked about the squaw around headquarters."

"Did he?"

"Actually, he didn't call you a squaw. That's me talking. I think he called you an Indian goddess who had every guy in the bureau tripping over his own feet."

"That's flattering. An Indian I am, a goddess I'm not."

"Apache?"

"Passamaquoddy."

"I've never heard of that. I only know Apache and Navajo."

"It's a tribe from Maine. Let me ask you about your husband's activities the day of his death. What time did he leave the house that morning?"

"Eight, but not that morning. He hadn't been home in two weeks."

"Two weeks."

"Maybe four. He seldom slept here."

"You were—"

"Estranged? That's a kind word. The fact is we hated each other and saw as little of one another as possible."

"Were you separated? Legally, I mean."

"No. We just went our own ways."

Saksis nodded, then said, "You have a daughter."

"Right. I'm impressed with your investigatory prowess."

Saksis stifled a reaction. "Her name?"

"Beth. Elizabeth. Named after her father's sister."

"How old is she?"

"Sixteen, and never been kissed. Sure you don't want coffee?"

"I'd love some."

"Help yourself."

Saksis poured a cup. "Where is your daughter?"

"Sleeping, a teenage disease."

"Would she know anything of her father's activities the day he was killed?"

"The day he was murdered?"

"As you wish."

"No. He didn't spend much time with her, either." She leaned forward and exaggerated every word. "George Pritchard was a special agent of the FBI, a G-man, an undercover hero who worked day and night to keep America free, and to keep us womenfolk safe at night."

Saksis had started taking notes. She lowered her pad and pen and said, "You're very bitter."

"Me?" She laughed. "No, just realistic. Besides, what's to be bitter about? I chose to marry a servant of J. Edgar Hoover. I made my bed—"

"Was your husband *that* dedicated that it ruined your marriage?"

Helen Pritchard crossed one shapely leg over the other and dangled a sandal from her foot. "It had nothing to do with dedication, Miss—"

"Saksis."

"Nothing at all to do with it. If George was dedicated, it was to living the undercover life with impunity from his family. Think about it. You walk around with unlimited cash in your pocket, you tell your wife you'll be away for a few months on 'official business,' but don't ask questions. It's for my country, for my leader. You run with all sorts of women, but God help your wife for questioning it. It's always official business. Little boys playing cops and robbers and being paid for it." She saw the tiny smile on Saksis's face and added, "And little girls, too. Fem lib. You've come a long way, baby."

Saksis finished her coffee and placed the cup and saucer on the table. She looked directly at Helen Pritchard and said, "There's nothing you can tell me that might help the investigation?"

Helen Pritchard shook her head. "Nope, nothing. You want a personality profile of George? That I can give you. He was handsome, self-possessed, and never should have married or had a kid. The FBI was his life, not because of some inner spirit, but because it gave him the freedom to chase broads and to stay away from this one. Add to that his growing paranoia over the past few years and you have a picture of a thoroughly despicable man."

"I'm—I'm sorry."

"Don't be. There were compensations." She indicated the room with a sweep of her hand. Saksis noticed the heavy, expensive-looking rings on her fingers. Obviously, money was not a problem.

Saksis hesitated, then asked, "Was there family money, Mrs. Pritchard?"

"Family money? No. You're asking because you've gotten the feeling that we lived slightly higher than what an FBI agent brings home."

"Yes, as a matter of fact, that *is* why I asked."

"I used to wonder about it, too, but I stopped asking. George told me years ago that he had 'business dealings' on the side. When I asked what they were, he told me to mind my own business. I did."

"What about personal effects?"

"Here? I told you he spent very little time here. What there was, one of your earlier teams took with them."

"They did?" Saksis was surprised. If Ranger was to be the only unit investigating the death, it didn't make sense to have others confiscating potential evidence. She asked the names of the other agents.

Helen Pritchard shrugged and lit another cigarette. "They all look the same to me. Morris. Norris. One of them had a name like that."

"Okay. Could I see the bedroom?"

"Site of the connubial bed? Sure." She pointed to a door that led to a hall. Saksis thought she'd accompany her, but Mrs. Pritchard didn't move. Saksis passed a closed door off the hall that she assumed led to the daughter's room. At the end of

38

the hall was the master bedroom. It was large, a vast expanse of pink and white. A king-size bed was covered by a spread the color of pink begonias. A frilly white canopy covered it. A dressing table was laden with expensive bottles of perfume and cologne. There were two closets. Saksis opened one of them. It was filled with female clothing. Same for the other closet. It was as though a man had never been there.

Saksis started toward the living room when the door that previously had been closed opened. Standing there was a teenage girl. Her face was puffy with sleep, and long, mousy brown hair hung in disheveled strands over her face. It was a pretty face, pale and round and pensive, a few freckles on each cheek. She wore a man's T-shirt that barely reached below her behind.

"You must be Beth," Saksis said pleasantly. "I'm Christine Saksis. I'm with the FBI."

"Oh."

"I'm sorry about what happened to your father. I didn't work closely with him, but I knew him."

"Uh huh. Is my mother here?"

"Yes, she's in the living room."

Beth picked up a robe from the floor, put it on and walked past Saksis.

"Well, sleeping beauty has arisen," her mother said.

"I was tired," said Beth.

"Of course you were. You can't sit up all night watching television and not be tired."

"Mother, I—do we have to stay here again today?"

Helen Pritchard looked at Saksis. "Ask her, my dear. She's big brother."

"Actually, I know nothing about the FBI watching your movements," Saksis said. "I'm not here to do anything but to meet you and ask some questions."

"Where's Ms. Busch?" Beth asked.

"In the kitchen," her mother answered.

Beth left the living room. Saksis sat and said, "I know how painful all this must be for the two of you, Mrs. Pritchard, and I don't enjoy intruding on personal lives. But, I have to. No matter what circumstances surround your marriage to George Pritchard, he is an FBI agent who's been murdered."

"Oh, now the truth comes out."

"That doesn't represent the truth, Mrs. Pritchard. I just used a word."

Helen Pritchard's laugh was the first indication of any warmth. "Don't worry about it," she said. "I know he was murdered, and so do you. So does everybody else in that ugly building, including the director himself. It'll all come out as soon as the embarrassment factor has been dealt with."

Saksis knew she was right but couldn't say it. She got up and looked out the window. The heat and humidity hung outside the glass like a dirty, gray wet sheet. It was the one thing she disliked about Washington, the summers. They were so unlike summers in Maine. Suffering a twinge of homesickness, she turned away from the window and said, "Thank you, Mrs. Pritchard, for talking to me. Here's my card. Please call me at any time if you think of something that could help, or if you just—well, just want to talk."

"Yeah, thanks. George was right."

"About what?"

"About you. You are a splendid-looking creature."

Saksis felt awkward. She absently smoothed down the sides of her khaki skirt and said, "Thank you for the compliment. We'll talk again, I'm sure."

Special agent Pat Busch was in the foyer with Beth. "Pat, could I talk to you for a minute?" Saksis asked.

"Sure."

They left the apartment and walked to the elevators. "What's the story?" Saksis asked. "Are they under house arrest?"

Busch shrugged. "All I know is that they're not supposed to leave or talk to anyone except bureau personnel."

"Whose order?"

"Gormley's."

"For how long?"

"I have no idea."

"What other agents have been here?"

"A dozen, in teams, in and out."

"Know any of them?"

"Sure." She named a few.

"What do you think of her?" Saksis asked.

"Mrs. Pritchard? Tough."

"That's for sure. There wasn't any love lost between them."

"That's a very kind understatement, Chris. I like the kid, though."

"I never really talked to her."

"Very quiet but smart. Sweet, too. Interesting the difference in how they viewed George Pritchard. Did you notice there doesn't seem to be a trace of him anywhere in the house?"

"Sure."

"Beth's room is different. She's got every award he ever received, pictures of him all over the place, letters from him. Poor kid, I don't think this has really sunk in yet. She's in shock. I feel sorry for her because her mother doesn't seem to be the comforting type."

"That, too, is a kind understatement."

7

AS CHRIS SAKSIS drove back to the Hoover Building, Ross Lizenby sat in Wayne Gormley's office with Gormley, special agent Charles Nostrand, and a high-ranking representative from the Justice Department, Robert Douglas.

Douglas had just come from a meeting with FBI Director Shelton. "It's our opinion at Justice," he said, "that too much is being made of this Pritchard matter. Instead of it being handled for what it simply is, an unfortunate murder of an FBI agent, it's turning into a national scandal."

Gormley grunted. "You have to admit, Mr. Douglas, that there are circumstances surrounding this 'simple murder' that make it difficult to contain, at least from the standpoint of the press and public. If it had happened in some office or house somewhere, that would be one thing. But this simple murder happened in front of two hundred American tourists on hand to witness our firing-range exhibition. That adds a bizarre element that the press loves."

Gormley looked to Nostrand, who realized the assistant director wanted him to say something. He shifted in his chair and said to Douglas, "Sir, the press is a vindictive bunch. Mr.

Nixon found that out with Watergate. Keep something back from them, stonewall information, and they camp outside your door and make a cause célèbre of it."

"I'm well aware of that," Douglas said.

Gormley coughed, rubbed his eyes, and said, "You have to realize, Mr. Douglas, that we've been operating under orders from Director Shelton that, I understand, originated with Justice."

"Of course," Douglas said. He was a small, slight man with a pinched face and disproportionately large ears. He wore eyeglasses with stainless steel rims and might have been the chairman of the board of a medium-size manufacturing company except for the rumpled, inexpensive tan wash-and-wear suit just a little too small for him. It was a junior executive suit. "Initially, it was prudent to keep a lid on things until the facts could be ascertained," he said, "but now, there's no question that agent Pritchard was murdered. It's our opinion that steps should be taken immediately to get this thing off the front pages and the nightly news."

Gormley said, "If my orders are to reveal to the press all we know at this juncture, then that's what we'll do." He looked at Lizenby. "Will that hamper or hinder the investigation?"

"I haven't given that much thought, Mr. Gormley. Off the top of my head I'd say it might get in the way, but not seriously so."

"That's really not a consideration," Douglas said. "What we want at Justice, and I'm sure Director Shelton agrees, is to get the spotlight off this mess. Any investigation into the murder should be low-key and without fanfare. By the way, how *is* the investigation progressing?"

All eyes turned to Lizenby, who said, "We're in the information-gathering phase of it now. We're trying to develop a list of possible suspects from which to work."

"I know one thing," Douglas said.

"What's that?" Gormley asked.

"There had better be a complete evaluation of security in this building. Obviously, someone from outside the bureau

43

killed agent Pritchard. There was a lapse somewhere along the security line."

"Exactly," Gormley said. "A review is already in the works."

"Good." Douglas stood. "Thank you for your time," he said to Lizenby and Nostrand.

They stood and shook his hand. "Good luck," Douglas said to Lizenby. "It's a most unusual case."

"Yes, sir, it is. We're doing our best."

When Douglas was gone, Gormley told Nostrand to prepare a release stating that Pritchard had, in fact, been murdered, and that a full-scale investigation was under way. "Stress that all preliminary indications point to someone outside the bureau as the perpetrator, and focus on the security review we're initiating to see that it doesn't happen again."

Nostrand left. "Sit down," Gormley said to Lizenby. "Would you like coffee?"

"No, sir, thank you."

"I think I'll have some." He called his secretary, settled back in his high-back leather swivel chair, and slowly turned left and right. He made a pyramid with his fingers, leaned his chin on it, and said, "Well, you heard. We've gone from dark secrecy to total disclosure. Your name will be part of the statement we release, which will put the media pressure on you. I suppose that's good, but it causes me some concern."

Lizenby laughed. "Me, too, sir."

"Yes, I suppose it would, considering your background with the bureau."

Lizenby straightened up and asked what Gormley meant.

"Well, Mr. Lizenby, I've reviewed your file and was struck with how much of a loner you've been over the years, all the special assignments without ever staying one place very long."

Lizenby said, "That's mostly because the bureau found me more useful in those situations and, frankly, I—"

"You enjoyed it."

"Yes. I like being on my own."

"Being here with SPOVAC must have been confining."

"Yes. That's why I asked for a transfer."

"And Pritchard promised it to you."

"Yes."

"What about Pritchard? You worked closely with him. What'd you think of him?"

"Well, I—I respected him."

"Liked him?"

"No."

"Why not?"

"Probably because—sir, is there a reason for these questions?"

Gormley laughed. The door opened and the secretary delivered his coffee. "Sure?" he asked Lizenby. Lizenby shook his head. "Thank you," Gormley told the secretary, who backed away from the desk, turned, and silently left the office.

"Okay," he said, sipping his coffee, "back to the question of your opinion of Pritchard. I would have assumed you two would have hit it off. His career with the bureau was pretty much that of a loner, too, undercover a lot of the time, using disguises, staying away from this bureaucracy as much as possible."

"Maybe that was the problem, sir, that we were *too* much alike."

"Maybe so."

"Again, sir, I wonder why you're exploring this."

"Because I might have made a mistake in assigning you to head Ranger. It made sense in the beginning because you knew him well and worked in similar ways, but I'm trying to anticipate the critics. I can hear one questioning why we didn't go with a completely impartial investigator, one who didn't have any bones to pick with the deceased."

Lizenby sat back and smiled. "You know, sir, you could make me a very happy man."

Gormley's eyebrows went up. "How?"

"By listening to that unknown critic and assigning someone else."

"Nobody wants to be involved in this. Agent Saksis requested being taken off it."

"I know."

"I denied her request."

"I know that, too,"

"I'm denying your request."

"It wasn't a request, actually. You brought up the possibility of criticism at having me involved."

"Just venting thoughts, Mr. Lizenby. I suggest we get on with it. You can use Nostrand where the press is concerned, but not on an exclusive basis. Maybe he can assign somebody to you out of Public Affairs. Mention it to him. And remember what Douglas said . . . keep it low-key, no fanfare, and no public statements without clearing through me. Understood?"

"Yes, sir."

"Check in with me twice a day. I hate surprises."

"Right. Is that all?"

"Yes. Thank you. At least I feel better about one aspect of this."

"What's that, sir?"

"That it wasn't someone from the bureau who killed George Pritchard."

Lizenby thought, He's believing his own press releases. He said, "We'll keep working on that assumption."

Chris Saksis filled Lizenby in on her interview with Helen Pritchard. He was unimpressed; he already knew of the strained relationship between Pritchard and his family, knew that Pritchard spent very little time at home. What did interest him was that teams of agents had removed Pritchard's personal effects from the apartment. "Who?" he asked. Saksis gave him the name she'd caught—Morris or Norris.

Lizenby called Gormley's office but was told the assistant director had been called to a meeting and was not expected to return until the following morning. He went through a directory of special agents until finding the one Chris had mentioned. The agent confirmed over the phone that he'd been part of a team dispatched to Pritchard's home. "What did you get?" Lizenby asked. "Can't tell you," the other agent said. Lizenby reminded him that he was in charge of Ranger. The other agent said, "I just work here, Ross, like you do. Check with Gormley."

Barbara Twain poked her head into the office and told Saksis she'd finished a computer run on .22 caliber pistol permits issued to FBI personnel who were known to be in the building the day of the murder, or had been in Washington, D.C., that same day. The length of the list didn't surprise anyone. Although special agents were not issued .22 caliber handguns, most agents purchased them on their own, for two reasons—they were easier to carry, and they were more effective in certain situations. That lesson had been learned from the mob, whose hit men found that the' smaller bullet did more internal damage because of its tendency to tumble within the body. The list ran to more than a thousand names and included George Pritchard, Ross Lizenby, Assistant Director Wayne Gormley, and virtually every other special agent assigned to headquarters.

"That sure narrows it down," Lizenby said, shaking his head.

Saksis laughed. "It eliminates me," she said.

"What about the list of people who signed in to see Pritchard that day?" Lizenby asked Barbara Twain.

"I gave it to you," Twain said to Saksis.

"I have it," she said.

"Let me see it," Lizenby said.

"Sure. I forgot."

She returned minutes later with the list and handed it to Lizenby. He quickly scanned it. "Who's this Raymond Kane?" he asked.

"Beats me," Saksis said. "He signed in at 11:30 that night and signed out at 2:30." She handed Lizenby a second list. "This is what we got from Shelly up in SPOVAC. She really doesn't keep a detailed roster of everyone who comes in to talk to SPOVAC people, but she put this together from the appointment book and memory."

"She has the mind of a rock," Lizenby said.

"Shelly? She's okay," Saksis said.

"She's a birdbrain."

The list drawn by SPOVAC's head secretary contained twenty names, most of them familiar to Lizenby. "Doering was there that day?"

"Evidently," said Saksis.

Bert Doering was a CIA operative who functioned as liaison between the Central Intelligence Agency and the FBI on a program that brought foreign law enforcement professionals into the United States for training. George Pritchard's objections to the program were well known, as was his disdain for Bert Doering.

"Loeffler, Nariz, and Teng, the fearsome foreign trio. What did they talk to Pritchard about?"

Saksis held up her hands. "Ross, I have no idea. Obviously, they have to be questioned, along with everyone else on that list."

"What are we waiting for?"

"For the list to be completed. Want me to do it?"

Lizenby shook his head. "No, put Perone and Stein on it." He realized Barbara Twain was still there and said, "You have something else?"

"I'd like to get together with you, Chris, about the next step."

"Sure. I'll catch up with you in a minute."

"You look exhausted," Saksis said to Lizenby when Twain was gone.

"I couldn't sleep last night thinking about this. Christ, all I wanted was to escape Washington and get back to the field. Now, this comes up. I hate it."

"I don't blame you. Look, I'll do all I can to help. Just tell me what you need and I'll be there." She heard herself speaking not as an assistant but as a woman standing beside "her man." It filled her, simultaneously, with pleasure and doubt.

"I appreciate that," he said.

"It does make me a little uneasy, you talking about leaving."

"Why?"

"Well, Mr. Lizenby, we do have a certain relationship that might make the person being left behind somewhat unsettled." She was sorry she'd said it the moment it passed her lips.

"Yeah, well, sometimes my mouth works overtime and the mind is on vacation. I didn't mean anything by it."

She smiled and said, "What you mean is exactly what you're thinking, and I have no business reacting the way I did. There are no strings either way. Forget I brought it up."

"Like hell I will," he said, going to the door and closing it. He came to her, looked into her eyes, and asked, "What do you have on for tonight?"

"Nothing special, unless duty calls."

"It won't. Dinner? Stay at my place. We both need an early night together."

Her immediate reaction was to decline, for reasons she couldn't, or didn't want to, identify. Instead, she said, "Yes, that would be nice."

They were about to leave the Ranger offices at six when Assistant Director Gormley appeared in the reception area carrying a large, sealed interoffice envelope. "Thought you'd want to have this," he said to Lizenby.

"What is it?" Lizenby asked.

"Various things from Pritchard's office and house. There's a personal phone book that should be checked."

Lizenby weighed the envelope in his hands and grappled with the question of why it had taken so long to deliver it. He opted not to ask. Gormley wished him a pleasant evening and left.

"What's that?" Saksis asked when Lizenby walked into her office carrying the envelope.

"Gormley just delivered it. Pritchard's personal effects."

Her eyes opened wide. "Really? Let's take a look."

"Tomorrow. We have an early night for us, remember?"

They put the envelope in the safe, turned off the lights, and went to Le Pavillon, recently relocated to the second floor of a new office building on Connecticut Avenue, where they dined on galette of wild mushrooms with a ballottine of pigeon, fillet of lamb with white asparagus and sage butter, and dense, rich raspberry tarts.

"So expensive," she said after they'd gotten in his car.

49

"We deserve it," he said. "I missed you."

She slid closer and rested her hand on his leg.

They made love for a long time that night. He seemed perpetually ready, and constantly asked her what he could do to please her. Once, he suggested he play one of a number of XXX-rated videotapes he had in his library, but she said, "We don't need that, Ross. We're doing fine all by ourselves." He had dozens of tapes, and when he first made Chris aware of them she'd been surprised and disappointed. She certainly wasn't a prude, but some of them were kinky and featured sadomasochism. She'd refused to watch those, but she had watched a few of the milder tapes. She hated to admit it, but they had generated erotic feelings in her.

As they were falling asleep, he asked, "Do you ever hear from the guy in Arizona?"

"Bill? He calls. We're good friends."

"That's all?"

"There was more once, not anymore. Friends, that's all." He said nothing. She leaned over him and asked, "Are you jealous?"

"No."

"I hope not, because there's no reason to be."

"I just know what he meant to you."

"He meant a lot and still does, but not in the same way."

"Do you miss him?"

She laughed. "Yes, as a friend. We share something, an American Indian heritage. He works hard to expose what happens on reservations. I admire him."

"You loved him."

"Once, yes, but now . . . this is ridiculous."

"Hey, Chris, understand me. *We're* together now. I just don't—"

"Don't what?"

"Forget it. Let's get some sleep. Are you happy?"

"Ross, I'm happy, about some things, about—"

"Satisfied?"

"Sexually? Do you have to ask?"

"Good. I want you to be happy."
"I am." She kissed his forehead. "Good night."
"Good night. Pleasant dreams."

8

DAWN BROKE AS hot and sticky as the previous seven dawns, although the forecast promised relief within forty-eight hours.

Ross Lizenby went directly to the Hoover Building. Chris Saksis went home for a change of clothes and to check on her mail. She arrived at the Ranger offices at 8:15 and poured herself a cup of coffee in the makeshift kitchen. Lizenby poked his head in and asked her to come to his office.

"Shut the door," he said. She sat across the desk from him as he placed in front of her the contents of the envelope Gormley had delivered the night before. Pritchard's wallet and keys were there, along with gold cuff links, a watch, scraps of paper, an appointment book, and a wallet-size address book.

"Have you gone through it?" Saksis asked.

"No. I can't get past wondering why Gormley sat on it so long."

"Is this all there was?"

"Yeah."

"What about the items they took from the apartment? His desk must have had more than this."

Lizenby shook his head. "I'll ask Gormley when I see him later this morning. In the meantime, go through everything and see if it rings any bells. Are Perone and Stein interviewing the people on the list?"

"I'm going to talk to them now. You want to start with the German and Teng and Nariz?"

"Might as well. Leave Doering for me."

"Okay."

She started to leave.

"You know, Chris, how much I appreciate having you on this assignment."

"Sure."

"It's going to fall more and more on your shoulders. I'm a lousy administrator. Besides, there are a couple of SPOVAC commitments I have to follow through on."

"I'll give it my best."

She went to her office, where Perone and Stein waited. She filled them in on their assignment—to interview the three foreigners who'd been training with the FBI over the past months, and who'd been in the building the night Pritchard was killed. Stein drew Walter Teng, Perone would talk to Hans Loeffler. They'd get to Sergio Nariz later in the day.

Once they were gone, Saksis refilled her cup, settled back behind her desk, and slowly started to go through Pritchard's phone book. Most of the entries were initials. There were few addresses. Most initials were followed by a single telephone number.

She went to where Barbara Twain and the second computer operator were at work in front of their terminals. "Barbara, can you break away?" she asked.

"Sure." The chubby blonde followed Saksis back to her office, where Saksis handed her the small phone book. "Set up a program to compare the initials and names in here to the list of people who signed in to see Pritchard that day, or who were known to visit him in his office. Will it take long?"

Twain shook her head and smiled. "Not long at all."

* * *

53

Hans Loeffler was a large, square man with sparse hair that he combed in wet strands across a bumpy bald head. He had high color in his cheeks and a bulbous nose. He wasn't fat, but it was obvious that keeping his weight down was not easy for him. Back home in Munich, Germany, he was deputy commissioner of that city's *polizei*, with its undercover division under his direct supervision. He'd been in Washington attending a special training program offered to foreign law enforcement officials at the bureau's Quantico academy. He'd completed the Quantico phase of his training, but instead of returning directly to Germany had been invited by Assistant Director Jonathan Mack, who headed up the bureau's law enforcement division, to spend two weeks at headquarters coordinating Munich's link-up with the FBI's CLIS program (Criminalistics Laboratory Information System), which shares a massive general rifling characteristics file with national and international agencies. Loeffler had a special interest in weapons and often bragged of his personal collection at home.

Perone and Loeffler met in a small conference room on the Tenth Street side of the Hoover Building. Perone took a seat at one end of a six-foot-long teak conference table and invited Loeffler to sit in the first chair to his right. Instead, the bulky German sat at the opposite end of the table. He was overtly nervous. His face was moist, and Perone noticed that when he lit a cigarette—which he seemed to do constantly—his hand trembled. The small tape recorder Perone had placed on the table didn't help.

"Well, Mr. Loeffler, I'm sure you know why I wanted to see you this morning," said Perone.

"Pritchard," Loeffler said bluntly.

"Yes. We're interviewing everyone who was in the building the night he—he died."

"You have a lot of interviewing to do. There must be thousands here at night."

"Yes, that's true, but we're starting with those who aren't employees of the FBI."

"I see. Well, I can tell you nothing you do not already know."

Perone smiled and leaned back. "Frankly, Mr. Loeffler, I don't know anything at this stage except that you were here that night. What were you doing?"

Loeffler lit another cigarette and tried to make his large body more comfortable within the arms of the narrow chair.

"Can't you remember?" Perone asked.

"Yes, yes, of course I remember, but I am not sure I am free to tell you."

"Why not?"

"Because it involves secret matters."

Perone raised an eyebrow and leaned forward to see that the cassette tape was running. He sat back again and stared at Loeffler.

"Please, Mr. Perone, try to understand the position you place me in. I wish to cooperate but . . ."

Perone continued to stare. He'd been told over the years with the bureau that his stare could melt a diamond, and he used it effectively during interrogations. It had unglued the coolest of suspects.

"I do not wish to break trusts," Loeffler said. "I feel privileged to be here and to have been taken into the confidence of Assistant Director Mack and the others. Please, it is not right to ask me to betray that trust."

"That's not what I'm looking for from you, Mr. Loeffler. I understand what you're saying, and I respect it. Let's forget about the nature of what kept you here so late that night. Just tell me who can vouch for your movements."

Another cigarette. "Many people, those I met with."

"Names?"

He mentioned three people.

Perone squinted. Smoke from Loeffler's chain of cigarettes floated in his direction and caused his eyes to sting. He said, "I don't think we have anything more to discuss, Mr. Loeffler. I'll talk to the people you've mentioned and confirm what you've said."

Perone shut off the tape recorder and slipped a narrow notebook back into his jacket pocket. He glanced up at Loeffler, who looked as though he wanted to say something.

"Is there something else?" Perone asked.

Loeffler, who'd just ground out a cigarette and was lighting another, wiped his brow with the back of his hand, shook his head, and said, "No, nothing else." He stood. Perone came around the table and shook his hand. "Thanks," he said. "I understand you've had a successful stay here."

Loeffler smiled for the first time. "Yes, yes, most successful. What a tragedy this thing that happened to Mr. Pritchard. Shameful."

"Did you know him very well?"

"No. Oh, yes, he taught one of the classes I took at Quantico but—no, not well."

"Did you like him?" Perone asked as they opened the conference room door.

"Well, no, there was some trouble. Minor trouble."

Perone drew a breath, looked at the German, and asked, "Should we go back in and talk again?"

Loeffler shook his head. "No, of course not," he said. He laughed. Perone read it as forced. "It was a little conflict of personalities. Mr. Pritchard was—how shall I say it?—not the easiest man to like. Please, do not misunderstand. I had the highest regard for him as a colleague. It was more personal."

Perone decided to drop it for the moment. He'd check out Loeffler's witnesses and ask around about any problems between him and Pritchard. "When are you due to go back to Germany, Mr. Loeffler?"

"In two weeks."

"That's good. You'll be here in Washington, here in the building for the next fourteen days?"

"Yes."

"We'll catch up again. Thanks." He left him with a remnant of his famous stare and returned to the Ranger offices.

Jacob Stein interviewed Walter Teng in an office adjacent to Director Shelton's suite. Determining the place where the meeting would take place proved difficult, which Stein hadn't bargained for. Obviously, there was official concern from high up that the Chinese gentleman be dealt with in a delicate and courteous manner.

When Stein arrived at the office, Teng was there with a tall, slender, professorial man wearing a colorful madras jacket, white buttondown shirt, and bright yellow bow tie. He introduced himself as Hoyt Griffith.

Stein shook his hand and asked. "Do you plan to be present during the interview?"

"Yes," Griffith said pleasantly. "It's been cleared with the director."

"I wasn't told," Stein said. "Are you with the bureau?"

"Yes."

"May I see your credentials, please?"

"I don't think that's necessary. Your director—"

"I don't want to be difficult, Mr. Griffith, but I'd be derelict to allow you to be here without instructions from someone in authority."

Teng said nothing during the exchange. He sat in a red leather easy chair and glared at Stein. Stein tried to ignore him, finally said, "Mr. Teng, I'm special agent Jacob Stein. I'm the one who'll be talking with you. Maybe you can help straighten this out."

The severe expression of Teng's face never changed as he said in perfect English, "Mr. Gormley wishes Mr. Griffith to be present during our talk."

"That may be true, sir, but I can't proceed without his direct authorization."

Griffith, who'd sustained his pleasant facade, now appeared to be losing patience. He said, "If that's true, Mr. Stein, I suggest you obtain it or conclude this little get-together. Mr. Teng and I have busy schedules."

"So do I, Mr. Griffith. I'll see what I can do in the next ten minutes."

Stein hurried to the Ranger suite and found Chris Saksis in the computer room reading a print-out Barbara Twain had just given her. He quickly explained the situation and they went to Lizenby's office. He wasn't there.

"I don't know what to tell you," Saksis said. "Maybe Griffith is from the CIA. They're the ones who brought Teng over here."

One of the secretaries came to the door and said, "Mr. Stein, there's a call for you. Assistant Director Gormley."

Stein looked at Saksis. "He's never called *me* before," he said, going to a phone and picking it up. "Special agent Stein here."

"This is Assistant Director Gormley, Mr. Stein. The interview with Mr. Teng can go forward as scheduled *with* Mr. Griffith present."

"Yes, sir, I just wanted to hear it from higher authority."

"I appreciate that. You now have it from higher authority."

"Yes, sir. Mr. Griffith—is he agency personnel?"

"No, but that doesn't impact on you or your interview. Simply proceed and treat Mr. Teng with tact and courtesy."

"Yes, sir, I intended to do that from the beginning. Sir."

"Yes?"

"I would like to call you back just to confirm that I'm speaking with you."

"Mr. Stein, that's . . . Yes, of course."

The return call to Gormley's number was picked up immediately.

"Thank you, sir," Stein said as he hung up.

Saksis, who'd been standing behind Stein, started laughing.

"What's so funny?" he asked. "Standard procedure. How the hell do I know it isn't somebody talking like Gormley and—?"

"I'm not arguing, Jake, it's just a first for me."

"Me, too," he said, grinning. "I'll be back."

Walter Teng's face defined the word impassive, a flat mask of noncommitment. He wore a cream-colored Mao suit. On the pinky of his right hand was a large diamond ring. There was a small tattoo on the back of his right hand. It was blue and green, and looked to Jake Stein like a large dog, or wolf with its fangs bared.

The first time Stein had seen Teng walking around the

building he could think only of old war movies in which a Japanese camp commandant extracted information from downed American flyers. Of course, Teng was Chinese, not Japanese, but that was a minor hitch in Stein's vision of the squat, powerfully built Asian.

Stein knew why Teng had been in the Hoover Building for the past two months. The Central Intelligence Agency had arranged for Teng to receive training, first at Quantico, then at headquarters, so that he could return to China to update its own version of the FBI.

It had been a top-secret project until columnist Jack Anderson broke the story and questioned whether the training would be used to enhance the secret and powerful police force to carry out Communist policies. George Pritchard, before his demise, had voiced loud objections to the project, which had not endeared him to the bureau hierarchy. He'd confined his comments, of course, to within the bureau, but he'd been vocal enough to receive a reprimand from Assistant Director Gormley, and to prompt a heated and not very private argument with the CIA's liaison at the bureau, Bert Doering.

Hoyt Griffith carefully arranged himself in a stuffed chair and quietly observed as Jacob Stein placed a yellow legal pad on his lap, cleared his throat, and said, "Mr. Teng, I appreciate you sitting down with me like this. As you know, one of our special agents, George L. Pritchard, recently died in this building under unusual circumstances. I've been assigned to a unit investigating that death, which is why I wanted to talk to you." He checked Teng for a reaction. There was none.

"We know, Mr. Teng, that you were in the building the night of special agent Pritchard's death. Would you mind telling me why you were here, and what you were doing?"

Teng looked at Griffith, who said, "Mr. Stein, it's no secret that Mr. Teng is here on a very important mission for his country, and for the United States. His activities are the concern of those who are responsible for the success of his visit."

Stein looked at Griffith and smiled. "I'm well aware of that, but I'm sure you understand that it's my job to pursue certain avenues of investigation regarding the death of agent Pritchard."

Griffith returned the smile. "I'm not suggesting that you not investigate this matter, Mr. Stein. What I *am* saying is that interviewing Mr. Teng is, at once, unnecessary, unfruitful, and perhaps foolhardy."

"Foolhardy? Why is that?"

"Because you are crossing the line into areas that are beyond your limited scope."

Stein let the comment go. He said to Teng, "Do *you* mind telling me of your movements the night Mr. Pritchard was— died?"

"It is my position that I am not to speak of things within this bureau. I will tell you this, however. I did not kill your agent Pritchard."

Stein laughed. "Of course not, Mr. Teng. I never suggested that."

"Then why talk to me?"

"Because you were here, and you are not a member of the FBI."

Griffith chuckled. "That's it, is it?"

"What's it, Mr. Griffith?"

Griffith sighed and shook his head. "The old protect-your-own syndrome."

Stein sensed his temper rising. He put the cap on his pen, stood, and offered his hand to Teng. The Asian shook it without getting up. Stein glanced over at Griffith, decided not to bother, and left the office.

"How did it go?" Saksis asked him when he'd returned to Ranger.

"Wonderful. Mr. Teng told me he didn't kill Pritchard, and I think it's hands off our Asian colleague for the duration. He had a spook with him." He told Saksis of Griffith's participation, and of his picking up on looking outside the bureau for a suspect.

"He's right," Saksis said.

"I know. I just don't like people like him being right. You know what crossed my mind while I was sitting there?"

"What?"

"I doubt if Walter Teng would have murdered George Pritchard, but what about the CIA?"

"Why?"

Stein sat on a couch and examined the fingers of his right hand. He said, "George Pritchard had a reputation of being a big mouth around here. I also happen to know that he'd been slapped down a few times for giving interviews to the press without clearance."

"So?"

"So, maybe it was Pritchard who leaked the China story to Jack Anderson. Maybe he was talking out of school to other people. Maybe he had to be shut up."

Saksis wanted to dismiss the theory as pure James Bond, but she couldn't. The same scenario had flashed through her mind a few times. In her version, however, there was an added incentive for the CIA. By creating an incident that pointed to an FBI agent being murdered by one of its own, it cast a long and dark shadow over the bureau.

"Remember," Stein said, "the CIA is not one of our biggest boosters."

"I'm remembering, Jake, I'm remembering."

An hour later Ross Lizenby received a call from Assistant Director Gormley. "Walter Teng is not to be approached again," he said.

"Well, sir, he was included on the list because he was in the building and was *not* bureau personnel."

"I don't care about the 'whys,' Mr. Lizenby, I'm simply telling you to leave Mr. Teng alone. That comes from the director himself."

"Yes, sir."

Joe Perone interviewed Sergio Nariz at four that afternoon. Nariz was Paraguayan who was also attending the FBI academy training program for foreign law enforcement professionals. Physically, Nariz came off to Perone like a young Caesar Romero, very handsome and smooth, impeccably dressed in a dark blue vested summerweight suit, shoes shined to a mirror finish, every salt-and-pepper hair perfectly in place.

Nariz lacquered his fingernails, a habit Perone disliked in men. He also wondered whether Nariz wore facial makeup. It looked it, although if he did he was skillful at it. You couldn't be sure.

They talked for an hour. Nariz was expansive in his answers, gregarious, charming. He frankly admitted that he disliked Pritchard.

"Why?" Perone asked.

"Because he was an arrogant and abusive man, Mr. Perone. He insulted me on a number of occasions. Because I am a guest here, I did not retaliate, but had it happened in my own country, I would have."

"How would you have retaliated?" Perone asked.

Nariz smiled broadly and offered Perone a cigar. Perone accepted it. They both sat back and enjoyed the taste and aroma.

"Excellent," Perone said.

"Cuban," Nariz said, "but don't tell anyone."

Perone laughed. "I wouldn't even consider it."

"Good. How would I have retaliated? Not by murdering him and hanging him in a target range."

"No?"

"No."

Perone thanked Nariz for the cigar at the end of the interview, packed up his recorder, and returned to Ranger.

"Well?" Saksis asked.

"He can account for his actions that night, but I'll check it out. By the way, I asked the people Loeffler, the German, said he was with that night.

"What'd they say?" Lizenby asked.

"He disappeared for about an hour, said he was sick."

"He didn't tell you that?" Saksis said.

"Nope."

"Ask him about it," Lizenby said.

"I intend to. By the way, Nariz carries damn good Cuban cigars."

Later, Lizenby sat with Saksis in his office. He was pensive, and she asked why.

"I was just thinking about George Pritchard and his life.

You know, he just about single-handedly infiltrated and disrupted that terrorist group operating out of New York. Remember, when he was with the Long Island field office?"

"I only heard bits and pieces. I do recall Director Shelton giving him a commendation."

"Yeah. Funny, but what sticks in my mind is that the terrorists had ties to Paraguay."

"They did?"

"Yup, and George maintained a contact within the group, a Paraguayan. In fact, I think they got together the day he was killed."

She sat forward on her chair. "How do you know that?"

"I don't *know* it for certain, but I'd bet on it. Just something he said that morning before he went to lunch that made me think he was meeting up with the guy."

"Do you have his name?"

"No. George Pritchard had refined to an art form the concept of keeping it to yourself. Even mentioning that the guy was a Paraguayan was a slip. I did a little research on the group he infiltrated. There's strong evidence that it's hooked up with a faction of Paraguay's national police force that's dedicated to overthrowing the government down there."

"Nariz?"

"Maybe. What about the others on the list?"

"Nonbureau types? There aren't many. I had Barbara run a comparison of the initials and names in Pritchard's phone book with everyone who was known to have seen him that day."

"Anything?"

"No, except for that set of initials, R.K., which matches up with Raymond Kane, who signed in to see Pritchard at 11:30 that night."

"Who is he?"

"I haven't the slightest idea. He listed himself as a consultant. I checked with the guard who was on that night and he remembers that Pritchard had left word to admit Mr. Kane the moment he arrived."

Lizenby leaned his head far back and stretched his arms in front of him. "Check out the number in the phone book."

"I am. There was no area code, and the exchange isn't from around here. We'll try them all tomorrow."

"Okay." He got up and did a series of waist bends. "What are you doing tonight?" he asked.

"Going home, soaking in a hot tub, and getting to bed early. I had a tennis game tonight but I canceled."

"Maybe you'd feel better if you played."

"I doubt it. You?"

"I need gym time. I'm tight. Want to meet for breakfast?"

"Sure. Au Pied De Cochon?"

"Sounds good to me."

Chris Saksis decided to jog once she got home. She ran for an hour along Massachusetts Avenue, past the stately mansions of Embassy Row, then back by way of Dumbarton Oaks Park. As she was letting herself in her apartment, the phone started ringing. She ran to it and picked it up. "Hello," she said.

"Chris. It's Bill."

"Bill, it's so good to hear from you."

"I wanted to touch base and let you know I'll be in Washington in a couple of days."

"That's wonderful. Tell me about it."

Bill Tse-ay and Chris Saksis had been lovers. His father was an Apache, and had started a national newspaper covering American Indian affairs. When his father died, Bill continued to publish it. He was even more of a crusader for Indian rights than his father had been, and it was his single-mindedness that contributed, in part, to the relationship with Chris ending. Bill had been quietly critical of Chris's decision to join the FBI. He considered it, in some symbolic way, selling out. She saw it differently, felt that a good way to help her people was to achieve status and influence within the prevailing power structure. There were other factors, of course, that caused them to drift apart, at least romantically, but there remained a strong bond that each of them understood.

Bill gave her his travel plans and said he'd call the minute he arrived. They started to exchange stories about their current lives but decided to save them for when they were together. He did ask before hanging up whether there was anyone new in her life.

"I guess not, Bill, although I have met someone who—well, I *am* interested, but it's early in the relationship. You?"

"Afraid not. Once you've met a Christine Saksis, everybody else pales, if you'll pardon the expression."

They laughed. "I forgive you. Can't wait to see you."

9

"BILL CALLED LAST night," Chris said as she and Ross lingered over a second cup of coffee at Au Pied De Cochon.

"Bill?"

"Bill Tse-ay."

"Really?"

"He's coming to Washington in a couple of days. I'd love you to meet him."

Lizenby looked past her to an adjacent table.

"Ross."

He returned his attention to her. "What?"

"I said I'd like you to meet Bill."

"Why would I want to do that?"

"Because—because he's a nice guy and he's part of my life and—"

"We'll see. What are you doing today?"

"Specifically? Well, I'm running down the phone number for Raymond Kane and following up on some other aspects of the list of people who'd seen Pritchard the day he was killed and—"

Lizenby waved for a check.

"Ross, are you angry about something?"

The waitress brought the check and Lizenby pulled money from his wallet. When the waitress was gone, he stood and said, "Let's go."

She started to ask again whether he was angry, decided to drop it, and walked to her car.

"This thing is dragging on too long," he said as she put the key in the lock.

"What thing?"

"Pritchard, this whole Ranger crap. The guy wasn't worth it."

She cocked her head and looked at him. "What does that matter?"

"It matters to me. I want this resolved fast so I can get the hell out of this fiasco called Washington, D.C."

She was hurt, but she fought against demonstrating it. "I'll see you at the office," she said curtly.

"Yeah. Let's have a meeting and shake up the troops."

"I don't think that's necessary. Everyone's doing what they're supposed to be doing."

"Are they? I'm not sure about that."

He turned and walked away. He hadn't bothered to close the door behind her, to kiss her on the cheek, to display anything that might have smacked of caring. She watched him walk, erect and sure, eyes straight ahead. She hoped he'd look back, wave, do something to acknowledge her. He didn't.

She felt the sting of tears in her eyes, willed them away, and started the car. It doesn't matter, she told herself as she joined the flow of traffic on Wisconsin. But then she had to admit that it did. She was in love with him. "Damn it all," she said as she cut off a cab and made a right turn.

10

FOR IMMEDIATE RELEASE

An autopsy performed by FBI forensic specialists on the body of deceased special agent George L. Pritchard has confirmed that the cause of death was a .22 caliber bullet wound to the heart.

Numerous other bullet wounds found in the body had been inflicted accidentally after the initial fatal wound.

Special agent Pritchard's assailant has not, as yet, been determined. At the time of death, a number of individuals not employed by the Federal Bureau of Investigation were present in the J. Edgar Hoover Building. Strict security measures insure that each of these individuals had some valid and official reason for having been admitted. However, because they are not under direct bureau control, the background of at least one was of a nature to provide a motive for killing special agent Pritchard.

A full-scale investigation is under way to determine the perpetrator and to bring him to justice. The investigation is headed by special agent Ross Lizenby, a ten-year veteran of the Federal Bureau of Investigation and a former attorney, who has been directly involved with numerous difficult investigations in the past.

All inquiries should be directed to the Office of Congressional and Public Affairs. Progress reports will be issued on a regular basis.

Chris Saksis scanned the release when she arrived at Ranger, tossed it aside, and concentrated on the name Raymond Kane. The phone number next to the initials R.K. in Pritchard's phone book did not include an area code.

She asked Barbara Twain to pull up from the bureau's central computer a list of cities where the first three digits of the number were used as an exchange. Once she had it she instructed Melissa Edwards, the tour guide and fledgling special agent, to start calling, and to tape-record each call.

Lizenby spent the morning in his office with the door closed. He emerged at noon, casually mentioned to those within earshot that he was going to lunch, and started to leave.

"Can I have a contact?" one of the secretaries asked.

Lizenby shook his head. "I'm not sure yet where I'll be. I'll call in."

Fifteen minutes later Saksis told the secretary, "I have an appointment at the academy at Quantico." She laid a neatly typed itinerary on the desk and left.

As she drove the forty miles south on I–95 she thought about the confusion she'd been experiencing since breakfast. Her instincts about not working so closely with Ross had been right. She should have insisted on being removed from Ranger. She knew, of course, that Gormley would not have changed his mind unless she had admitted the personal relationship with Lizenby. That probably would have done it, but it would also have tainted her in Gormley's eyes. The bureau was not a place for romance. A lecturer had made that point during her training. "Keep the boy-girl games out of the office," he'd said. "Keep them far away from the bureau. It can cause potential embarrassment." To say nothing of personal anguish.

She drove through rolling woodlands until reaching the entrance to the United States Marine Corps base at Quantico, a sprawling facility that had been the center of all FBI training since June 1972. The facilities constructed on the bureau's end of the base were ultramodern—two seven-story dormitories, a well-stocked library that also contained the latest in audio and video equipment, cafeterias and a large dining room, indoor and outdoor rifle ranges, a thousand-seat auditorium, a bank, post office, dry cleaner and laundry, and a physical training center all linked together by enclosed walkways.

Saksis found a parking space near the administration center, turned off the engine, and looked around, recalling vividly her training as a special agent. She'd enjoyed it, found its intensity a stimulating challenge physically and mentally. She'd done well—right up near the top of her class—and she'd nearly burst with pride the day FBI Director R. Bruce Shelton shook her hand in the auditorium and welcomed her to the bureau.

She'd been back every six months since graduating three years ago, for refresher courses and twice to lecture on FBI jurisdiction over American Indian reservations. She felt she'd found a home at the FBI, a tight-knit community of professionals who were the best in the world at what they did and who exhibited unbridled pride at it. Of course, many within the bureau had become jaded and cynical, which she understood. The bureaucracy could be smothering, and monotony was not unknown. Still, she accepted that. Maybe one day she'd be put off by it. Not now.

She went to the office of the academy's director of personnel, Barry Croft, a tall, handsome, gentle man who was like a dean of students to recruits. He could be tough when the occasion demanded it. She remembered a fellow student being summarily dismissed from the program because he'd lost his ID. At least they hadn't tacked "with prejudice" on his dismissal. There had been a few of those in her class, too, usually for breaking regulations, major or minor, or for failing to match up to bureau "image," as perceived by any member of the staff. Simply not being a "team player" was enough to do it. J. Edgar Hoover had promised that the FBI would only have the best.

Croft greeted her warmly and suggested they go to a small briefing room down the hall from his office. "Let's get away from the phone," he said.

Once they were seated in chairs with writing arms, Croft smiled and said, "They put you on a tough one, huh?"

"They sure did. To be honest, I tried to cancel the assignment, but no dice."

"Assistant Director Gormley told me."

She was surprised and showed it.

"He called yesterday and filled me in on things. You've got total cooperation from me. Here." He handed her file folders he'd carried with him. "George Pritchard's files from here. They go back to his student days and cover his teaching duties as well. He was down here about a week before it happened."

"Really?"

"Yes. You know, this whole SPOVAC project is hot. The director himself is high on it. We've been weaving aspects of it into the curriculum and Pritchard was the one who pretty much handled this end of it."

"He was good, wasn't he?"

"Pritchard? Yes, damn good. A strange man, as I assume you've already gathered."

"Strange? I suppose so. He wasn't especially liked, that's for certain."

Croft laughed. "A charmer he wasn't. A good agent, though. From what I understand there wasn't a better undercover man in the field. I remember him holding an impromptu seminar one night on the use of disguises. He was remarkable. He had his own collection of disguises and makeup to rival MGM."

"I didn't know that," she said, wondering where it was. She certainly hadn't seen any evidence of it in his home.

"Yeah, George Pritchard was a piece of work. Shocking what happened. Any leads?"

71

"Not a one."

"It couldn't have been a—well, it may sound naive but it couldn't have been someone from the bureau."

"We're hoping it wasn't."

"Yes, let's hope not. Had lunch?"

"No."

"Why don't you take a half hour and skim what's in the folders. I'll pick you up and we'll grab something."

In the brief time she had, Saksis focused on records of Pritchard's days as a student. At that time, the academy at Quantico didn't exist. Training took place in Washington's Old Post Office Building, in the Justice Department, and at scattered sites around the area. She was surprised to see how the training had changed over the years. In Pritchard's student days the course material was limited. Every time there was a new technological advance, it was incorporated into the curriculum. Still, some things stayed the same, especially in the areas of firearms and physical conditioning. Pritchard had been good with weapons, not great but respectable. He'd barely managed to pass the fitness requirements, was top of his class in courses dealing with psychology and covert activity, and did well in the investigative techniques program.

There were negative notes in his file. One had to do with his dress, which the critic felt was not up to bureau standards. Too, he'd been criticized for displaying a tendency to follow an individualistic path at times, and to be too outspoken.

It all fits, Saksis thought.

Croft returned and they went to the dining room.

"Interesting?" Croft asked after they'd been served chef salads.

"Yes, of course, but I feel guilty peeking into another agent's file."

"Never happens except under these circumstances. He was an interesting guy, Pritchard, a real loner, which got him in occasional trouble. Never seemed to be comfortable on the team."

Being in the dining room and eating a chef salad brought

72

back many pleasant memories. It had been her favorite thing on the menu when she was a student. Usually, she ate in the cafeteria, but once a week she'd splurge at a local restaurant. She smiled. "I enjoyed the training," she said.

"You must have," Croft said. "You excelled. I have an idea."

"Yes?"

"We have an instructor here named Joe Carter."

"I remember him," Saksis said. "He taught investigative techniques."

"Right. Joe's one of our best at the academy. He's almost got his Ph.D. in psychology, really knows his stuff. The reason I bring him up is that he was a classmate of Pritchard's during training. I think Joe is the only one who ever got really close to Pritchard. You might gain some insight from him."

"I'd love to talk to him."

"I told him you were coming today. He had to be in Washington for a briefing but said he'd be free tonight if you wanted to catch up with him."

"I'll make a point of it."

"Good. I'll get a hold of him. Want to meet at headquarters?"

Saksis started to say yes, then shook her head. "No, I think it's better to keep these interviews out of headquarters. Like you said, stay away from the phones."

"Got a suggestion?"

"Depends on what he likes to eat. I've been dying for Chinese all week."

"I'm sure that will be fine with Joe."

"Okay, tell him to meet me at Ted Liu's, on Twentieth, Northwest."

"Good. He said he'd be free by six."

"Six it is."

Chris stayed at the academy until four going through Pritchard's files. Then she drove to her apartment, changed into a plain taupe jersey dress, and reached Ted Liu's at 5:45. Joe Carter arrived at six straight up. They had a drink at the bar, then were ushered to a teal blue banquette where the table was set in pink.

"I've never been here before," said Carter. "Doesn't look like a Chinese restaurant."

Saksis laughed. "No red dragons here. I like it."

They ordered Hunan beef cooked with fresh ginger and pepper, and jumbo shrimp grilled in their shells and served with scallions, cashews, and a spicy tomato sauce.

"I couldn't believe it when I heard about George's death," Carter said. He was a short, stocky man with a square face and thick fingers, hardly the stereotype of the academician. Chris would have pegged him as an outside investigator, a special agent who hated desks and books and who liked to be where the action was.

"What's new on it?" he asked.

"Nothing, really. We have a special unit set up to investigate—"

"Ranger."

"Supposed to be top secret." She laughed.

He joined her. "No such thing in the bureau. Any leads?"

She shook her head. "No. We're building a list, and there are avenues to pursue, but as of now, nothing. I was hoping you could help."

"Probably not, unless you want my war stories with George Pritchard. We were pretty close during training. We naturally drifted apart, but we still kept in touch, especially when he'd come down to Quantico to lecture." He looked down at the table, then at her, and said, "Funny how much being his friend meant to me when we were recruits. He didn't seem to have friends in the class, didn't want any except for me. I was flattered. I respected him."

"For any special reason?"

"There was a confidence about him that none of the others had, including me. He was my age, but he always seemed older, as though he'd been around the bureau for a long time. He just had that way about him. He had old eyes."

"Old eyes."

"Yeah, and you were sure there were deep pools of wisdom behind them."

Their food was served and they shared it. "What about his wife?" Saksis asked.

"Helen? Not my favorite lady."

"Not his either, I gather."

"I wouldn't say that," Carter said.

"No?"

"No. He loved her, treated her better than she treated him."

"The daughter, Beth?"

"Nice kid as I remember. It was a long time ago. Once they drifted apart I never saw Helen and Beth again."

"Did he talk about them?"

"Not much."

"Mr. Croft said Pritchard was in Quantico the week before he died."

"Yes, he was. We had dinner."

"Do you remember anything he said or did that might have been different, or that indicated there was a problem?"

Carter laced his fingers together and slowly shook his head. "No, can't say that I can. He talked about SPOVAC most of the evening—he was very deeply into it, especially developing the psychological profiles of serial and mass murders."

"What about the terrorist group he'd infiltrated before coming to headquarters to head up SPOVAC? I've been told he still maintained an important contact within that organization."

The question caused Carter to stiffen. He glanced around the large restaurant before saying in low tones, "That's the sort of information that's best left buried."

Saksis looked at him quizzically. "Even when it might help solve the murder of an agent?"

Carter nodded. "Even then," he said, serving their final portions from covered metal bowls.

"You're saying it's true."

"I'm saying it doesn't matter."

"It does to me. It must have mattered to George Pritchard."

Carter dabbed at his mouth with his pink napkin, put an arm up on the back of the banquette, and drew up a leg on the seat. "George had contacts inside many groups. He was one of the best of the Unkempts." Special agents who worked undercover were nicknamed the Unkempt Bunch within the bureau. "He treasured those contacts, never shared them because he knew somebody would steal them. He understood the bureau game better than anyone I've ever known, even back when we were students. I suppose that was one of the reasons I was so attracted to him during training."

"But I wonder—"

"The point is, Miss Saksis, there are certain things that must be respected, and one of them is a man's contacts. I don't believe that it had anything whatsoever to do with George's murder, but even if it had, there are greater stakes to be considered than simply discovering who killed him." He poured green tea into two delicately painted China cups.

Saksis sipped, then said, "I understand that, of course, but in this case that bigger stake, that greater good would be achieved if the murderer were one of Pritchard's outside contacts. Ranger is operating under orders from up top that the bureau is not to be embarrassed. We're committed to finding out who killed George Pritchard from a list of suspects *not* directly connected with the FBI." She realized how foolish that sounded and added, "Provided, of course, that the person *is* an outsider."

Carter laughed. "You don't have to clarify for me. We all hope that George was killed by an outsider. It may not end up that way, though."

"I know. Again, about his contact with the terrorist group he'd infiltrated a few years ago. My information is that he might have had lunch with him the day he died."

Carter's eyebrows went up and he poured more tea. He said, "But he wasn't killed at lunch."

"But maybe whoever he had lunch with came back to see him that night. There are a number of names on the sign-in sheets that we can't trace. They were visitors to see Pritchard who might have used false names. Does Raymond Kane ring any bells?"

"No."

"How about anyone George knew with the initials R.K.?"

"No, sorry."

"His terrorist contact? R.K.?"

"Miss Saksis, you're a good interviewer. I admire that. But, I already told you that George kept his contacts to himself."

"But everyone shares information like that with someone else, at least one other person."

"Well, it wasn't me. Maybe Helen."

"His wife? No chance." She was sorry that a bit of an adversarial relationship had developed. Carter didn't have to talk to her. She said, "I really appreciate the chance to talk to you about George Pritchard. I'm trying very hard to understand the sort of man he was."

Carter motioned for a check. "He was one of the best, Miss Saksis, strange, a brooder and loner, but a totally dedicated and skilled special agent. That's why Director Shelton brought him in to run SPOVAC."

"There's a lot of questions about that, though."

"Why? Because the director was known to not like him personally? That's true, but Mr. Shelton is the type who can put personal feelings aside in the interest of the bureau."

He walked her to her car. "It was good seeing you again," he said. "I remember you from when you were training at Quantico."

"I loved it."

"You know, I've only heard scuttlebutt about how George died, but one thing bothers me."

"What's that?"

"That whoever did it would take the time to prop him on a target trolley hook. Why? Why not just shoot him, let him fall, and walk away."

"I've wondered the same thing, but there are so many questions at this stage that I can't deal with them all at once."

"I know what George would have said."

77

Saksis cocked her head.

"George would have said, 'You never eat a whole pie at once. You eat it piece by piece and pretty soon you've eaten the whole damn thing.' "

It occurred to Saksis as she drove home that Carter's final words were probably the best thing that came out of the evening. She was trying to eat the whole pie instead of in little pieces. It was time to start nibbling.

But then she thought of Ross Lizenby and everything seemed jumbled again.

11

SAKSIS ASKED THE secretary the next morning where Ross Lizenby was. "Coming in later," was the answer. She'd been tempted to call him when she got home from dinner with Joe Carter but resisted it. It wasn't easy. She hoped he'd call her, but that didn't happen, either.

She walked into the office shared by Joe Perone and Jake Stein. Stein had his feet propped up on a desk and was reading the *Washington Post*.

"Jake," Saksis said, "has anyone run a re-creation of the crime scene?"

"I don't think so. I do know that somebody's head's on the block for removing the body before they had a chance for pictures and sketches."

"I guess the panic was on."

"With the help of two hundred gaping tourists."

"Let's go down to the range," Saksis said.

"Sure." He checked his watch. It was 8:30. "We have time before they run the first marks through."

Special agent Paul Harrison was there when they arrived. "How goes it?" Stein asked.

"Not bad, but every time a group comes through I get the feeling they're looking for another spectacular."

The three of them walked to where the paper target hung forty feet from the firing station. "This is where he came through," Harrison said.

Saksis looked past the target to the far wall. She approached it, with Harrison and Stein following. The target trolley originated against the wall. A platform approximately four feet high and six feet square was directly beneath where the targets were attached to the trolley.

"Why the platform?" Saksis asked.

"Makes life easy, especially for short agents."

"Careful," Stein said.

"No offense, Jake," said Harrison.

"Maybe he was killed here," Saksis said.

"They ruled it out," Harrison said. "No blood."

"The .22 shell never exited his body," Stein said.

"What blood there was dripped from the wound down onto his coat and pants," Saksis said, "which meant he must have been leaning forward after he died."

Harrison shrugged, said, "All I know is that rushing the body from here to Forensics wasn't the best idea. The brass isn't happy."

"Yeah, we heard," Stein said.

"Jake, do me a favor," Saksis said.

"What?"

"Sit up there on the platform with your back facing the wall."

"Why?"

"Please."

Stein perched on the platform's edge. "Want me to really back up against the wall?"

"No, just stay where you are." She came around in front and faced him, then glanced up at an empty target hook that dangled behind him, a foot over his head. "What about this, Jake? Whoever shot Pritchard is standing where I am. Pritchard is sitting where you are. They're arguing. It's dark here, quiet, all the sound-absorbing materials taking care of that. Whoever killed him made a point of getting him down here because of the circumstances and surroundings. *Or,* maybe Pritchard suggested it because *he* intended to kill the other person. Either way, he's sitting just like you. I pull out a .22 revolver and shoot him in the chest. He leans forward and clutches at the wound. I'm not sure which way he's going to fall but I see the empty hook, slide it forward the short distance needed to reach his body and jam it under his jacket collar. The point had come right through the fabric, remember?"

"Yeah, I read the report."

Saksis looked at Harrison. "But what happens then?" she asked.

"What do you mean?" Harrison asked.

"Would the body, supported by the hook, naturally slide forward until it reached the target down the trolley?"

"Probably not," Harrison responded. "The trolley's level with the ceiling. Everything moves electronically. I control it from the firing station."

She looked at Stein.

He jumped down from the platform. "Don't get ideas," he said. "The suit's new."

Saksis laughed, turned to Harrison, and asked, "Do you have a bulletproof vest down here?"

"Sure."

Ten minutes later Jacob Stein had removed his jacket and replaced it with the vest, and was again sitting on the edge of the platform. Saksis climbed up behind him and brought the target hook to where it could be attached to the portion of the vest behind his neck. She did it, then said to Stein, "Go ahead and dangle. Slip off the edge."

"Come on, Chris, this is—"

"Please."

"Okay. Just make sure I get a letter of commendation in my file."

Saksis and Harrison watched as Stein allowed his body to hang from the hook. His feet barely touched the ground. Slowly, the hook on the trolley started to slide forward, dragging Stein along with it. They followed him until he came to rest against the paper target Harrison would use for the first firing range demonstration that morning.

Harrison helped Stein down and handed him his suit jacket. "Maybe," Stein said, "but so what?"

"Thanks, Paul," Saksis said. "Really appreciate it."

When they were back in Ranger, Stein again asked her what point she'd made.

"It makes it less bizarre and crazy," she said, "for someone to go to the trouble of hanging him up there. It wasn't any trouble."

"True."

"And, it means we don't rule out a woman."

"I didn't know we had."

"Not literally, but there's always been that question in my mind whether a woman was capable of hoisting him up onto that hook. Now we know there's no hoisting involved. I did it. Any woman could."

Stein smiled and put his feet up on the desk again. "Got one in mind?" he asked.

"No, but it's nice to know there won't be any discrimination based upon sex in this case. Thanks, Jake. You're a trouper."

Ross Lizenby arrived an hour later. Saksis asked if she could see him. "In a half hour," he said brusquely.

Thirty minutes later she sat in his office and filled him in on what she and Jake Stein had done that morning on the firing range. He looked at her blankly.

"It resolves the question of whether it had to be a man to hook Pritchard up to the trolley," she said. "And, it explains why anyone, man *or* woman, would have bothered. It wasn't difficult."

"Yeah, okay. What else have you got?"

She debated telling him about her dinner with Joe Carter and decided to. "Sounds like a waste of time," Lizenby said.

"I don't think it was. I learned a little about George Pritchard, what made him tick."

"I knew what made him tick. I worked with him."

"I know that but—"

"Why didn't you ask me about him instead of Joe Carter? We're supposed to keep this inside Ranger."

"Ross, I was told to follow whatever leads I felt might be fruitful."

"Fine, fine. What else?"

"Pritchard's .22. Where is it?"

"I don't know. It wasn't in any of his effects."

"Why?"

"How the hell do I know? Check it out."

"I will. I also wonder where that elaborate disguise and makeup kit Barry Croft mentioned ended up."

Lizenby shrugged.

Joe Perone knocked. "I talked to Hans Loeffler again," he said. "He admits he disappeared for an hour that night, claims he found an empty office with a couch and took a nap because he wasn't feeling well."

"Do you buy it?" Lizenby asked.

"Sounds reasonable enough," replied Perone. "I just wish he'd told me up front."

Perone left and Saksis was about to follow.

"Dinner?" Lizenby asked.

Just as though nothing had happened between them.

"I don't think so," she said.

"Why? Is your friend in town?"

"No."

"Then let's have dinner. I'm sorry if I've been testy this morning. There's a lot on my mind."

"I can understand that." She paused. "Okay."

"Let's make it late, around eight. I don't see getting out of here before then."

"That's fine with me."

"Want to stay at my place, or yours?"

"Ross, I—let's just plan on dinner."

"Oh, come on, Chris, get rid of the pout. It's not becoming."

"I'm not—dinner at eight. I'll talk to you later."

*   *   *

Saksis kept calling Helen Pritchard all afternoon but didn't get an answer until seven that evening.

"Mrs. Pritchard, this is Christine Saksis from the bureau."

"Yes?"

"Your husband had a .22 caliber revolver registered to him."

"He did?"

"You didn't know that?"

Helen Pritchard laughed. "Oh, sure, I forgot. George bought it for me because I was alone so much."

"You had it at home?"

"That's right. But it disappeared."

"Disappeared?"

"Yup. One day it was gone."

"How long ago?"

"Must be a year at least."

"You never reported it?"

"I told George. He said he'd take care of it."

"And? What did he do?"

"I have no idea. I never gave it another thought until now."

"I see. Thanks. I take it the bureau people with you have been recalled."

"Yes, thank God. Things are back to normal around here again."

"That must be a relief. Thanks again."

Lizenby stopped by Saksis's office at eight. "Another fifteen minutes, okay?"

He was no sooner gone than her phone rang. It was Bill Tse-ay. "I tried you at home but no luck. Thought I'd take a chance at the office."

"I was just on my way out, Bill."

"Putting in overtime, huh?"

"Yes. It's been this way since—well, it doesn't matter. You're in town?"

"Uh huh. I got here a couple of hours ago. Had dinner yet?"

"No. As a matter of fact, that's where I was going when you called."

"Damn. I should have called earlier. Any chance of getting out of it?"

"No, Bill, it's—it involves a case I'm on. How about tomorrow?"

"Sounds good. I'm staying at the Gralyn on N Street."

"Free for lunch?"

"No. I'm tied up with some people from Interior. I'll call you later in the afternoon and we'll set something up."

"Fine. I'm glad you're here."

"So am I. We have a lot of catching up to do."

Saksis and Lizenby went to Suzanne's, a noisy but pleasant café that Chris Saksis liked when she was in the mood for something light. They stood around the downstairs take-out section until a table was available, then went up a narrow staircase to the restaurant, where they had a cold platter of smoked chicken and beef fillet with herbed mayonnaise, two individual portions of cold pasta with pesto, and a bottle of white wine. Lizenby was in good spirits, more gregarious than usual. He was affectionate during dinner, frequently holding her hand across the table and complimenting her. "You have such a great smile," he said.

"So do you, but you don't use it enough," she said.

He appeared to be hurt at her comment, then broke into a wide grin. "Yeah, I suppose I don't. It's the Scandinavian in me."

He talked a little about his childhood in Seattle, about his father, who he characterized as humorless and unbending, in contrast to his mother, a nervous, giddy woman who he remembered as always laughing. "She had to placate the old man all the time," he said. "She was good at it, which was good for me. It took the edge off."

Chris knew he'd been married once and that it had ended in divorce. She'd asked on a couple of occasions about it, but he offered little: "It didn't work," or, "We were too young," or, "It was a mistake we caught in time." When she asked where his former wife was now, he shrugged and said, "I don't know and I don't care."

Over coffee he brought up the question of where they'd stay

85

that night. To Chris the question was not *where* to stay but whether to spend the night with him at all. Until dinner, she had been determined not to, but now . . . it was a tough decision.

"Ross, would you mind terribly if we didn't stay together tonight? I really need time at the apartment to catch up on some personal things."

She searched his face for a sign of anger or disappointment, but saw neither. Instead, he smiled, took her hand, and said, "Of course I don't mind. We both need some time alone. I'm just glad we had a chance for dinner together. I miss you."

His words touched her. She squeezed his hand and said, "I miss you, too."

"You know what I'd like to do when this Pritchard mess is resolved?"

"What?"

"Go away together for a couple of weeks, maybe Mexico, Europe, just the two of us."

"Sounds wonderful. I've got lots of vacation time accrued."

"So do I. Let's plan on it."

They returned to the Hoover Building to pick up her car. He took her in his arms and kissed her with an urgency to which she readily responded. "I love you," he said.

He'd said it before, very early in their relationship, but hadn't for a while. The first time he'd said it she found it strange, unsettling. They'd only been out together twice, a concert and dinner, and a party for a friend who'd retired from the Interior Department. It was so premature, and it caused her to wonder at his stability. But those doubts quickly dissipated and she enjoyed hearing him speak those words to her. Now, after a period of time during which they'd not been said, she reveled in hearing them again, and returned the kiss with equal fervor.

"See you in the office," he said. "Have anything on for tomorrow night?"

"Yes, I do."

"What?"

She would question herself all the way home why she lied to him. She had her reasons—not wanting to break the pleasant mood of the evening, not wanting to upset him—but none of it served to justify her actions. She told him that she was getting together with a college friend.

"Who?" he asked.

"Oh, you don't know her. Her name is Laurie."

"Well, have fun. See you in the morning."

She didn't see the hardness return to his face as she drove off. All she knew was that she'd been stupid to lie to—to a man with whom she'd fallen in love.

She called him when she got home to tell him the truth, but there was no answer. She tried a few more times, the last call at one in the morning. He wasn't home.

By the time she arrived at the office the next day, the compulsion to correct the lie was gone. Maybe it was better to let it go, chalk it up as a prudent white lie that could be corrected later on, in the proper setting and when the mood was conducive. There was also a parallel resentment that had developed by the time she awoke that morning. The reason she'd lied was that he'd established an atmosphere in which the truth—that kind of truth—was unacceptable.

They'd have to talk about that one day soon.

12

SAKSIS SPENT THE morning analyzing the results of calls around the country to exchanges with the first three numbers listed next to R.K. in Pritchard's phone book. It didn't turn up much—most calls reached housewives or small businesses. There was one, however, that interested her, the Hotel Inter-Continental in New York City.

She called, was put through to an assistant manager, and asked whether a Raymond Kane had recently been a guest. He had not. Saksis asked whether their computers could run a program in which all guests with the initials R.K. would be highlighted. "Of course," she was told. "I'll get back to you this afternoon."

The return call came in at four. The assistant manager expressed some concern at releasing guest information. Saksis said she understood but explained that this was a murder investigation and that a subpoena could be issued. The assistant manager said that they saw no need for that and were happy to cooperate with the FBI.

The list contained about fifty names, with addresses, phone numbers, and the occupation or business affiliation that had been listed on the sign-in card. It covered all registrations over the past six months, but Saksis was assured that if it became necessary to go back farther, that could be accomplished, too. She had Barbara Twain run the names through the bureau's central computer. As she waited for the results, she dwelled on one name that was familiar to her, Richard Kneeley, a best-selling author of nonfiction books, most of which dealt with esposés of government agencies. He'd written one a few years ago based on secret documents from the Defense Department that were extremely damaging to its secret program of arming rebel armies in Africa. Kneeley had made the talk-show rounds, and Saksis remembered seeing him on the Cable News Network's "Sandy Freeman Reports." She'd been impressed. Kneeley was a smooth, confident journalist, about sixty, with a full head of silver hair and a deep voice. There was no doubt in her mind after watching the interview that he knew what he was talking about and did, indeed, have the papers upon which he'd based his book.

She called the hotel again and asked how recently Kneeley had been a guest. A few minutes later she was told, "Mr. Kneeley is a regular here, Miss Saksis. He's been in and out a lot over the past few months."

"Does he live in New York?" Saksis asked.

"No. Well, actually he does, but not the city. He lists Fire Island as home."

"I would assume that's a summer address," Saksis said.

"I would, too, but I don't have anything else."

"That's not a problem. Mr. Kneeley is certainly well known. I can check on it."

"Again, Miss Saksis, just call if there's anything else we can do for you."

"I appreciate that. Thank you."

Jacob Stein stopped in a few minutes later, closed Saksis's door, and handed her a file with *Background—Foreign Nationals In-Training—Confidential* stamped in red across the folder.

"Where'd you get this?" Chris asked.

"A friend. Just skim. I have to get it back."

What she read caused her heart to pump a little faster. The material was obviously not meant for casual perusal, or even for official bureau dissemination. It contained highly sensitive and personal information about the backgrounds of Hans Loeffler, Walter Teng, and Sergio Nariz that had been provided by the Central Intelligence Agency.

"Nice crowd, huh?" Stein said.

"Not very," said Saksis.

Loeffler, according to the report, was a neo-Nazi with strong ties to an organization known as *Stammesbruder*, an anti-Semitic group dedicated to the precept of rule by "racial brethren." Although it was not considered by the German government to be large enough to warrant active concern (the CIA likened it to America's Ku Klux Klan), there was interest in the fact that a disproportionate percentage of its members were from German law enforcement agencies. Hans Loeffler, the report said. was one of Stammesbruder's most effective recruiters.

Sergio Nariz was characterized as a "strong man" within Paraguay's military and law enforcement structure. The Washington-based Council on Hemisphere Affairs had branded him one of the most flagrant violators of human rights in Latin America. The military and police actually ruled, and thousands of Paraguayans were thought to be in prison because of their political beliefs. Nariz, claimed the report, was directly responsible for the program of identification and detention of political dissidents.

Walter Teng was considered by the CIA to hold a powerful position within the law enforcement arm of mainland China's People's Liberation Army. The "revolutionary committee" from which he'd gained his initial power was one of the strongest in the People's Republic of China. (Saksis had to smile as she read that Teng had received one of the nation's highest awards for spearheading a program to provide flyswatters to every citizen to rid the country of flies and mosquitoes. It had worked; China boasted of a fly- and mosquito-free society.)

He'd also helped stamp out political dissent in the large cities. The blood of thousands of Chinese was on his hands, according to the CIA.

All three men had previously attended the CIA's Office of Public Safety school, which, according to insiders, had little to do with public safety, focusing more on teaching the latest torture and interrogation techniques.

"Fascinating," Saksis said as she handed the file back to Stein.

"Yeah, I thought so. Hey, whatever came out of questioning Bert Doering?"

"I don't know. Ross was taking care of that personally."

"Did he talk to him?"

"I have no idea, but I'll ask."

She was going through a list of George Pritchard's personal effects when Bill Tse-ay called. They arranged to meet for dinner at the Market Inn, an eclectic seafood restaurant on E Street, beneath a highway. It offered two distinctly different rooms, a busy one with jazz music and a quiet one with dimly lit booths. She opted for the latter when she made the reservation.

Ross Lizenby had been away from Ranger for most of the day, for which Chris was grateful. She didn't want the question of where she was going that night to come up again. She knew he was in the building; she'd seen him getting into an elevator an hour ago. She packed her briefcase with papers pertaining to the Pritchard case, locked her desk drawer, and went out to where Ranger's secretaries sat. "I'm leaving," she said. "I'm going to New York Monday. I'll be back here the next morning."

"Contact?" the secretary asked, poising a pencil over a sheet of paper.

"The Hotel Inter-Continental in Manhattan for lunch and early afternoon. The Garden City field office on Long Island in the morning."

"Right. By the way, who's in charge when you and Mr. Lizenby are away?"

Saksis shrugged. "You'd better check with Mr. Lizenby."

"He's gone, too."

"Where?"

"He's been at a SPOVAC meeting most of the day, out of the building. No contact tonight, Quantico tomorrow."

"I just saw him a little while ago."

"That's all I know, Miss Saksis."

"Well, if you can't reach him, Mr. Stein will be in charge, unless Mr. Lizenby has another suggestion."

"God, it's good to see you." Bill Tse-ay sat across the booth from Chris and held her hands. "You look wonderful."

"So do you," she said, "better than ever."

They'd first met at a rally in Denver sponsored by the American Indian Movement (AIM), an organization founded to build public awareness of the American Indian's plight. Chris had been a speaker at the rally, and Bill was covering it for his father's newspaper, *Native American Times*. She'd noticed him in the crowd, tall and slender, a warm and understanding expression on a face with fine features and liquid brown eyes. He was of American Indian parentage, no question about that, but there was an absence of typical Indian features that she found interesting. She assumed that one of his parents had been white, but found out otherwise later. They'd both been Apache.

His father had had little formal education. He'd found work with a newspaper that was published in a town adjacent to his reservation, starting as a handyman and messenger, carrying materials to and from the printer, cleaning offices, and acting as a part-time chauffeur. The publisher took a liking to him and suggested he report news from the reservation in the paper. Bill's father was amused at the notion that he could report anything, but the publisher encouraged him to try, and he started a monthly column, with considerable editorial help from the newspaper's staff. He was bright and soon needed little help preparing the column.

One day the publisher took him aside and announced that

the readers weren't happy having a column on Indian affairs in the paper. A few advertisers had threatened to pull their advertising unless the column was dropped. "I have to listen to them," the publisher said. "I'm sorry, but I have an idea. Why not start your own newspaper devoted strictly to American Indian news and issues?" He offered to bankroll Tse-ay in return for a percentage of revenues. Tse-ay agreed and founded the paper that his son inherited upon his death.

Native American Times had never been a financial success, although it always managed to break even. It had few advertisers; its major income came from foundations and from funds the younger Bill Tse-ay could "steal" from federal grants to other American Indian programs. The publication was not popular with federal officials. Under Bill's leadership, it had become a strident and dedicated champion of the Indian's place in American society, and its editorials were often scathing attacks on the Bureau of Indian Affairs, Congress, the White House, and any other bureaucracy that worked against what he considered fair treatment for his people.

Bill Tse-ay's personality belied his fervent dedication to his cause. He was quiet, soft-spoken, even shy with most people. He'd attended Northwestern University, where he majored in journalism, and had received a master's degree from Columbia in the same field. He lived modestly on the Apache reservation outside of Phoenix, Arizona, and drove a battered Mercury station wagon. His wardrobe consisted of a dozen pairs of chino pants, drip-dry blue chambray shirts, and a couple of sports jackets, all purchased with his only department store credit card—Sears, Roebuck. He carried a gold American Express card issued to American Indian Times, Inc.

"So, tell me everything that's happened to you for the past six months," he said, laughing.

"It's not funny," Chris said. "I can sum up."

"Go ahead."

"Overworked, hate the summer heat, tennis game continues to improve and—"

"And? Who's the guy?"

"Oh"—she smiled and shook her head—"it's nothing, just a fleeting infatuation."

"It didn't sound that way on the phone."

"Well, maybe there was more to it then, but things change."

"What's his name?"

"Ross. Ross Lizenby."

"The guy from SPOVAC."

"How do you—?"

"I'm a journalist, my dear. I know everything." Her laugh was easy and genuine. "Come on, Bill, how do you know about Ross Lizenby?"

He sipped his Perrier water and leaned back, which removed his face from the circle of light shining from a red globe above them. "Chris," he said, "you know about SPOVAC's think tank in Phoenix, don't you?"

She shook her head. "No, I don't."

He came into the light again. "Yeah, they set it up about a year ago. It's inside that technological institute that opened up in '77. They've got a brain trust operating there that rents itself out for top-secret government projects."

"Fascinating, but that still doesn't explain why—"

"Your friend has been out there a lot. In fact, I tried to interview him about the murder of a teenager from the reservation. Remember? Six months ago?"

"Sure. You called when it happened. You were very upset."

"I knew her, a nice kid, typical Indian situation—an alcoholic father who beat her up for recreation, mother dead from drinking and one beating too many from whoever she was living with. Run-of-the-mill, the American Indian sit-com."

There was an edge to his voice. The plight of his people— *their* people invariably caused it. He would either become angry as he discussed it, or would cry. Chris reached out for his hand across the table and squeezed it. "You tried to interview Ross?" she said, wondering why Ross hadn't seemed to recognize Bill's name when she'd mentioned it earlier.

Bill said, "I know that SPOVAC is running its major operation out of Phoenix and I wanted to talk to somebody about what light they might shed on her murder. It sure fit the pattern of a serial murder, all the trappings. There'd been at least six others in the area, but this was the first from the reservation. There was some deviation in the M.O.—she hadn't been as brutally beaten as the others. Christ, whoever's doing it ends up carving weird symbols on their bodies. That didn't happen with Sue."

"That was her name?"

"Yeah, Sue White Cloud. Pretty thing. Anyway, I kept calling and they eventually decided I wasn't going to disappear, so they put on this FBI agent named Lizenby, Ross Lizenby."

He stopped talking and sipped his drink. She said, "And?"

"Oh, he was pleasant enough I guess, but he basically told me to get lost. Everything's 'top secret' was the message. That's about it. I just think it's ironic that I happen to know who he is."

"I get the feeling that you'd like to say more but—"

"Nothing more to be said. You say it's not going well."

"I—I have very mixed feelings these days, Bill. I like him and . . . well, maybe that's an understatement but—"

"*But*, he's an FBI man. Hey, Chris, you know what comes with that territory."

"Careful. I'm one, too."

He laughed. "What are we eating?"

They ordered red snapper soup for both of them, a combination seafood platter for her, broiled bluefish for him from the four-page menu. They talked during the meal about many things—the worsening plight of the American Indian under the Reagan administration, baseball, the stories Bill was pursuing for his newspaper, Washington gossip, the weather, and a dozen other topics. He eventually asked about the murder of special agent George L. Pritchard.

"I really can't say much about it," she said. "You know, it's—"

"Top secret. I think that's what bothered me most about you joining an organization like the FBI. It's closed. I like openness."

She could see the beginning of an old and familiar argu-

95

ment, the one that eventually wedged them apart. She sighed and pushed a few scallops around on her plate. "Bill," she said, "you do know how I feel about you, don't you?"

"Sure."

"Seriously. I love you very much."

"Like a brother."

"Yes. And in other ways, too."

"That was a long time ago."

"Not so long."

"Too long. Tell me more about Ross Lizenby. He worked for Pritchard in SPOVAC, right?"

She nodded and frowned.

"Hey, Chris, I don't write about the FBI. I write about American Indians. Remember?"

"Bill, I just can't discuss it."

He shrugged. "I'm curious, like millions of other people. Think about it, a special agent of the Federal Bureau of Investigation is murdered in the J. Edgar Hoover Building in front of two hundred witnesses. Can you imagine what—"

"There weren't two hundred witnesses. There weren't *any* witnesses."

"Whatever. At any rate, the story was played up big all over the world. Are you working on it, directly, I mean?"

"Please."

"With Lizenby?"

She leaned over the table and said, "My only assignment is to play the token American Indian special agent."

"Hooray for a little basic honesty. They do use you, you know."

"And I used them, Bill. Besides, there are almost forty of us within the bureau now."

"That many? That's a good story."

"Maybe it is. Want to talk about that? I'm ready."

"Another time. Right now I'm torn by internal debate."

"Over what?"

"Over whether to fight for the woman I love, to attempt to rekindle the old flames, or to bow out graciously and congratulate the better man."

She giggled. "It wouldn't work. Remember? Two different worlds."

"The same world—savages, redskins, selling scalps for bounty."

"Are you sure that's Perrier water you're drinking?"

"It ain't firewater, dearie," he said. "Us injuns don't tolerate whiskey too good."

"You haven't changed."

"And you have. I wish *we* hadn't."

"But we did. I have to call it a night, my dear brother and friend. I have a long, tough weekend of paperwork, and I'll be leaving first thing Monday for New York."

"What's going on up there?"

"Routine. Do I get to treat, or would that represent compromising a journalist?"

"If you were with the Bureau of Indian Affairs, I'd decline, but since you're with an agency I don't cover, I accept."

"What's new at BIA?" she asked when they'd reached the parking lot.

"Nothing much. They're solving the American Indian problem by cutting every program that keeps us alive. Another couple of years and they'll be out of business because there won't be any American Indians."

She drove him to the Gralyn Hotel.

"Any chance of enticing you upstairs?" he asked.

"No."

She slid close and embraced him, accepted his kiss, but stiffened when his hand found a breast beneath her cotton dress.

"Sorry," he said.

"Don't be. Will I see you again before you go back?"

"You'd better. When will you be back from New York?"

"Late Monday night."

"Breakfast the next day?"

"Sure, why not?" She thought of Lizenby and their breakfasts together, almost begged off, then decided to stick with what she'd said.

He was halfway out of the car when he turned and said, "I forgot to tell you, Chris. We got six more computers."

"That's marvelous." She'd worked with him to find funding to equip the school on his reservation with a couple of computers for the kids. It hadn't been easy, but they'd finally raised enough money to purchase two.

"Yeah, I got the computer manufacturer to spring this time. You know, good PR for them, all that stuff. They'll be coming in next week."

"Congratulations," she said.

"Now all we need is food, doctors, housing—"

"I know. Good night, Bill."

13

SAKSIS'S EASTERN SHUTTLE flight to LaGuardia Airport arrived in New York a little after eight. She picked up a rental car, checked a map, and headed for Garden City, on Long Island, where one of the bureau's 416 resident agency offices was located.

The special agent in charge of the Garden City office, Terry Finch, was waiting for her with fresh coffee and Danish pastries. He was a big, pleasant man with sparkling blue eyes and pronounced jowls, someone who'd feel at home in an authentic Irish bar. "What can I do for you?" he asked once they were seated in his office.

"I'm not really sure," Saksis said. "I'm trying to get a handle on George Pritchard, what he was like, who his contacts were before he was killed, his activities leading up to the day of his death, anything that might help."

"Let me give you what little input I can on George Pritchard. Of course, he left this office a long time ago."

"A year."

Finch laughed. "That's a long time for some people, especially guys like George. He never was comfortable staying with one assignment too long."

"So I've heard. He must have hated being assigned to SPO-VAC."

"That's right. Once he wrapped up his work here, he wanted to head on to another undercover operation. He balked at going to headquarters, but Director Shelton wouldn't budge."

"Tell me about the undercover project he worked on out of this office."

"Tricky assignment, but he seemed to thrive on it. The terrorist group originated somewhere up in Vermont, but it moved down here to Long Island when things got too hot up in New England. We knew they'd set up some base of operations here but didn't know much more than that. George came in from San Francisco and established a cover. He played the disgruntled former military adviser who was looking to sell weapons to Third World countries."

"Or to a terrorist group."

"Whoever had the money. It took him about six months to make the contact. Once he did, he moved fast. Unfortunately, some details got screwed up and we lost convictions on most of the group's leaders; but it did disrupt them."

Saksis glanced at notes she'd made on the plane, then asked, "Who was his main contact in the group?"

"I'd have to pull the file on that."

"We can do that later," she said. "What I'm *really* looking for is the name of someone from that organization with whom George Pritchard might have kept in touch right up to the night he was murdered."

"I wouldn't have any knowledge of that," Finch said.

"The terrorist organization. Where on Long Island?"

"Up on the north shore mostly, Roslyn, Manhasset, Port Washington. They rented a big house in Roslyn. At least that's where they were when George made his move."

A tiny smile crossed Saksis's face. "You know, Mr. Finch, you're the first person I've talked to who calls Pritchard 'George.' There's a certain affection in the way you say it."

Finch smiled. "Yeah, I know, he was a son-of-a-bitch, a foul ball who didn't get along with anybody, but I liked him—even though the feeling wasn't reciprocated. I admired George Pritchard. Maybe I envied his freedom. I've spent my FBI career behind a desk, which suited me, I suppose, suited the wife and six kids. I retire in three years and I've never fired my gun except on a range."

"I hope I can say the same," said Saksis.

"I'm not complaining. It's just that people like George and the other Unkempts are what we envisioned ourselves being when we joined up. Anyway, I really don't know much about the contacts George made in the terrorist group. Everything was close to the vest with him."

"How about others in this office? Anybody get close to him?"

Finch nodded. "One of our agents worked directly with him on the Roslyn Project. That's what it was called, by the way. His name's Bill Dawkins, a Young Turk who butted heads with George, damn near got booted because of it."

"Really? I'd like to talk to him."

"I told him you were coming. He said he'd be back before noon. What are your plans?"

"I was going to have lunch in the city. There are some possible links to the case there. While I'm waiting for Mr. Dawkins, is there anyone else I can talk to?"

"Who knew George? I don't think so. This is a small office. They come and go depending on specific cases. No, Dawkins is your best bet."

"I'll wait."

"Fine."

She took a walk and browsed in the elegant shops along Garden City's Franklin Avenue. Every once in a while a pretty dress in a window or a passing face on the street captured her interest, but her thoughts never strayed far from the purpose of her visit to Long Island. It occurred to her that the more she learned about George Pritchard, the more enigmatic he became, especially in light of the prevailing philosophy of the bureau—that it was a team, with little room for individuality.

Obviously, Pritchard didn't fit that mold. It was as though he worked for an agency within an agency, and under a different set of rules.

As she returned to the Garden City office, she found herself wondering why Pritchard would have been the one chosen to administer SPOVAC. It was fairly common knowledge that Director Shelton didn't like him. Too, he'd never had administrative experience within the bureau. It just didn't make sense. She made a mental note to pursue the question when she got back to Washington.

Bill Dawkins was of medium height and well built. Saksis pegged him at about thirty-five, although he could have been younger. He wore a nicely cut but inexpensive brown suit with a subtle stripe in it, white buttondown shirt, and muted green paisley tie. His sandy hair was short—almost a crew cut. He wore a wide gold wedding ring, which drew attention to nails that were chewed to the quick.

"Feel like some lunch?" Saksis asked after they'd been introduced by Terry Finch.

"I have a date," he said, "but it's not for an hour. If you want a drink, we can go where I'm meeting the person."

"Fine with me," Saksis said. She'd intended to be in the city by noon but decided to stay with Dawkins. She followed him in her rented car until they passed a sign that read *Village of Roslyn—Historic District*, then proceeded up a busy, narrow road that led to a restaurant called the Jolly Fisherman. Dawkins turned into the parking lot, and Saksis followed. The parking valet greeted Dawkins by name. "Hello, Richie," Dawkins said. "Take care of her."

They went to the bar. "Hello, Mr. Dawkins," the bartender said. "The usual?"

"Yeah, George, thanks." He didn't introduce Saksis. She ordered a club soda with lime. Dawkins downed half his martini, smacked his lips, and said to her, "Finch says you want to talk about Pritchard."

"That's right."

"What about him?"

"Whatever you want to tell me. I understand you worked closely with him on the terrorist case here on Long Island."

Dawkins guffawed and finished the drink. "Nobody worked closely with George Pritchard," he said. "Look, I know you're working with Ranger and trying to find out who killed him, but I'll be honest with you. I hated the bastard, and whoever killed him ought to get a recommendation in his file."

Saksis allowed what he'd said to sink in. She looked around the bar—most tables were taken. A couple of men had acknowledged Dawkins as they came in, but he'd ignored them. Dawkins was obviously a regular here. Had he used the establishment as a base of operations during the terrorist investigation? Agents often did, meeting people at bars and restaurants, becoming familiar faces in communities, hanging around until they were accepted—and trusted.

This was not the sort of place where terrorists congregated. It was too genteel, too middle-class. But, if she were trying to establish herself as a disgruntled high-roller and former member of the military establishment, she might try it here.

Then again, she realized, Dawkins might simply have latched on to the Jolly Fisherman as a watering hole and pleasant spot to have lunch.

"You come here often?" she asked.

"No."

"They all seem to know you."

"That's *their* business."

The bartender served him his second drink.

"Why did you hate Pritchard so?" she asked.

He didn't hesitate. "Because he tried to railroad me out of the bureau."

"Why?"

"Read the file."

"I'll do that when I get back, but that'll only represent his version."

"It doesn't matter," he said, drinking again. "I'm leaving anyway."

"Oh? Because of George Pritchard?"

103

"No, because the FBI is a sham."

She wasn't sure how to react, decided to keep asking questions. "Why do you say that?"

He swiveled around on his bar stool and faced her. "The FBI sells one thing to the public, deals another way with its own people. I was really gung-ho when I applied, worked my ass off at Quantico, put in twenty hours a day on my first assignments. You know what that does to a marriage?"

"I can imagine."

"I gave it everything I had. You know the result? A wife and two kids down the drain, a ton of debt, and a lousy letter in your file that gives them the right to walk all over you."

"All because of George Pritchard?"

"Yeah, Pritchard, with the blessing of Shelton and Gormley, and the other fat cats who don't know what the . . . Ah, look, I'm not out to spill on you. You like working here, that's your business. All I know is I'm getting out."

"Does Mr. Finch know that?"

"Nope. I plan to tell him tonight. We're having dinner. Finch is a good guy, only he's too used to shuffling papers and counting the days to retirement. I've got a new wife and a new job with a private security agency. Screw the FBI."

Saksis started to say something, but he interrupted. "What's the real story on Pritchard getting it? Who's the smart money on?"

"No bets so far."

It was a sardonic laugh. "You know something, Miss Saksis, I don't feel even a twinge of sadness that the son-of-a-bitch got it. I've met a lot of people in my life who I didn't like, including real scum, but nobody was as bad as George L. Pritchard. The worst thing was that he was such a goddamn phoney, the dedicated agent of the Federal Bureau of Investigation who wasn't above selling out his own mother if it put a buck in his pocket."

"I'm sorry, Mr. Dawkins, but you're presenting a side of him that doesn't match up with what I've learned. I know he wasn't personally popular, but everyone I've talked to claims he was a dedicated and principled special agent."

"That's your decision to make."

"Yes, it is. How close did you work with him on the terrorist case?"

"Damn close. He gave me all the dirty work, then turned around and slammed me with an unfavorable evaluation. It was worse than that. He went down to Washington and demanded that I be dismissed with prejudice."

"On what grounds?"

"Incompetence, insubordination, gross negligence, you name it." When she didn't respond, he said, "Did I deserve it? Who cares? I've got a nice job lined up, and the bureau, the precious bureau, can take Pritchard's evaluation of me and shove it."

"I'm sorry you're so bitter," Saksis said.

"I'm not bitter. I just got smart, that's all."

"Before I go, could you tell me about the terrorist group Pritchard infiltrated?"

"It's all on paper."

"A contact. My information is that he maintained a contact inside that group, that it was linked in some way with Paraguay, and that the contact he kept might have been in Washington the day he was murdered."

"Impossible," Dawkins said.

"Why?"

"His contact—the one who blew it open for him—is dead. Pritchard arranged it."

"He killed his contact?"

"Maybe, maybe one of his people."

"What people?"

"The army."

She paused, then said, "I'm sorry, but I don't understand. The army?"

"The Unkempts, the dirty dozen. Come on, you know about them."

"No, I don't, I really don't."

Dawkins finished his drink, put his glass on the bar. "Ask your boss about it," he said.

"My boss?"

"Lizenby. He's one."

She was about to ask another question when a tall platinum blonde approached them. Dawkins stood and kissed her. The blonde gave Saksis a "Who the hell are you" look.

"Chris Saksis," Saksis said, extending her hand.

"This is Carol. It was good to see you," Dawkins said. He reached in his pocket and handed her a business card: WILLIAM P. DAWKINS—SPECIAL INVESTIGATOR. The name of a private detective agency was below it.

"Thanks," Saksis said as she got up and prepared to leave. "Nice meeting you, Carol."

"Likewise," Carol said.

Chris drove directly into Manhattan, parked in a lot on Forty-eighth Street across from the Hotel Inter-Continental, and entered the large, sprawling lobby that was dominated by an elaborate bird cage beneath a huge Tiffany glass skylight. She stopped to admire the exotic birds, then went to the information desk, where she was directed to the administrative offices. The same assistant manager with whom she'd spoken on the phone came out of her office and asked, "Was anyone expecting you?"

"No," Saksis said. "I'd originally intended to not bother anyone officially and just spend a little time downstairs, but I thought better of it. Could we talk in your office?"

Saksis showed the assistant manager a photo of George Pritchard she'd brought with her. "What I'd like to do is show this to the people on your staff who have public contact to see if anyone remembers him being here recently."

"That's no problem. Where would you like to start?"

"The restaurants, I suppose, the bar, the front desk."

"I'll send our PR director with you to smooth the way."

A few minutes later, accompanied by a personable young blond woman named Linda Kam, Saksis started making the rounds. They started in the bar, a handsome masculine room with aubergine suede on the walls, large leather chairs, and plush velvet semicircular banquettes. It had the distinct feeling of a private club; men in dark business suits spoke in hushed tones over drinks. The bartender and waitresses looked at the

106

photo of Pritchard and shook their heads. "He looks pretty much like everybody else who comes in here," said the bartender.

They moved on to La Recolte, the hotel's four-star and spectacularly decorated *nouvelle cuisine* restaurant, where people lingered over late lunches in Mozartean splendor. None of the staff recognized Pritchard, so they went to the third restaurant in the hotel, the oak-paneled Barclay, where they met with the same result. It wasn't until they'd joined dozens of well-dressed men and women on the Terrace that the photograph brought a spark of recognition. It was an older waiter in a black tux who carefully positioned half-glasses on his nose, squinted, and adjusted the photo to catch just the right light. "Sure," he said, "I've served him. I think he had a moustache and glasses, but I recognize the eyes and the ears."

"Eyes and ears?" Saksis asked.

"Yeah. You get to notice those things dealing with people all the time. I've been here thirty years." He began to recount experiences, when Linda Kam pleasantly interrupted him. "Is there anything else you'd like to ask?" she said to Saksis.

Saksis looked at the waiter. "Do you recall the circumstances when you saw him—the time, date, who he was with?"

The waiter frowned. "Let me see. I'd say it was late afternoon. No, no, now I remember, it was late at night. They came in here, took a seat over there by the piano, and ordered a Blanton's for him, a—I can't remember what she had. Might have been—"

"Blanton's?" Saksis asked.

"Bourbon, the best. Expensive though. That's why I remember him ordering it. It's not that popular because it costs so much."

"You said he was with a woman."

"Yes, nice-looking gal, tall, good figure. I notice those things. Good-looking woman with lots of red hair." He laughed. "I've seen lots of redheads here over thirty years, but this one was—" He suddenly appeared to be embarrassed. "Maybe I shouldn't be—"

Saksis said, "Could you describe her in more detail for me?"

107

He shrugged. "Sure. Let's see, very pale skin, milky-white like redheads usually have, tall, dressed like a million bucks. He tipped good. I remember a ring she was wearing, took up half her finger, great big oval-shaped diamond with little rubies around it. He went for big bucks on that."

Chris asked the waiter, "Did you hear the red-headed woman talk at all?"

"Yes, I did. I like talking with my customers, establishing a rapport because—"

"Was she southern?" Saksis asked.

He grinned. "I was just about to say that. I think she was, had a little bit of an accent like that."

"One more thing," Saksis said. "Do you know the author, Richard Kneeley?"

"Sure, he practically lives here," the waiter said.

"Was the man in the photo ever with him? Did you ever serve them together?"

"No. I'd remember if I did. I serve Mr. Kneeley all the time. He's a good man. He always tells me I should write a book about my experiences here. I will some day. He said he'd help me."

"But you've never seen them together?" Saksis said.

"No, ma'am, I don't think so."

"What about the red-headed woman?"

He shook his head. "I've only seen her once, with the man in the picture. Just once."

"Was she a guest?"

"I don't know."

"Was he?"

"I wouldn't know that, either. He didn't sign the check. He paid cash."

There were two messages on her answering machine when she arrived back at her apartment that night, one from Bill Tse-ay asking where they would meet for breakfast, the other from Ross Lizenby asking the same thing. She returned Bill's call first and said, "I'm sorry, Bill, but something came up while I was in New York that fouls up tomorrow. I have to cancel."

He didn't try to hide his disappointment.

"Let me square things away," she said, "and I'll get back to you later tomorrow. We'll find some time, I promise."

There was no answer at Lizenby's apartment until eleven. He was brusque, almost angry.

"Is something wrong?" she asked.

"No. What about breakfast. Usual place?"

"Yes, usual place."

"Feel like company?" he asked.

"Now? No, Ross, I'm beat."

"What happened in New York? Why didn't you tell me you were going?"

"Because you weren't around. I'll fill you in tomorrow morning."

14

ROSS LIZENBY CALLED Chris Saksis as she was leaving her apartment the next morning. "Let's break the habit," he said pleasantly. "I made a reservation at Joe and Mo's. See you there."

The steak house had only recently begun catering to the increasingly popular Washington "business breakfast," but it was almost filled to capacity when Saksis arrived. She was led to a table against the far wall, where Ross was already seated. He stood, kissed her cheek, and held out a chair.

"Breakfast with the high and the mighty," she said, looking around the room and recognizing familiar faces from politics and the media. "What made you decide to come here?"

He smiled and covered her hand on the table. "I just think we've gotten into a rut, Chris, and I'd like to get out of it—for *our* sake."

She was on guard. He was so unpredictable, so up or down, angry one moment, charming and loving the next. She certainly preferred the latter mood but found herself increasingly ready to defend against the swing that was almost sure to follow.

"You know what I think," he said.

"What?"

"I think we should chuck everything next weekend and go away, maybe down to the shore or even up to New York, catch some theater, a couple of good dinners, just relax and get off this treadmill."

"It sounds appealing but—"

"Then let's do it. Look, Chris, I know that I've been neglecting you lately, but it doesn't represent how I feel. That's why I want some time together, time alone so that we can discover each other and see where we're headed."

When she didn't immediately respond favorably, he said, "Maybe you'd rather make it a tennis weekend, some sauna time, sweat out all the crap that gets in our way."

"Are you talking about *this* weekend?"

"Yes."

She wanted to say yes, the idea of getting away was immensely appealing. She looked into eyes that were disconcertingly boyish. He was right, of course, that if they were ever to find out about each other, and whether a deeper relationship was in the cards, they'd need to get away from the tensions of the investigation and of working together. She wanted to know where they stood, if only to avoid a time down the road when she'd regret not having given it a running chance. His unpredictable actions over the past few days could be chalked up to the pressures and responsibilities of his job. She had to give him that benefit of the doubt. Besides, when he was like he was at that moment, any cognitive analysis of the situation was short-circuited by a pure rush of emotion, a tiny internal switch tripping off the conduit to the head and opening a valve to the heart.

Still . . .

He seemed to recognize it was prudent to back off and to let her think about it a while. He picked up a menu and said, "Whatever happened to breakfast?" There was the "Dave Butz Breakfast," a twenty-ounce steak and ten eggs for $32, and a "George Starke Stack," twenty large pancakes for $15.

111

They settled on smaller steaks and two eggs for him, an omelette for her.

"Tell me about New York," he said. "Who did you see up there?"

"A couple of people." She told him about Terry Finch, Bill Dawkins, and the Hotel Inter-Continental. He listened intently, an occasional nod or grunt his only response. "I have a couple of questions for *you*, Ross,"

"Shoot."

"Why did they choose George Pritchard to head up SPO-VAC? Director Shelton didn't like him, and Pritchard had no interest or experience in administration."

Lizenby shrugged and sat back as a waiter delivered their juice and coffee. "He was one of the best undercover people in the bureau," he said, then added with a chuckle, "The Peter Principle at work."

"Could there have been another reason?" Saksis asked.

"Like what?"

"I don't know, but I can't get rid of the question. Did Director Shelton want him in headquarters to keep him close, to keep an eye on him?"

"I doubt it, but it doesn't matter, does it? Drink your juice."

She picked up her glass and looked at him over it. He dismissed what she'd said too quickly. She decided to go on to another topic. He obviously wasn't about to offer more on that subject.

"Ross, what do you know about Richard Kneeley?"

"The writer? Nothing."

"He must have a substantial file with us considering some of the books he's done in the past."

"Probably does. Why do you ask?"

She explained what she'd come up with so far.

"Doesn't fly for me, Chris. I'd suggest we concentrate on more viable things." He said it with an edge to his voice that stung her. She decided to drop that line of inquiry, too, and to simply proceed with her own background check on Kneeley. She asked about the CIA liaison, Bert Doering.

"Nothing there. There's no link."

Finally, when they were well into their food, she asked, "What do you know about Pritchard and Rosemary Cale?" He was about to bring a forkful of food to his mouth. He slowly lowered it to the plate and sighed, like an impatient parent. "Chris, what does that have to do with the case?"

She, too, lowered her fork. "They'd had an affair, and she was in the building the night he was murdered."

"That affair was over long ago. Are you suggesting that she's a suspect?"

"I didn't realize that *anyone* had been ruled out."

"I'm not ruling her out, Chris, I'm just saying that there are better places to direct energy. That affair was over long ago."

"You're sure of that?"

"Yeah, I'm sure. George talked to me about it. Besides, it wasn't some full-blown thing they were into. She was one of many. What brings her up? Oh, the woman that waiter said was with Pritchard, the redhead. Pritchard was partial to redheads. Drop it."

"Every point I've brought up this morning you've waved away, dismissed without even a modicum of consideration. Why?"

"Because I don't have time to chase stupid leads and to run down blind alleys."

"I didn't consider these things—"

He grabbed her hand. "*This* is why we have to get away from Pritchard and the bureau and everything else except us."

She wasn't sure what to say next.

"Look, Chris, I'm sorry, but to be honest with you, I'm having a lot of trouble concentrating on Ranger. I'll be off it pretty soon."

"Oh."

"SPOVAC's been neglected since Pritchard died, and the director wants me back on it full-time, which, frankly, is fine with me."

"When?"

"Maybe next week. I have a meeting with Gormley this af-

113

ternoon to discuss it. Chances are I'll be out of town all next week if he decides to take me off Ranger."

"Who'll take over?"

"You."

"I don't want that."

"You have a choice?"

"I suppose not, but I'm beginning to resent not having choices. Where will you be going next week? Phoenix?"

"Yeah, maybe, but how do you know?"

She smiled and turned her hands outward. "Well, you used to spend a lot of time in Arizona and I know there have been a number of SPOVAC conferences out there."

"I don't know where I'll be." He started to eat again. Then he looked up and said, "That's why I want this weekend together."

"Let's talk about it later."

"Okay. Tonight. Let's have dinner and stay at my place."

She closeted herself in her office and spent an hour writing down every thought she had about the Pritchard case. The final item on her list was Rosemary Cale.

Cale was a senior laboratory technician in the bureau's fingerprint division. She certainly didn't *look* like someone at home in a laboratory. Tall, voluptuous, with a thick mane of red hair that she usually allowed to fall loose down her back and to her waist, she could easily have been mistaken for a model, or actress—anything but a highly trained and skilled researcher. She'd received her master's degree in computer science from the University of Maryland and was halfway finished with her doctoral studies at American University. Because she was so stunning, there was always the object of rumors around headquarters, including one that she was intimate with Director Shelton. All of them remained unsubstantiated rumors, except for the one about George Pritchard. She seemed to be truly smitten with him and talked openly with a few friends about their relationship. It was said that her openness was what caused Pritchard to end it, and it was the consensus that it was, indeed, over. But Saksis's conversation with the waiter at the Hotel Inter-Continental caused her to view it in a different light. She was hesitant to approach Rosemary Cale about it. They'd never been friends. In fact, Cale had made it obvious after they'd first been introduced that there would be no friendship. Comments had been passed to Saksis that Cale resented having another good-looking woman around headquarters. Saksis dismissed those remarks, but as time went by she wondered if indeed there was some truth to them.

Rosemary Cale had made an open play for Ross Lizenby, but according to office scuttlebutt, he'd walked away from her advances. Saksis knew, of course, that he'd been involved with other women from headquarters, but they didn't bother her. Rosemary Cale would have.

She decided that no matter how unpleasant approaching Cale about George Pritchard might turn out to be, it had to be done, despite Lizenby's admonition to drop it. It was a matter of three things, she decided. One, the questions had been raised in her mind. Natural curiosity was at work. Two, she had to admit to herself that *she* wanted to be the one to solve the Pritchard case, just as she'd always wanted to finish first in the track meets that brought her public attention. She was a competitor, pure and simple, and she wouldn't be comfortable with any other approach to life. And three, it was her job.

She stopped by the fingerprint labs at noon and was told that Rosemary Cale had taken a personal day, but would be in tomorrow. She left a note asking Cale to call her and returned to her office, where she ordered in something from the cafeteria and went back to sorting out her thoughts, and the information that had been collected to date. Lizenby poked his head in at four. "What about tonight?" he asked.

She hadn't thought about being together. "Sure," she said.

"I'll pick you up here at six. Feel like Japanese?"

"That'll be fine."

"Good. Oh, by the way, you might as well have this." He handed her an eight-by-ten manila envelope.

"What's in it?" she asked.

"Some more personal effects from Pritchard."

"More? Ross, why haven't these things been given to us sooner? How are we supposed to—?"

"Not to question, kid. It's junk anyway. Just put it in the safe and forget about it."

He left and she opened the envelope. Inside were a dozen scraps of paper, laundry receipts, a membership card for a San Francisco private club, a wallet-size faded and wrinkled photo of his daughter when she was quite young, two parking receipts from a Washington lot, and a parking receipt for the ferry that ran from Bay Shore, Long Island, to Fire Island dated six days before he'd been murdered.

"Damn it," she muttered as she opened the safe and placed the envelope and its contents with other materials from the Pritchard case. "I don't understand."

She wanted to talk to Lizenby about it that night, but each time she started to raise a question about Ranger and Pritchard, he shushed her with a kiss, a touch, an "I love you." Eventually, she was able to put the FBI out of her thoughts and concentrate on the pleasures at hand, the intense feelings that accompanied their lovemaking.

But after he'd fallen asleep, she sat up against the headboard and grappled with the confusion that had been there all day. Something was wrong, and she desperately wished she knew what it was.

15

SAKSIS AWOKE WITH a start the next morning. She'd forgotten to call Bill Tse-ay. She looked over at Ross, who was still asleep, quietly slid from the bed, and was halfway to the bathroom when he said playfully, "Get back here. I'm not finished."

She turned and smiled.

"God, you're beautiful," he said, sitting up and propping his head on one hand as he took in her naked body.

"Duty calls," she said as she continued to the bathroom.

He was anxious to make love again, but she dissuaded him in the interest of getting to work early. "We'll have the weekend," she said.

They had melon and coffee in his kitchen after showering and dressing. "Let's do it again tonight," he said.

"Ross, I'm not available tonight," she said. "My friend, Bill Tse-ay, is in town and I owe him some time."

He didn't look up as he said, "What the hell is this, some kind of a game?"

"Pardon?"

His eyes were cold as he focused on her face. "That's right, a goddamn game. You sleep with me, plan a weekend together, and then go off and sleep with your Apache."

"I don't believe you," she said, incredulous.

"You'd better start. I'm serious."

"I don't sleep with—he's my friend, Ross, that's all. There used to be more, but that's over, and he's not—not an Apache."

He grinned. "I thought he was. You told me he was."

"What I mean is I resent the way you said it."

"Great. And I resent being played with like this."

"I told you I'm not . . . I want to go."

"Go."

"My car's at work."

He slammed his spoon down on the table and went to the bedroom. Ten minutes later he was back. "Come on, I'm ready," he said.

They did not talk on their way to the Hoover Building, continued their silence on the way up in the elevator, and went to their respective offices without breaking it.

Saksis didn't know which emotion to play out—anger or sadness, to cry or to throw the telephone through the window. She didn't have a chance to do either because Rosemary Cale called.

"I wondered if we could find an hour together today," Saksis said.

Cale replied with a cynical laugh. "My turn, huh?"

"If you want to look at it that way," said Saksis. "Feel like stopping up here at my office?"

"No. I'd rather get out of the building."

"Fine with me. Lunch?"

"No. Why don't you stop by my apartment this afternoon."

Saksis thought of Bill Tse-ay. She was hoping he'd be free for dinner and didn't want anything to interfere with it. "What time?" she asked.

"Any time after two," she said.

"Four?"

"That'll be fine." She gave Saksis an address on N Street, in Georgetown. "Don't be late. I have an appointment at five."

"I'll be on time," Saksis said, wondering why she'd be off so early.

Rosemary Cale's slight southern accent stayed with Saksis for the rest of the day. She managed to reach Bill Tse-ay and apologized for not getting back to him the day before. They made a six o'clock date for dinner at Tandoor, in Georgetown. She had lunch in a local sandwich shop with Barbara Twain and Ray Okawa, the pathologist, who was leaving Ranger because there was nothing more for him to do on the Pritchard case.

After lunch, she went through the lastest batch of Pritchard's personal effects once again, put the Fire Island ferry ticket in her purse, and carefully read the computer print-out Barbara Twain had run on Richard Kneeley. It was long; the nature of his books had certainly brought him to the bureau's attention over the years. But there was more, a detailed section on his personal life. The report pegged him as a homosexual despite two marriages. Transcripts of conversations he'd had in hotel rooms that had been bugged by the bureau supported the homosexual allegation, although most of them dealt with mundane telephone calls concerning his business—talks with his agent, a couple of publishers and assorted friends, male and female. There was nothing in his file that touched upon government contacts he might have made to gain the classified information he used as the basis for his books.

Kneeley's politics were left of center, and there was a page in the report about his involvement years ago with a writer's group that had been branded "subversive" by the FBI.

For Saksis, however, the most important piece of information came from a list of all the books Kneeley had written. He'd used a variety of names early in his career, and one of them was Richard Kane, a pseudonym used for a series of paperback westerns. That item, coupled with the ferry ticket, helped make up her mind. She'd return to New York the next day, this time with Fire Island on her itinerary.

Rosemary Cale's apartment was on the second floor of an elegant row house on Georgetown's sedate and fashionable N Street, where the Kennedy House, a gift from Senator John F.

119

Kennedy to his wife upon the birth of their daughter, Caroline; and Cox Row, named after Georgetown mayor Colonel John Cox, who built its string of houses in 1817, stood as understated testimony to the neighborhood's gentility.

Cale's apartment was large, sunny, and tastefully furnished. She wore a powder blue terrycloth robe when she opened the door to Saksis, and was obviously in the process of getting ready for a date. She was barefoot; the ends of her red hair were still moist from the shower. Usually, Cale wore quite a bit of makeup, at least compared to Saksis. Now, there wasn't a trace of it, and the result was a naturalness that only enhanced her beauty.

"Sit down," Cale said. "You'll have to excuse me for a minute. I was in the middle of something."

"Sure," Saksis said.

"If you want somethin' to drink, it's over there. I'd offer coffee but I'm in too much of a rush. There's juice in the refrigerator, and milk. Help yourself."

"I'm fine," Saksis said. "Take your time."

Saksis took the opportunity to look around the living room. Built-in bookshelves contained an array of leather-bound editions of classics, probably from a club, she decided. The overall impression was a collection for show, rather than for reading. One wall was covered with prints in heavy frames. The furniture was obviously purchased in one swoop, as a set, a conversation pit formed by a series of modular pieces in a chocolate brown corduroy fabric. The parquet floor was partially covered with a large, authentic Oriental rug in yellow and red tones. A large piece of furniture housed a 26-inch color TV monitor, VCR, and a Sony component stereo system with a dual cassette deck and graphic equalizer. The room was, at once, tasteful, yet packaged, one call to a furniture store, a swing by a print gallery, and a fast stop at an electronics outlet—functional, comfortable, and lacking in personal touches.

Rosemary Cale returned. "Nice apartment," Saksis said.

"I like it, especially the neighborhood. The neighborhood's more important than the place, don't you agree?"

"Yes, of course. It's a pretty street."

"An *expensive* street, but it's worth it for peace of mind." Saksis sat in the conversation pit. "Rosemary, you obviously know why I'm here."

"George L. Pritchard." Cale stood in the center of the pit, hands on her ample hips, the robe falling open to her waist, giving a generous view of her milky-white breasts. "Did we have an affair? I suppose so, if a sexual fling qualifies for that nice term. How long did it last? A month, maybe two. Who broke it off? George L. Pritchard. Was I unhappy? For a day or two. Was it a satisfyin' affair? Oh, yes. The man knew what a woman likes, could sustain the interest and mood, if you get my drift."

Saksis smiled. "I think I do."

"Of course you do, a knock-out woman like you."

"Thank you. What I wanted to ask was—"

"Whether I killed George L. Pritchard. Hell, no. He wasn't *that* good." She tilted her head to one side and grinned. "Any further questions?"

"Yes."

"Ask away."

"When did the affair end?"

"Too long ago to remember."

"That long ago? The way you describe Pritchard, I'd think it would be etched into your memory."

Her laugh was raucous. "Come on, Miss Saksis, I'm sure there have been enough good men in your life to blur the dates of their comin' and goin'."

Saksis could only smile.

"See, I'm right. Look, I really have to get on the road. Maybe you didn't hear. I've resigned from the bureau."

"No, I hadn't heard that."

"Oh, yes. My time with the house that Hoover built is over. It's amazin' how much more the private sector is willin' to pay for talent."

"Congratulations."

"Thank you. So, if you don't mind, I really have to ask you to—"

"I'll go," Saksis said, "but there's one point that we haven't covered."

"Which is?"

"It's my information that you and George Pritchard were in New York together the week before he was murdered."

"That's your information?"

"Yes, at the Hotel Inter-Continental on Lexington and Forty-eighth."

"Well, Miss Saksis, your information is wrong." She gestured with her left hand to emphasize her point, flashing her oval diamond-and-ruby ring in Saksis's face.

"You're sure it is?"

"Very sure."

"The affair with Pritchard didn't continue until recently?"

"That's what I said."

"What were you doing in the Hoover Building the night he was killed?"

"Giving the Federal Bureau of Investigation another drop of blood for minimum wage. Working late. That's why I'm leaving. Too much work and not enough pay."

"I have someone in New York who'll testify that you were there with Pritchard the week before he died."

Another hearty laugh. "Then, by all means have him testify. Have we reached that point? Am I about to be accused of murder?"

Saksis shook her head and stood. "Of course not. By the way, have you ever met the author Richard Kneeley?"

Cale thought for a moment, then shook her head. "Can't say that I have, although I wouldn't mind. He's a very handsome and successful man."

Cale walked Saksis to the door. "Give my best to Ross," she said.

"Ross? Oh, of course."

"He's such a divine-looking man. You're lucky."

"Meaning what?"

It was a knowing smile between sorority sisters that formed on Cale's lips.

Saksis almost challenged her, but knew that it would only compound the embarrassment she was feeling. She asked, "Besides being good with—"

"You're referring to George?"

"Yes. Besides—"

"Besides bein' good in the sack, he was a swine. I always felt sorry for his wife and daughter."

"Did you?"

"Yes, I did. You know, Chris, I always intended to get a little closer to you, become more friendly. I'd love to know more about American Indians. I'm interested in those things."

Saksis stifled a smile. "I would have been happy to educate you," she said.

Cale pressed her index finger against her lips, removed it, and said, "I'll give you one more bit of information for your files."

"I'm listening."

"I did go to bed with Director Shelton."

Saksis looked at the floor before saying, "I really don't care about that, Rosemary."

"But I do. Between us girls, he wasn't very exciting."

Saksis wanted very much to bring up Ross Lizenby's name again, but successfully fought the urge. "Thanks for seeing me, Rosemary."

"You take care, Chris. The FBI is a dangerous place for little gals like us."

Saksis got to Tandoor an hour before Bill Tse-ay. She nursed a Pimm's cup, absently stirring it with its cucumber stick until he arrived.

"I feel as though I've been granted an audience," he said as he kissed her.

"No shtik tonight, Bill. I need a serious ear."

"Have you ever seen ears more serious than these?" he said. "You look troubled."

"You're very observant. Could we go back to my apartment instead of having dinner here? I can make something."

He smiled. "Actually, I've been in deep Apache prayer all day that we could skip dinner. I can't stand Indian food."

They finished talking at four the next morning. Chris told Bill everything, including the details of her relationship with Ross Lizenby. Bill provided the serious listening she needed. His final words as he left the apartment were, "Let me do a little checking. I was going back to Arizona tomorrow night, but I think I'll stay around a few more days."

16

SAKSIS'S SEVEN A.M. flight the next day to LaGuardia Airport was delayed twenty minutes because of deteriorating weather up and down the East Coast. It was drizzling as she started her drive to Bay Shore, but by the time she reached it the rain was coming down in wind-blown sheets. She parked the car in a lot adjacent to the ferry slip and was given a receipt identical to the one found in Pritchard's effects. It was stamped with the date and time by the Fire Island Terminal Company.

She leaned into the wind and went to the ticket window, where she was told the next ferry to Cherry Grove would leave in forty-five minutes. She bought her ticket, spotted a coffee shop across the parking lot, and allowed the wind to propel her in its direction. It was crowded with Fire Islanders waiting for the ferry, and with local fishermen who ate clam chowder and discussed the weather.

Saksis ordered coffee and a Danish, found a table near the window, and leaned against it. Her purpose in returning to Long Island was to show Pritchard's picture around in the hope someone would remember having seen him with Richard

Kneeley. She'd originally intended to simply contact Kneeley and ask about a link with Pritchard, but she'd learned long ago from her lawyer and investigator friends that the best way to ask a question was to already know the answer. If Kneeley denied knowing Pritchard, she wanted to be able to come back with something solid. It was helpful to know when someone was lying, as in the case of Rosemary Cale. Saksis didn't have a doubt in the world that it had been Rosemary with Pritchard in New York, not with the red hair and southern accent and distinctive, expensive ring. Why had she lied? Pride? Embarrassment? Guilt? She hoped the answer would make itself evident soon.

Now, it was time to build a case for the truth where Richard Kneeley was concerned.

She went to the counter and showed Pritchard's photo to the women behind it. They didn't recognize him. She tried several men sitting at the counter but met the same response. No one asked who she was or why she was showing the photo. If they had, she'd decided not to mention her FBI affiliation, simply to chalk it up to a sister looking for a missing brother. No sense having them gossiping on Fire Island about an FBI agent snooping around.

She paid her bill and ventured out into the rain. The girl at the ferry's ticket counter didn't recall ever having seen Pritchard, nor did two young men who were loading cargo onto the boat.

Because of the rough weather, everyone was crowded into the enclosed lower deck. The wind buffeted the craft as it backed away from the slip, turned, and headed across the choppy expanse of water that separated Long Island from the smaller Fire Island. Saksis showed Pritchard's photo to a couple of deckhands. Nothing. The man next to her was obviously a regular commuter.

"Ever see this man on the ferry before?" Saksis asked.

The man laughed. "Lose a husband?"

"A brother," Saksis said.

"Oh, I'm sorry. Didn't mean to make light of it. Nope, never saw him before." He showed the photo to his friends, none of whom recognized Pritchard. Now, of course, Saksis was asked myriad questions about the disappearance of her brother. She answered some of them, eventually said, "It's all too painful."

"Leave the girl alone," the man next to her said to his buddies. His final word was, "He doesn't look like you." Saksis smiled and said, "Stepbrother."

Her raincoat and rainhat provided scant protection against the wet wind that swept across Fire Island. The tiny streets of Cherry Grove were virtually empty, except for a few young, handsome, well-built men, scurrying between stores and bars, darting out into the elements and escaping from them as quickly as possible. Saksis was disappointed. She'd hoped to stroll sunny streets and show the picture to people she bumped into. That wouldn't be the case today.

She started with a bar at one end of the main street, showing Pritchard's face to employees and patrons. The bartender seemed to recognize the man in the picture, but he couldn't be sure. "Something about him," he said, "a look, an expression."

"He might have been with Richard Kneeley," Saksis said.

"With Dick? He's always got somebody with him," the bartender said. "Let me see it again." He held the photo in better light. "Could be, but I can't be sure. Why are you looking for him?"

"He's a stepbrother who disappeared."

"Oh, gee, that's rough. Here, having something on me. What do you drink?"

"Nothing, thanks."

"Sure? Something soft?"

"All right, club soda, with lime."

"You know Dick Kneeley?" the bartender asked as he placed the glass in front of her.

"No, but I certainly am a fan of his books."

"He's big, huh? Good guy."

"So I've heard. My stepbrother used to know him, which was why I wanted to come here."

"Have you called Dick?"

"No."

127

"Your brother—he was—?"

"Was what?"

"I mean your stepbrother. Well, this *is* Cherry Grove."

She knew he was referring to Cherry Grove's reputation as the popular homosexual village on Fire Island. She wasn't sure how to play it. The bartender didn't appear to be gay, although that didn't prove anything. She decided to go along with the idea he'd introduced.

"My stepbrother was gay. He announced it one day and took off for San Francisco. Then, he vanished. We used to hear from him pretty often, but not for the past year. The California police couldn't locate him, so I thought I'd give it a try."

"That's pretty gutsy," the bartender said. A wide grin broke over his flat face and he extended his hand to Saksis. "Name's Paul. I work here every summer, then take off for Florida. I'm not, uh—"

"My name's Chris," she said, "and I'm not, either."

"You know, it's funny, you don't look anything like him. Oh, right, he's a stepbrother. You look . . . you look sort of Indian, American, I mean."

"Just half. Passamaquoddy."

"Huh?"

"It's a Maine tribe. My father was. My mother wasn't."

The bartender nodded seriously and looked around the bar. "You going out to Dick Kneeley's house?"

"Yes, eventually."

"Call first. He's got this thing about security. The whole place is wired, and he's got dogs and Jubel."

"Jubel?"

"Sort of a houseboy and bodyguard. Used to be a professional wrestler, goes about three hundred pounds, mean as hell. We don't let him in here."

"That bad, huh?"

"A nasty drunk. Damn near destroyed the place one night. He's an ox, but Dick likes him. I suppose he gets the job done."

"What job?"

"Protecting Dick. Hey, when you write the kinds of books

128

he writes, there's got to be all sorts of spooks after you, CIA types, FBI, who knows what else?"

"I suppose so. Got any suggestions who else I might show the picture to before I go to Kneeley's house?"

"Not really. Maybe there was another place he hung out in more than this, but I don't know of one."

Saksis drained her glass and thanked him.

"My pleasure. Sure you don't want to stay? It's rotten out there. I've got an apartment here for the summer. Comes with the job. I get off at six and—"

"Thanks, but I've got to get back before then. I really appreciate your help, and the drink."

"Any time."

The rain had let up a bit, but the wind had picked up. She held her rain hat as she proceeded in search of another bar, then stopped and looked across the street, where a young man and woman were taking pictures. The man held a large striped golf umbrella over the girl's head. Saksis crossed the street and stood next to them. The girl looked up from the camera she was holding and said, "Hi."

"Hi," said Saksis. "Rough day to take pictures."

The girl looked in the view finder again, then back at Saksis. "Doing a photo feature on Fire Island in the rain."

The young man laughed. "You can see how strapped we are for news," he said.

"You're with the local newspaper?" Saksis asked.

"One of them," the girl said.

"There's more than one?"

The young man laughed. "There's been one for a while but it's not very good. We started our own."

"That's terrific."

"Not very profitable but fun," said the girl. She told the young man, "Let's wait until that guy in the yellow slicker walks into the frame. It'll give the shot some dimension."

Saksis watched as the yellow slicker hopped a puddle and the girl grabbed the shot. "Hey, can I ask you something?" Saksis said.

The man and woman looked at her.

"Ever see this person?" She handed them Pritchard's picture.

They huddled together and carefully scrutinized the photo.

"Nope," the young man said.

"I've seen him," the girl said.

"Really? Where? When?"

"Why?"

"Why—because he's my stepbrother and he disappeared a year ago. He was a friend of Richard Kneeley and—"

"That's where I've seen him," the girl said.

"With Kneeley?"

"Yes. I was shooting street scenes here in Cherry Grove a couple of weeks ago and spotted Kneeley coming down the street. There was somebody with him. I decided to grab a shot. Kneeley is a big name, and names sell newspapers. I took the picture and the guy with Kneeley—the one in this photo— wasn't too happy. He started to make a fuss, but Kneeley told him to forget it and they moved on."

"You're sure it's the same person?"

"Pretty sure. The one with Kneeley had a moustache, I think, but it's the same face. It was funny. Right after it happened, he put on sunglasses and walked away with his back angled at me, like something out of an old movie."

"Did you publish the picture?" Saksis asked.

"No. It was blurry, and we had better stuff."

"Do you still have it?"

"Sure, back in the office."

"Here in Cherry Grove?"

"No, Ocean Beach."

The young man said, "This is a good story, searching for a long-lost brother on Fire Island. It might even help you find him."

"Well, I'm not sure I—can I see the picture you took?"

They both shrugged. "We're heading back now," the girl said, "*if* the water taxi is running in this weather. Otherwise, it's a long walk."

The water taxi that linked the communities on Fire Island

was running, but barely. Saksis wondered if it weren't about to flip over as it skimmed the breakers and twisted in the severe wind that blasted in from the northeast. They eventually arrived at Ocean Beach, and the young couple led Saksis to their apartment a block up from the dock. It was also their newspaper office. It took ten minutes of rummaging through piles of papers and pictures until the girl, whose name was Sharon, came up with the shot she'd taken of Richard Kneeley and his friend.

"It's him," Saksis said almost inaudibly.

"It is?" the young man, Mitch, asked.

"Yes, I think so."

"Boy," Mitch said. "Can we do a story on it? How about sitting down and telling us the background, the circumstances surrounding his disappearance, all of it?"

"I'd like to but . . . Can I come back? I'm very distraught about all of this and—"

"Sure you can," Sharon said.

Mitch looked at her as though she'd just performed a monumental social blunder.

"Look, I really appreciate your help," Saksis said, feeling a little guilty about using such a sincere young couple. "Let me pursue this a little further before I decide to go public. I promise you one thing. When I'm ready, it'll be your exclusive."

"That's great," Sharon said.

"Can I take the picture with me?" Saksis asked.

"Sure," Sharon said.

"Wait a minute," Mitch said. "It does belong to us. We can sell it to you."

"That's fine," said Saksis. "How much?"

"Te——"

"Would fifty—"

"Sure, fifty's fine."

Saksis went to a restaurant and dialed Richard Kneeley's unlisted number, which she'd gotten from the central computer print-out on him. She reached an answering machine: "I'm unable to come to the phone at this time. Please leave your name, number, and a brief message after the tone, and I'll get back to you. Thank you." She hung up.

She had a choice—to go to Kneeley's house, wait around in the hope he'd return, introduce herself as a special agent of the Federal Bureau of Investigation, and ask questions, or return to Washington, digest what she'd learned, and take the steps in slower cadence. She chose the latter, rode the wind-swept ferry back to Bay Shore, drove to LaGuardia and was in her apartment by nine.

17

"WHERE'S MR. LIZENBY?" Saksis asked the secretary the next morning.

"In Arizona. He won't be back for at least three days."

"Did he leave any messages for me?"

"Just this." She handed Saksis a sealed envelope.

In the envelope was a formal memorandum:

> TO: *Special Agent Christine Saksis*
> FROM: *Lizenby*
> SUBJECT: *Command—Ranger*
> *In my absence, you will be Case Officer In-Charge. All matters pertaining to Ranger will be your responsibility.*

"Okay," she said to herself as she tossed the memo on her desk and picked up the phone. She punched in the extension for Jake Stein and Joe Perone. Perone answered.

"Joe, Ross is away and I've been left in charge. Let's have a meeting with everyone in an hour."

"Fine with me, Chris, but Jake's gone."

"Where is he?"

"Beats hell out of me. He left a note saying he'd been put on another case for a few days."

"Who put him on it?"

"I just gave you all I've got."

"Okay, grab anybody who *is* around and we'll meet in Ross's office in an hour."

"See you then."

She took from her briefcase the photo she'd bought on Fire Island and stared at it for a long time. There was no doubt that the other man was George Pritchard, and that he was with Richard Kneeley. She dialed Kneeley's number but got the same recorded message and hung up.

She made a list of things she wanted to cover in the meeting and was about to leave when Melissa Edwards, the tour guide and aspiring special agent who'd been assigned to Ranger, knocked. "Can I talk to you for a minute?" she asked.

"Sure, but I'm heading for the meeting. Did Joe tell you?"

"Yes, he did, but this is something I'd rather discuss with you privately."

"Tell you what, let's go to the meeting and then come back here."

An hour later Saksis and Melissa Edwards sat in Saksis's office. Edwards had been visibly nervous during the meeting and continued to be as she sat across from Saksis. Saksis liked Edwards, with her open moonface that projected a Missouri honesty you couldn't help but respond to.

"What's up?" Saksis asked.

"I'm not sure how to approach this," Melissa Edwards said.

"Try being direct."

"I'm not beating around the bush. It's just that . . ."

Saksis waited.

"It's just that I'm uncomfortable passing along third-hand information."

"Who's the third party?"

"Linda Gaffney."

"I don't know her."

"She's a guide, like me, and looking to get into the special agent program. She's a nice girl, and smart as the devil. She's going to law school nights."

"Sounds like a go-getter."

"Yeah, she really is. Look, Miss Saksis, maybe the reason I'm having trouble just coming out with this is that I'm not sure what it will mean to my application."

"Sounds serious. Are you in trouble?"

"No, not at all, but I'm doing this as a favor to Linda and . . ."

Saksis smiled. "Tell me what's on your mind, Melissa, and I promise it stays right here. Fair enough?"

"I guess so. Linda knows that Mrs. Pritchard was in the building the night he was killed."

Saksis sat back. "That's not what Mrs. Pritchard told me."

"I know. I read your notes on your interview with her. The problem is that Linda claims Mr. Pritchard came down and personally escorted his wife into the building at about eleven that night."

"There was no record of it on the sign-in sheets."

"That's right, because Mr. Pritchard convinced the guard to ignore her visit. He said it was personal and he'd just as soon not have it on the record."

Saksis grunted. "That's serious. Who was the guard?"

"I—you see, Miss Saksis, I shouldn't be sitting here telling you this."

"Linda should."

"Exactly. I told her that, but she thought that since I work with you and Ranger, you'd be more likely to listen to me."

"I would have listened to her. All I care about is getting to the bottom of George Pritchard's murder."

Melissa Edwards fiddled with her fingers. "Linda hopes that by coming forward with this information, her application for special agent training will be enhanced."

"Is your friend Linda suggesting that if it doesn't enhance her application, she won't tell us what she knows, which could very well help resolve a very serious murder investigation?"

Edwards laughed nervously. "Oh, no, of course not. I think I'm doing a lousy job of presenting this."

"I think you're doing a fine job. What else did Linda tell you?"

"That's about all. She said she'd be happy to give you a statement if you were interested, and if you—"

"I'm interested. As for Miss Gaffney's aspirations to become a special agent, that will take its own natural course, just as yours will."

"I understand."

"Send your friend up here."

"Now?"

"Whenever she's available. This information could be very important, Melissa, very important."

Edwards stood, her face somber.

"Can I give you some advice?" Saksis asked. She came around the desk and put her hands on the girl's shoulders.

"Sure."

"The next time something like this crops up in your bureau life, tell the other person to take care of it herself."

Melissa looked relieved. "I already figured that out, Miss Saksis, but thanks for putting it into words."

"Get your friend up here and forget about it. You're doing a good job, Melissa. I intend to make that point in your file."

"Gee, thanks."

"Now, go on, get her up here."

Linda Gaffney was tall with stringy blond hair and a slight tic in her left eye. She shook Saksis's hand with enthusiasm and looked around the office. "It looks permanent," she said.

"It isn't."

"But it looks it. I always admire people who can turn something temporary into a permanent place overnight."

"Yes."

"I've been in my apartment for more than a year and there are still unpacked boxes in the middle of the living room."

"I know what you mean. Sit down, please." When she had, Saksis asked, "Are you giving tours today?"

"Yes."

"Do people still ask about agent Pritchard's death?"

"They sure do. There are always a couple of questions about it."

"How do you answer them?"

"Oh, we have a script we go by. Public affairs wrote it."

"I see. Well, Linda, Melissa tells me you have information that might help us in the investigation."

"I hope it's helpful, Miss Saksis. I'd like very much to help."

"Go on."

"One of the guards, Sam, admitted Mrs. Pritchard to the building the night her husband was murdered. She didn't sign in because Mr. Pritchard personally came down and escorted her inside. Sam asked that she sign in, but Mr. Pritchard told him it was highly personal and that it would be awkward if her name appeared anywhere. Sam went along with it because he knows—*knew* Mr. Pritchard, and knew that he was very important around here."

Saksis shook her head and sighed. "It was still a major breach of security," she said.

"I know, bad judgment on Sam's part, but he meant well. He's been with the bureau fifteen years."

"I'll have to talk to him. What's his full name?"

"Sam Quince."

"Okay. What else?"

"That's all, really."

"How long have you known about it?"

"Just a couple of days. I wasn't sure what to do. I didn't want to get Sam in trouble. He's a very nice man. But then I started thinking about the murder and about my responsibilities to the bureau. I have my application in for special agent training."

"So Melissa told me."

Gaffney smiled. "Frankly, I was jealous when she was assigned to Ranger. I know she's just a gopher, but being so close to a major investigation must be exciting and helpful on your application."

"Yes, I suppose it will help Melissa. And she's more than a gopher around here."

"I didn't mean anything disparaging. Miss Saksis, could I make a suggestion?"

"Sure."

"Why not rotate those of us who are working as guides and have applied for agent training? If each of us could work a week in something like Ranger, it would teach us a lot and give you a chance to evaluate us."

"That might not be a bad idea, Linda. Why don't you put it in writing and submit it to administration?"

"Sure, but I thought I'd run it by you first. I'd really like a chance to work here while Ranger is still operational. Would you consider letting me replace Melissa?"

"No."

"All right. I suppose I was hoping my coming up with the information about Mrs. Pritchard would—well, I was hoping—"

"To be rewarded. Maybe you should be. Thanks for coming up. Would you find Sam Quince and ask him to see me."

"I'd rather not. I wouldn't want him to know I was the one."

"Okay. I'll contact him, and don't worry, I won't mention you."

Saksis learned that Sam Quince was on nights and wouldn't be in until midnight. She tried Richard Kneeley's number with no success, then called Helen Pritchard. "Could I come see you?" Saksis asked.

"Whatever for?"

"A few more questions, that's all."

"It's really inconvenient today. I'm packing Beth up."

"Oh? Where's she going?"

"Is that an official question?"

"No, just simple curiosity."

"She's going to New York to visit her cousins."

"Sounds nice, a little trip before school starts."

"Yes."

"Mrs. Pritchard, I really need to talk with you. Today."

The sigh on the other end was deep and long. "We're leaving here at two."

"I can be there by noon."

"Fine." She hung up abruptly.

Beth's suitcases were in the foyer when Saksis arrived at the penthouse. Helen Pritchard answered the door, flashed a tight, cursory smile, and led the way to the living room, where Beth sat on the couch reading a magazine. Her mother sat next to her, crossed her legs, and gave Saksis a "Let's get it over with" look.

Saksis asked Beth, "Would you mind if your mother and I had some time alone?"

"No, I guess not," she said, tossing the magazine on the floor, slowly getting up, and walking with deliberate nonchalance toward her bedroom.

Saksis said to Helen Pritchard, "When I was here last time you said you were at home the night your husband was killed."

"That's right."

"And Beth corroborated it."

"Why shouldn't she? It's true."

"I don't think it is, Mrs. Pritchard."

The woman's face hardened. "I don't have to put up with this."

"I'm not asking you to put up with anything, Mrs. Pritchard. Just tell the truth. On the night your husband died, you visited him at the Hoover Building. You didn't sign in because your husband convinced the guard to let you in without a signature."

"Nonsense. Whoever told you that is a liar."

Saksis suddenly had a sense of being on shaky ground. She'd acted impetuously, should have waited until she'd had a confirmation from the security guard before barging in to Pritchard's home with an accusation. All she had to base it on was the story of an ambitious young tour guide with special agent aspirations. But it was too late now to back off. Besides, she couldn't imagine Linda Gaffney coming in with such a tale and naming the guard if she wasn't sure that it had happened. At least she hoped that was so, for her own sake.

"Look, Mrs. Pritchard, I don't like being in this position. I accepted what you and Beth told me without question, but now I've been told something else by very credible sources. They'll testify to the fact you were there at the time someone murdered your husband."

Helen Pritchard stood and ran her carefully manicured hands down the sides of the yellow silk caftan she was wearing. She looked down at Saksis and said, "Then you'd better arrange for that testimony, and you'd better charge me with killing George. Otherwise, leave this house and never come back. You may be an FBI agent, Miss Saksis, but you're a lousy investigator."

She walked across the living room and disappeared into the bedroom wing. Saksis heard the bathroom door slam. Moments later, Beth appeared. She crossed the room to Saksis, glanced back over her shoulder, and quickly handed Saksis a slip of paper. "This is where I'll be on Long Island," she said. "You can call me there, but don't say you're from the FBI. You're just a friend, okay?"

"Okay. I'll call you tomorrow."

"No, a couple of days," Beth said. She'd been crying. Her eyes were red and puffy, and one cheek was stained with a tear. She turned and quickly went into the kitchen.

Saksis left the condominium and drove back to the Hoover Building.

18

CHRIS SAKSIS MET Bill Tse-ay for dinner. He was agitated about a report that had been released by the SPOVAC unit in Phoenix. In it, the women of that area who'd been murdered by a so-called "recreational killer" were alleged to have had certain things in common, one of them being prostitution.

"It's crap," Bill said as they sat at the bar in Georgetown's Place Vendome. "I knew Sue White Cloud and she wasn't a whore."

"Did the report say they were all professionals? I mean, full-time prostitutes?"

"No, just that each of the victims had had some experience with area prostitution. What they're claiming is that the psychological profile of the murderer includes some pathological hatred of hookers, but damn it, Sue wasn't like that."

"Maybe she was the exception. The basic report can still be valid."

"Yeah, maybe, but here we go again with painting a good kid a bad one because she's Indian."

Chris took his hand. "Bill, I don't think anyone is trying to do that, especially in a report like this."

"I don't care what they're *trying* to do, it's the end result that counts. I was going over the latest statistics at BIA this afternoon. You know what they're putting out, that Native Americans have three times the national arrest rate of blacks, and ten times that of whites."

"That's true, isn't it, but we know that it's because nobody cares. Even the blacks, as far away from equality as they may be, at least have voices in the establishment standing up for them."

He snorted. "Yeah, you and I know that, but BIA doesn't bother explaining it. The fat cat over there told me that by releasing these kinds of statistics, white America will become better educated about what has to be done to help us. I don't see it that way. The way I read it, the average American reads the stats, shakes his head, and says, 'They're still savages.' And he reads about Sue White Cloud and he shrugs and says to his wife, 'These young women who get into prostitution are asking for it.' Damn it, Chris, it's wrong."

"It always has been," she said, "but it'll get better, if you keep bringing it up."

"I sometimes wonder."

"No, you don't. You'll write a brilliant, scathing editorial about this and somebody will agree and take some action. Hey, my good friend, think about the computers we managed to get for the kids. And the clothes, and the commitment from Housing to repair all those houses on my reservation up in Maine. It's slow but one day—"

"I'll be up in the happy hunting ground long before that."

She giggled. "And so will I. Let's eat."

They talked about computers for much of the meal. Both of them had developed an intense interest in them, although Chris's was on a much more personal level. Bill had installed them at *Native American Times,* and on his recommendation Chris had purchased one for personal use and had begun writing her own programs as a hobby.

"Let me tell you what I'm trying to develop," he said over their salads. "I want a national bulletin board for all the reservations, a system link-up where kids—hell, or adults, for that matter—can connect with other Indians anywhere in the country. Wouldn't that be great? If we come up with some idea that works in Arizona, we can tell our brothers and sisters immediately about it, how to do it, who to see. It'd be almost like a Native American radio network, exchanging information, ideas, making us all one instead of 287 different tribes."

"Is that the latest count?"

"Yeah, a million and a half of us. If we could be hooked up together and working in concert, maybe the clout would be there." He was becoming increasingly animated as he outlined his plan for a computer network between reservations. "It wouldn't take much. All we'd need is 287 computers, one for each tribe, and a modem for each of them so we could use the phone lines to connect. Once we had that in place, we could . . ."

Chris had to smile as she listened to his plans. It was what had attracted her to him in the first place, his fire and dedication to a cause. She could never match him in his fervor, which was one of the contributing factors in the erosion of their relationship. It wasn't that she didn't have her causes, her passions. It had been track and field, and her studies, the combination of which often left her with an aching brain and leg muscles that screamed out in pain. Underneath it all was a commitment to her Indian heritage, although it was difficult to explain to Bill. For him, the only way to prove your dedication was to work at something active and visible where Native Americans were concerned. She didn't see it that way. For her, excelling within the American society did more for the image of her people than all the charity work she might get involved in. She'd told Bill once that he might be of greater service by using his education and talents as a writer for a major publication, to win awards, to make the point to the general public that the American Indian was *not* the stereotypical drunkard and lout. But he never saw it that way. And they drifted apart.

Now, in the restaurant, she found herself caught up in his zeal. "What can I do to help this along?" she asked.

He shrugged. "Got any high-placed friends in the computer business?"

"No, but I can look around. What about the people who got you the units for the kids?"

"Possibly, only I had to twist arms back so far to get those few machines that I'm not sure they'd be overjoyed to see me again."

"Well, maybe we can make it work together."

A puzzled frown crossed his face. She knew what he was wondering, whether what she'd just said had greater meaning than simply working together.

"Dessert?" he asked.

"Never touch the stuff," she said.

"I feel like splurging," he said. "It's good for the soul every once in a while."

"An old Indian proverb?"

"No, a new one. Sure you won't join me?"

"All right."

They had rich chocolate cups filled with genoise and mousse, and coffee. They said little. It had been a long time since they'd been intimate, and there was a mutual, unstated fear of rekindling something that was probably doomed to end again. Their breakup had been painful. They'd discussed it often in the months following it, which served to vent the frustration and hurt. They'd finally gotten over it and had gotten on with their lives and other relationships. But though the hurt had dissipated, the positive feelings about each other lingered, coming to the surface in aching bursts, then quickly ebbing in the business of daily life.

Chris waited for him to bring it up, to suggest that they extend the evening. When he didn't she said, "Want to come back to the apartment?"

"Yes. Very much," he said. "I'll get the check."

The waltz toward the bedroom began almost as soon as they'd entered her apartment. The familiarity of it came back immediately, and it was welcome. It crossed Chris's mind a few times how different making love with Bill was from her experience with Ross Lizenby. With Bill, there was a patience and tenderness that was missing with Ross, a gentleness that contrasted with the almost desperate hardness of the act with Lizenby. One word kept coming to her as they played out the passionate ritual of touching and kissing, fondling and whispering terms of endearment in each others' ears. *Caring.* That was the word that summed up, for her, the difference.

When they both were spent, they sat against the headboard and held hands, thinking but not speaking. Finally, Bill turned and said, "I'm not sure this is the time to bring this up, Chris, but it has to be said."

She'd hoped they could avoid a discussion of their past, and of this new beginning. But you couldn't control those things. She faced him and said, "Go ahead, Bill. What's on your mind?"

"Ross Lizenby."

The name seemed, to her, to flip a switch that sent a bolt of blinding white light into the darkened bedroom.

"I've done some checking on him."

"Checking?" This was not what Chris had expected.

"I called an old friend of mine, an attorney in Seattle. His name's Bob Miko. He's part Zuni, and he handles a lot of reservation cases in the state of Washington."

"And?"

"Well, you know Lizenby's from there, started a law practice years ago and—"

"I know all that, Bill. What are you getting at?"

"He was married for a short time, which you also know, but maybe you don't know the circumstances of his divorce. His wife brought him up on charges at least twice for assault. Bob checked back through Seattle PD records and came across a photo of her that was taken after she'd come in to file a complaint. Your friend really worked her over."

Chris felt a knot form in her stomach. She forced herself to say, "Go on."

"Lizenby had made it known that he intended to fold his practice and to apply to the FBI. The practice, what there was

145

of it, never got off the ground. A deal was struck with his wife. He'd give her an uncontested divorce and whatever alimony she was asking for, in exchange for dropping the criminal charges against him."

"I was wondering about that. He would never have been accepted into special agent training with that kind of background."

"That aspect of his background was buried, at least officially, but there's more."

She didn't want to hear.

"About a month after the divorce, Lizenby's wife—ex-wife—disappeared. The missing person file stayed open for a year. She was never found."

When Bill stopped talking, Chris said, "I have a feeling there's more you'd like to say."

He squeezed her hand and said, "I feel like a jealous suitor digging up dirt on my competition in order to come out the winner."

"Don't," Chris said. "I know that's not why you're doing this."

"I'm glad you understand. It makes it easier. Look, Chris, your friend doesn't shape up, at least to me, as the world's nicest guy, but that doesn't mean a hell of a lot. I'm just concerned that you've gotten deeply involved with the kind of man who might not be good for you. That's presumptuous, I know, but besides being madly in love with you, I *do* respond to that brother-sister relationship we fell into after it came apart between us. I care."

That word again. "I know you do, Bill, and I treasure it." She wrapped her arms around him and they slid down the headboard to the bed, their bodies pressed together, mouths finding each other, the passion swelling to another crescendo of satisfaction and release.

He did not stay the night. She kissed him gently on the lips as he left her apartment at three in the morning, then returned to her rumpled bed and lay awake until the first light of dawn filtered through the blinds.

146

The phone rang at six. She quickly picked it up and said, "Bill?"

There was a long silence before the voice said, "No, it's not Bill. It's Ross."

"Oh, I—I was expecting a call from him and—"

"Did I wake you?"

"No, I was—I was just about to get up."

"Are you alone?"

"Yes. Are you in Arizona?"

"Yes. I'm calling because . . ."

She waited.

"Because I miss you. I'm sorry I left with anger between us. I don't like that. We should never be apart from each other when we're angry. It's like the old adage, never go to bed mad." He laughed.

She didn't know what to say. Her mind was still filled with nasty visions of him based on what Bill had told her. She suddenly felt very cold, as though the air conditioning had been turned down to its lowest setting. She pulled the covers up and said, "I really should get in the shower, Ross. We can talk about this when you come back."

"I'll be back Sunday, probably early evening."

Sunday seemed so close. She said, "That's good."

"Can't you muster up a little more enthusiasm about it? This was the weekend we were supposed to go away together."

"I know, but when I heard you'd gone to Arizona I assumed that—"

"Of course. Look, I'll try to catch as early a flight as I can on Sunday. Things are pretty much wrapped up here. this series of serial killings in Arizona is over. Whoever did it sure hasn't stayed around. We'll be sending his M.O. over the system, but there's nothing left to do here. I'll try to get back in the afternoon on Sunday. We'll play some tennis, have an early dinner, and try to make up for the lost weekend."

She desperately groped for something to say. "Ross, I'm not sure I'll be here over the weekend. I may go to New York."

"For what?"

"The Pritchard case. There are some leads there that—"

"Screw the Pritchard case. I want you there when I get back."

"I don't think I—"

"I'm counting on it. Damn it, Chris, I've done a lot of thinking out here, and I know—just *know* deep down inside that you and I are right for each other. Let's give it a decent shot. Hey, by the way, I bought you a very fancy present."

"You did?"

"Yeah, I think you'll love it. In fact, I know you will. I can't wait to give it to you."

"That's—Ross, please, try and understand. I'm very confused at this point in my life and—"

"Of course you are, but you can't keep in touch with some former lover and expect to see things clearly. That's over, isn't it?"

"Yes, but . . ." She couldn't believe she'd said what she had, nor could she reason why she was so reluctant fo face up to him, to tell him about Bill and their night together, to tell him that she didn't want to see him anymore.

"I know it is, Chris, because you probably can see what we could have together as clearly as I do. This is all dumb, talking like this on the phone. I'll be back Sunday and come directly to your apartment. Just do one favor for me and don't plan on wearing any of your usual jewelry."

"Jewelry?"

"I never could keep a secret." Another laugh. "See you Sunday, and don't forget between now and then that I love you." He hung up.

19

IT WAS BUSINESS as usual Saturday morning at the bureau, and in Ranger's offices. Another attempt by Saksis to reach Richard Kneeley on Fire Island paid off at ten o'clock. He sounded as though he'd been awakened by the call, saying in a thick, slurred voice, "Hello."

"Mr. Kneeley?"

"Who's this?"

"My name is Christine Saksis. I'm a special agent with the Federal Bureau of Investigation."

She heard him try to clear the hoarseness from his throat before he asked, "What's this about?"

"I'd like very much to be able to talk to you in person concerning an ongoing investigation."

"What investigation?"

"We can discuss that when we get together. I'm willing to come out to your house if that would make things easier."

"I don't know. Do you have a subpoena, a warrant?"

"No. Do I need one?"

"Depends on what you're fishing for."

"I'm not fishing, Mr. Kneeley, I'm simply asking some

questions to help me in this investigation. I'd hoped you'd co-operate without the need for papers."

"I don't know. Am I being accused of something?"

"Not that I know of. Look, if you want to make it difficult, I'll come up with any papers I need to force the issue. This is a murder investigation, Mr. Kneeley, and you might have information that can help me, and the bureau."

He grunted. "Write a couple of books about the bureaucracy and you get called for everything."

"I've never called you before."

"Yeah. All right, Miss—"

"Saksis. Christine Saksis."

"Interesting name."

"American Indian."

"Really. How long have you been with the bureau?"

"A few years. Can I see you tomorrow?"

"I had plans."

"I won't take a lot of your time. Perhaps you'd prefer to come down here to Washington instead."

"I make it a point to spend as little time as possible in Washington.

She laughed. "Wish I could say the same. I could meet you in the city, say, at the Hotel Inter-Continental."

"What are you tryng to do, Miss Saksis, make the point that you've done your homework?"

"I'm not in the business of making points, Mr. Kneeley. I just know that you spend considerable time there. You are, you know, a somewhat public figure."

"I try not to be. It's not good for business."

She was tiring of the chitchat. "I'll be at your home on Fire Island at noon tomorrow, Mr. Kneeley. I trust you'll be there."

"I'll be here, but I'll be making a few calls to friends of mine in the bureau to make sure a Miss Christine Saksis has reason to pay a visit."

"I'd be pleased if you would, Mr. Kneeley, if it'll put you at ease."

Jake Stein stopped in a few minutes later. "What's new?" he asked.

She wasn't sure how much to share with him. She said, "Not a lot, Jake." She decided not to mention her planned interview with Richard Kneeley. It was happening on the weekend, which meant she didn't have to account for her time. Besides, Lizenby had left her in charge. But there was more to her reluctance to share with Stein—the fact was she simply didn't know who to trust anymore.

He sat across the desk from her, propped his feet upon a low table, and asked, "What's this I hear about George Pritchard's widow having been here the night he got it?"

Saksis was surprised that he knew. She asked where he'd heard it.

"It's making the rounds. The guard, Sam Quince, is evidently quaking with fear. Talked to him yet?"

"No. How about you handling that?"

"Sure. Hey, Chris, can I ask a couple of questions and make a couple of unsolicited comments?"

"To me? Of course."

"I'm a little uneasy about the way this Pritchard investigation is heading."

"Why?"

"Well, since Ross is pretty much out of the picture, you're sitting in the driver's seat. Not that that's bad, but I get a feeling that this has now become a one-woman show, everything kept close to the vest and that the rest of us might as well pack up and get back to the real world."

"I'm sorry that's the impression I've been giving out, Jake. I don't mean to, it's just that with Ross gone and by being handed it, things have gotten a little loose. That's my fault, and I'll do what I can to correct it."

"I'm not blaming anybody, but you know how things work around here. All of a sudden somebody upstairs yells for input and the only person with any is away somewhere."

"Meaning me."

"Right." He shook his head and smiled. "Chris, I never

thought I'd see the day when Jake Stein would be suggesting a meeting, but I think it's in order, a regular meeting every day, maybe twice a day, to keep the troops filled in."

"I agree. We'll start this afternoon."

"Good. Three?"

"Four."

"You've got it. I'll tell Joe. Maybe we ought to keep it between the three of us, you know, on a need-to-know basis."

"That makes sense. The three of us at four, right here."

"Okay. What are you doing for lunch?"

"Maybe something brought in."

"I'm offering a *real* lunch, my treat."

"I don't think so, but check me about noon. I may be desperate for something real by then."

Stein did come back at twelve, but she begged off. At 12:15 she left the building, went to a phone booth a few blocks away, and called Bill Tse-ay at his hotel.

"Good timing," he said. "I was on my way out the door."

"Bill, I'm going to New York for the weekend. I'm catching an early shuttle in the morning."

"Feel like company?"

"I don't know, I—"

"I wanted to get to New York this trip east. Hey, why fly? Let's drive up together tonight."

"That sounds nice but—can you leave by seven?"

"Sure."

"Any ideas on where to stay?"

"I can stay with friends, I suppose, but after last night I—"

"I liked it, too, Bill. We can stay together. I'll book something."

"Fine. Pick me up at seven?"

"Right, and thanks for being a friend. I need one more than ever."

"Where are you calling from?" he asked. "It's a lousy connection."

"A booth. I'm trying to keep a low profile around the office." She could have admitted that she wanted to avoid having her telephone conversations recorded but didn't want to ac-

152

knowledge that such a thing was possible with one of the bureau's own. The fact was she knew the possibility was more than distinct, and that the cases of it were as well known in the bureau gossip mill as who was sleeping with whom.

The four o'clock meeting started on time. Chris Saksis, Jake Stein, and Joe Perone sat behind her closed door and went over what they had. It was a sham, Saksis realized, because she was determined to not mention certain developments to which only she was privy. She wondered whether Stein or Perone were playing the same game, keeping something back in their own self-interest. Probably, she decided. It was the way things seemed to work in the bureau. She only hoped that when all the dust settled and there was a resolution of the case, none of them would be hurt, especially not her. She wasn't especially proud at that bit of self-preservation, but there was no sense denying it existed, and that it was growing stronger every day.

She had decided before they arrived to introduce the question of Rosemary Cale's affair with Pritchard. When she did, not mentioning the fact that her information had come from the waiter in New York, Joe Perone grinned and said, "My understanding was that they kept seeing each other right up until the time he died."

"That's my understanding, too," Saksis said. "Does anyone know where Pritchard was staying the last few weeks of his life?"

"I read your report on the interview with Helen Pritchard," Stein said, "and I wondered the same thing. Rosemary's place?"

"That crossed my mind," said Saksis.

"Did you ask her?" Perone said.

Saksis shook her head. "It didn't occur to me then, but maybe we'd better pursue it."

"My pleasure," said Perone. "I always wanted to get close to the redhead."

"She's leaving the bureau," Saksis said.

"So I heard," Stein said. "Succumbed to the lure of private industry."

"Bigger bucks," said Perone.

"I prefer upward mobility," Stein said.

"You would," said Perone.

"What about the foreigners-in-training?" Saksis asked. "And Bert Doering?"

"It's hands-off all the way around," Stein said.

Saksis sat straight up. "That's official?"

"Yup."

"Why hadn't I heard about it?" she asked.

"Why haven't any of us heard everything everybody else has heard?" Stein asked. "That's what I meant this morning, Chris. Instead of Ranger being a unified investigation into a murder, it's a group of individuals going their own separate ways, the group be damned."

"That's not true," she said.

"Yes, it is," said Stein. "For instance, Chris, you chase after Rosemary Cale, interview her, and pretty much come to the conclusion that her affair with Pritchard was still going hot and heavy even though she denies it. You didn't share that with us. If you had, I could have added that Miss Cale met Pritchard at a local hotel and went to bed with him the week before he died. Instead of conjecture, that pooling of information could make a difference."

Saksis sat back. What he'd said hadn't surprised her. It was the meaning behind it, the tacit accusation that she'd been holding back evidence, which, of course, she had. How much did Stein know?

"What else, Jake?" she asked.

"I don't know, not much, I suppose, but the point is that—"

"You don't have to explain, Jake. You've already said it very nicely."

He said, "It's the same situation with Helen Pritchard. You find out that she was in the building, but that's as far as it goes. It stay with you. No good, Chris, not if we're going to get to the bottom of things. By the way, the guard, Sam Quince, got axed."

Saksis registered her dismay. "He didn't deserve *that*," she said. "He had fifteen years in."

"He deserved worse," Stein said.

Saksis was intensely uncomfortable. She glanced at Perone, looked down at her hands, then said. "Nothing will be held back again, I promise. I can make the excuse that Ross's in-and-out stature has contributed to it, but I won't." She also wondered how Stein knew about Helen Pritchard. She'd ask at another time.

Stein laughed. "The jury will disregard the statement. Hey, Chris, don't look so glum. I'm not coming down on you. I just don't want to see any of us, including you, wind up on the short end, that's all."

"I know, I know, Jake. Thanks."

"What about this Richard Kneeley?" Perone asked.

Saksis covered her surprise by asking in a flat voice, "What about him?"

Perone looked at Stein before he said. "That print-out Barbara Twain ran on him is interesting, especially since there was that R.K. in Pritchard's book, and a Raymond Kane on the sign-in sheet."

"I found it interesting, too," said Saksis. "I was the one who asked Barbara to come up with it."

"What are we doing about it?" Stein asked.

"We'll follow up," Saksis said.

"Want me to do it?" Stein asked. "I've read his last couple of books, the best-sellers. He digs deep, that's for sure. He evidently knows how to get the goods out of the agencies." He asked Perone, "How do you figure he does it, Joe, finds some disgruntled employee, pays him off, and ends up with the files?"

"How else?" Perone replied.

"You know what I was thinking, Chris?" Stein said, lacing his fingers together and staring at the ceiling. "I was wondering whether Kneeley was involved in a book about us."

"Us? The FBI?"

"Yeah. Why not? He wouldn't be the first."

"And maybe Pritchard was mixed up in it in some way," Perone said.

Both men stared at Saksis. She averted their gaze, then deliberately met it. "That thought crossed my mind, too, but there's nothing to substantiate it."

"I'll see if I can come up with something," Stein said.

"No, not now," Saksis said. "I'd rather have you pursue the business of Helen Pritchard being here in the building that night."

"I thought you'd gotten close to her," Stein said.

"I did, but . . . Look, I've talked to Kneeley," she said.

"You have?" Stein said. "Did you tell me that?"

"You know I didn't."

"Why?"

"Because I want to follow through on it myself, that's why." It had reached a point where she was beginning to resent Stein's tone. She leaned on the desk and said, "Jake, I understand and appreciate everything you've said here, but I think there are two things to be considered. One, I have been put in charge of Ranger in Ross's absence. Two, I report to *him*."

"No argument about that, Chris. I just want to see Ranger succeed—for all our sakes."

"Yes, I know that." She lightened the mood. "Let's take what's left of the weekend and enjoy it, forget about Ranger and George Pritchard. I need time away from it, and I'm sure you do, too. We'll meet first thing Monday morning and really lay out every scrap of information that *we've* managed to gather."

"Ross will be back Sunday," Stein said.

"Yes, I was told. Maybe he can join us and—"

"Are we wrapped up here for today?" Perone asked, looking at his watch. "I have another thing to get to."

"We are as far as I'm concerned," Saksis said.

Stein and Perone went to the door. Stein looked back at Saksis and asked, "Plans for tomorrow?"

She shook her head. "Sleep late, some tennis, the gym, maybe even find time to finish a book I started before all this happened."

"My kid's seventh birthday is tomorrow," Perone said. "Fifteen little monsters at a bowling alley. I'd rather be in a shoot-out with the ten most wanted."

They all laughed, and Perone and Stein left, closing the door behind them.

"Oh, boy," Saksis muttered. She checked her watch. It was a few minutes before five. She'd have to go home and pack, gas up the car, and do it fast if she was to be on time to pick up Bill.

There was a knock on the door. "Come in," Saksis yelled.

Melissa Edwards opened it. "Miss Saksis, here's that photograph you wanted." She handed Chris a small envelope.

"Thanks," said Saksis. "Have a good weekend."

She opened the envelope. Inside was a photograph of Rosemary Cale from her personnel file. She put it in her purse, gathered up some papers she wanted to take with her, and was about to leave when the phone rang. She hesitated, then picked it up.

"Miss Saksis?"

"Yes."

This is Assistant Director Gormley. I'd like to see you in my office."

"Well, sir, I was about to leave and—"

"It won't take long, Miss Saksis, and it is important. I'd appreciate a few minutes of your time."

"Of course, sir."

Gormley was seated behind his desk when Saksis arrived. He didn't bother getting up to greet her. She glanced about the office, decided to take one of two red leather wingback chairs, and lowered herself into it. Gormley's expression hadn't changed since she entered his office. It was stern.

"Miss Saksis, what I have to say is extremely unpleasant, and I wish it weren't necessary. But it is."

"Yes, sir?"

He drew a deep breath, got up and stood behind his red leather swivel executive chair. He gripped its edges, moved it slightly back and forth. "Miss Saksis, it's come to my attention that your assignment to Ranger and to the Pritchard investigation represents a serious conflict of interest."

"It—how so, sir?"

"I'm sure you're aware, Miss Saksis, that there is a bureau

regulation against—how shall I say it?—against close fraternity between male and female special agents."

If the situation weren't so obviously serious, she might have laughed at his choice of terminology, but if there was one thing Chris Saksis wasn't interested in at the moment, it was humor. The affair with Ross Lizenby had surfaced. Of course it had. They'd played it out too publicly for it not to have happened. How could she have been so stupid? How did he find out? What were the official ramifications? Those questions, and a dozen others, managed to invade her thoughts during the few seconds of silence in the room.

"You do know to what I'm referring, Miss Saksis."

"No, sir, I don't."

"You don't? I'd like to believe that, of course, but considering the circumstances, it's difficult."

"Mr. Gormley, I'm not trying to be coy, but I would appreciate a clearer statement of what it is you're getting at." She hoped she hadn't been too forward.

A tiny smile formed at one corner of his mouth. "Yes, of course, I appreciate directness. I was just trying to be delicate.

"About what?"

"About your affair here within the bureau."

She realized that there was no sense in denying, in playing games with him. He knew, and that was that, and the only thing that might mitigate the situation was further directness on her part. She said, "If you're alluding to a relationship that has begun to develop between me and another special agent, I can do nothing except acknowledge it, chalk it up to a lapse of judgment, and assure you that it no longer exists."

What she'd said evidently amused him, judging from the smile that again originated at one corner of his mouth and almost made it all the way across to the other side.

"Is what I said funny, Mr. Gormley?"

"No, no, please forgive me, Miss Saksis. It's just that—"

"Yes?"

"It's just that when someone in a relationship dies, it's assumed that the affair is over."

158

"I—"

"Miss Saksis, the point is that your role as an investigator into the death of special agent George L. Pritchard is blatantly and inexcusably inappropriate."

"My role in—George Pritchard? There must be some mistake."

"Is there? I think not."

"Oh, no, you're wrong, sir, very wrong. Are you suggesting that Mr. Pritchard and I had an affair?"

"I'm suggesting nothing, Miss Saksis. I'm presenting you with an unfortunate fact that *you* should have made known the moment you were assigned to the Ranger unit."

"Why?" She stood. "Why would I have suggested such a thing when it never happened? I knew Mr. Pritchard, but only casually, in the halls, around the building, the cafeteria. We never so much as had a cup of coffee together."

He shifted into the role of the understanding uncle, coming around the desk and sitting on its edge.

"Mr. Gormley, I deeply resent this," Saksis said. She crossed the office to a far wall where framed photographs of Gormley with politicians formed a precise gridwork, every picture in line vertically and horizontally with the next. She felt tears begin to sting her eyes, and she was aware of a slight trembling in her legs. She summoned up what control she could, turned, and said, "You are very wrong, Mr. Gormley. I demand to know the source of your erroneous information."

" 'Demand?' I don't think you are in a position to demand anything, Miss Saksis. You've breached a serious bureau regulation. But, more than that, you've allowed a personal relationship to intrude upon an investigation that has serious meaning to this agency. The world is looking to us to clean up our own house, and it is assumed that we have used good judgment in pursuing that goal. Obviously, we've made a mistake." As he spoke, each word took on an increasingly hard edge.

"Mr. Gormley, *you are wrong!*"

"And you are in trouble, Miss Saksis. I offer you this. Pack up your things in Ranger and return to the Indian division. Do it quietly. Say nothing to anyone in the bureau, or outside. Otherwise—"

"Otherwise *what?*" Every other emotion had been replaced by intense anger.

"Otherwise, there might have to be a hearing on the ability of one special agent, Christine Saksis, to perform her duties with the Federal Bureau of Investigation to its satisfaction, based upon its high standards." He went behind his desk, looked up at an oil painting of Director R. Bruce Shelton and said, "You told me when I called that you were on your way somewhere. I suggest you go there now. Good evening, Miss Saksis."

20

CHRIS SAKSIS STARED straight ahead from the passenger seat of her car as Bill Tse-ay drove toward New York City. She'd told him of her meeting with Wayne Gormley when she picked him up at his hotel. He'd registered appropriate shock but hadn't pressed her with questions.

Now, as the first long shadows of evening crossed the highway, he glanced over and said, "Feel like talking more about it?"

She shook her head, said, "It's not even real, Bill. I mean, it's so farfetched that it's difficult to deal with. If he'd been talking about Ross—and I assumed he was at the beginning—I could at least accept it and try to figure out some strategy. But George Pritchard? Oh, God."

Bill passed a string of slow-moving cars, then asked, "Any ideas about who came up with the story?"

"No. It would have to be someone who was really out to hurt me, some personal vendetta. I told you about the run-in I had with Rosemary Cale. I thought of her, of course, but that doesn't add up any more than the others who come to mind. She's leaving the bureau. Besides, I didn't do anything to attack her personally. She knows I was doing my job."

"What about Pritchard's wife?"

"Helen? What would she gain from it?"

"You called her a liar."

"Not in so many words. She's a bitch, no doubt about that, but—no, not her. Not *anybody*, Bill."

He started to say something but caught the words before they came out of his mouth.

"I know what you're about to suggest. Ross Lizenby."

"Well, it's possible, isn't it?"

She sighed deeply and leaned her head back against the restraining yoke. "I suppose everything's possible, isn't it, when it's such a ridiculous story."

Bill said, "Maybe it's not a personal thing. Maybe somebody really wants you off the Pritchard case."

She snorted. "That's not hard. Reassign me."

"But what if it's someone who isn't in that position, who has to resort to passing a lousy rumor in order to bring about a reassignment?"

"Sure, I can buy that. But whoever did it sure didn't take into consideration the impact it would have on me. Gormley's not talking about simple reassignment, he's intimating big trouble for me. The bureau's a funny place, Bill. It has its own rules stemming from the Hoover days: the bureau first and individuals after. This could have a devastating effect on my career. From Gormley's perspective, I've breached a very important tenet of that code. I put myself in an investigatory capacity that's compromised because of my "affair" with the subject of that investigation. Add to that the fact that the Pritchard case reflects directly on the bureau and you have a wonderful reason to boot one Christine Saksis out the back door."

"Do you really think it could come to that?"

"I won't let it. I'll find out who set me up with the rumor and square it."

"Chris—"

"Yeah?"

"What if you don't?"

"Then—then I think I'm in big trouble."

It was almost midnight when they checked into the Hotel Inter-Continental. "Hungry?" Bill asked after they'd been shown to their room."

"Yes, but I'm too tired to eat."

"We'll have something sent up."

An hour later the remains of turkey sandwiches from the "Supper Snacks" menu sat on a tray on a coffee table in front of a couch. They'd changed into robes; their bare feet were propped up on the table.

"Feel better?" he asked.

"A little."

"We'd better get to bed. You have to be up early."

"Not that early. I told Kneeley I'd be there at noon."

"I'd like to come with you."

"No, that would only complicate things."

"Who's his publisher?" Bill asked as he finished a small piece of leftover pickle.

"Kneeley? Sutherland House, at least for the last couple of books."

Bill smiled. "I have a very good friend there."

"Really?"

"Yeah, a gal named Billie Wharton. Her mother was Navajo, and I knew her father from some work I did with the Arizona equal rights commission. Billie got herself a degree in English from Arizona State and was looking to get started in publishing. Perfect profession for her. She read more books faster than any human being I've ever known. Anyway, I'd given Sutherland some free publicity on a book they published on Indian affairs and they owed me one, so I recommended her to them. They hired her, and the last I heard from her, about three months ago, she'd been promoted to assistant editor." When Chris didn't respond, he added, "If you and I hadn't gotten together again, I would have stayed with her here in New York."

Chris looked at him through sleepy eyes. "She's a girl friend?"

"No, but we did have our moments. Hey, when you walked

away I had to choose between a lifetime of celibacy or normal me Tarzan–you Jane relations. I debated it for months before I—"

"Spare me the details."

"The only reason I brought it up was that I had planned on calling her as long as I was here, maybe grab some lunch. Interested in joining us?"

"When? I'll be out at Fire Island tomorrow."

"It's already today. Maybe we can make it dinner."

"Sounds fine."

"Good. I'll get a hold of her in the morning and set something up. I'll leave a message here at the hotel."

"I'm going to bed. I feel as though I've been stampeded by a herd of cattle."

He laughed. "You can take the maiden out of the wigwam but you can't—"

She poked him in the ribs. "What do you mean by that?"

"Here you are, big-city special agent for the Federal Bureau of Investigation, having forsaken your Indian heritage, and you use a stampede metaphor instead of a bus, or a fleet of runaway cabs, or—"

"Good night, Bill."

"I'm coming, too."

"Good, only this is a perfect night for you to reconsider your decision."

"What decision?"

"Whether to be celibate or not. It's a good time to give it a try."

Bill was still in bed when Chris was about to leave their room the next morning. She knelt on the bed and kissed his cheek. He opened his eyes, grinned, and said, "I made my decision."

"What decision?"

"Celibacy. It's not for me."

"Good. I'll be back by five, maybe six. Do me one favor."

"Anything."

"Don't tell your friend Billie why I'm here. Don't talk about the FBI or anything even remotely connected with it."

"Why?"

"Because. Just because. Promise?"

"Sure." He grabbed her around the neck, pulled her down next to him, and kissed her with passion.

"Brush your teeth," she said as she disengaged and went out the door.

It was a lovely day. The first faint hint of fall was in the air. She opened her windows as she exited the Queens Midtown Tunnel and headed east on the Long Island Expressway toward Bay Shore. Despite what had happened in Assistant Director Gormley's office the night before, despite the fact she was on her way to what undoubtedly would be a difficult interview, she felt free and at peace with herself. Something her father often said came to her: "Freedom is within each of us. What happens outside is of little consequence." He was right. She was alive, the air was cool-crisp, and the day was before her, rather than trailing behind.

This time, the crossing to Cherry Grove was smooth and tranquil. The narrow, twisted streets were filled with the village's primary inhabitants, homosexual men, most young and good-looking, some older—"old bucks," she'd heard them referred to. Some male couples walked hand-in-hand, or with arms over shoulders. A female friend who'd spent a day in Cherry Grove termed the overwhelmingly gay population "a terrible waste of beautiful manhood."

She walked until she realized she was lost, stopped a young man wearing a sweatshirt and jeans, and asked for directions to Kneeley's house. It was only a few hundred feet away, he told her pleasantly, on the other side of a long string of dunes.

She surveyed Kneeley's house and property from a distance. An imposing fence surrounded the house. It was at least six feet high, and a roll of nasty-looking barbed wire ringed the top. There were signs in red that warned against trespassers, and that the fence was electrically wired.

The house was three stories high and was covered with slats

of gray weathered board. Large windows on every level afforded unencumbered views of the ocean. The grounds were typical of a beach resort, mounds of wind-blown sand pressing against long strands of snow fence, pieces of gray and brown driftwood tossed casually into intriguing patterns on the beach. Gulls swooped low in search of food and announced their mission.

She approached a gate on which a doorbell was attached, pushed it, and waited. When nothing happened, she rang it again in a triplet and peered toward the front door. A shutter opened and a face appeared. The shutter closed, the door opened, and a man stepped onto the small porch. He wore a pair of cut-off jeans, a black T-shirt, and sandals. His head was shaved, which created the impression of a perfectly round ball resting precariously atop a pair of immense shoulders. His legs were as thick as redwoods, and the muscles of his chest prevented his arms from touching his sides. His gut was huge and solid. Saksis assumed he was Jubel, the bodyguard the bartender had mentioned. He'd been right—Jubel was made for professional wrestling. He stepped down from the porch, waddled toward the gate, and held Saksis in a long, questioning stare.

"Chris Saksis," she said through the gate. "I have an appointment with Mr. Kneeley."

"I know."

"You're Jubel?"

He hesitated, then mumbled, "Yeah, I'm Jubel." Then he inserted a key into the padlock that secured the gate to the fence. He swung it open and Saksis stepped through.

He closed the gate, attached the chain, snapped the lock, and led her to the house. She stepped into a foyer of blanched wood and Mexican tiles. Sprays of exotic plants rose gracefully from redwood pots to create an archway leading to a large living room at the rear of the house. Chris went to it and looked through sliding glass doors onto a swimming pool in the shape of a guitar.

She turned. Jubel stood in the doorway. He said, "Richard will be down in a minute. Coffee? Tea?"

166

She had to adjust to his voice. It was small and high, and didn't belong in such a bulky, muscular body. "Coffee," she said.

"You take sugar, milk?"

"Black."

He disappeared, leaving her alone in the room. She looked up. Rough planks weathered to a silver gray extended up two stories to a white ceiling dotted with skylights. A balcony ran the length of the wall opposite the sliding glass doors. Large abstract paintings of vivid red, yellow, and green circles and lines broke up the room's monochromatic color scheme. A gleaming black Steinway grand occupied one corner, an elaborate bar another. The furniture was a mix of white leather couches and love seats, and a dozen director's chairs in a variety of colors. The title of each of Kneeley's books was stenciled in black on the back of each chair. A large telescope on a tripod stood in front of one of the sliding doors. The soft strains of a Haydn symphony emanated from speakers in each of the room's four corners.

"Miss Saksis."

She looked up to the balcony where Richard Kneeley stood. "Yes, Mr. Kneeley."

"Jubel said you were here. Come. My study's upstairs." He pointed to a black wrought-iron spiral staircase. Saksis climbed it, emerged on the balcony, and was greeted with a firm handshake and a broad smile. Kneeley was taller than she'd expected, and heavier. His full head of silver hair was carefully combed. He wore a pale blue silk shirt open halfway to his navel, which allowed a mat of gray chest hair and a cluster of gold charms on a chain to poke through, tight chino pants, and white canvas deck shoes.

"It's a beautiful house," Saksis said.

"I like it, especially the view. Come on, let's talk."

He led her along the length of the balcony to another staircase. At the top, on the third floor, was his study, a huge room with one wall of glass overlooking the ocean."

Saksis let out what was almost a whistle. "It's breathtaking," she said.

"Thank you. Sometimes I wonder if I wouldn't get more work done without a view, but I can't give it up. Sometimes I close the drapes, but then my claustrophobia takes over and I open them. Sit down." He pointed to a modular setup of couches off to the side of his work area, which consisted of three long tables formed into a horseshoe. In the middle of it was an elaborate word processing system connected to modems and printers.

"You've entered the computer age, I see," Saksis said.

"My days sitting under a birch tree with a yellow legal pad are over. I suppose it's because I've been doing nonfiction lately. I'd go mad trying to keep track of source material."

"I can understand that." She got up and entered the horseshoe. "Impressive," she said.

"It works," he said. He came into the U-shaped area and sat in an expensive ergonomic chair in front of the computer's keyboard.

Saksis went to a wall of floor-to-ceiling bookcases and perused its contents. "Quite a library."

"I've been building it for a long time," he said.

She turned and surveyed the rest of the study. It was warmer than the downstairs area. The floor was covered with thick burgundy wall-to-wall carpeting. Every available inch of wall space contained books. There was a large safe in one corner. Next to it was a row of four-drawer file cabinets. She counted three telephones. The answering machine she'd reached on her earlier calls to him was next to two dictating units and other electronic equipment on a credenza directly behind where he sat. He was obviously fascinated with gadgets. There were a number of calculators on the credenza, as well as an automatic telephone dialing unit, a fancy weather-forecasting rig, and a high-speed printer that didn't seem to be connected to the main word processing unit.

"I always swore I'd never be seduced by electronic gadgetry, but I succumbed. You must spend some time with technology at the bureau."

She nodded. "Yes, we keep up. Do you write everything on the computer?"

"Sure. I have another complete set-up down the hall that's used when I have part-time help come in, but I do most of it myself."

"I can understand that," said Saksis, "considering the nature of your books."

"That's right. So, Miss Saksis, what can I tell you? What questions do you have for this aging writer?"

"First of all, Mr. Kneeley, did you reach your friends at the bureau to vouch for my authenticity?"

"Yes, I did."

"And?"

"You never offered to show me your credentials."

"I forgot. Here." She offered her ID.

"Legitimate, the seal slightly covering the picture. By the way, you should insist upon having another photo ID taken. This one doesn't do you justice at all. You're quite beautiful."

"Thank you."

"Compliments are so utterly wasted unless they're passed on. Okay, we've established that this gorgeous FBI agent named Saksis is who she said she was. I've welcomed you into my house. Now, it's your turn to do what you came here to do, ask questions."

"All right, I will."

"Before you start, would you like a drink, a sandwich, caviar, a pizza?"

"No, thank you."

"Nothing? I intend to."

"Go right ahead."

"Coffee?"

"I asked Jubel for some while I was waiting for you."

"And it hasn't arrived yet. He's slipping. Usually, he's very fast."

"It's all right. I really don't need it."

"Well, Miss Saksis, I need something. I think I'll have some caviar on toast, smoked salmon with onions and capers, and perhaps a drink. It is afternoon, isn't it?"

"That's right."

"And you?"

"The coffee, if it's convenient, and maybe a sandwich."

"Turkey, ham-and-cheese, egg salad . . . ?"

"Anything."

He picked up one of the phones and repeatedly hit the button. "Jubel, where's Miss Saksis's coffee?" A pause. "Fine, bring with it a nice, fresh sandwich for her, and caviar and salmon for me."

He hung up, went to a portion of the wall that swung open at the touch of a button, and removed a bottle in a brown chamois sack from a concealed bar. He placed the bottle on his desk, held a brandy snifter to the light, then carefully removed the small, delicately shaped bottle from its protective bag. "Bourbon?" he asked.

"No."

"Don't like bourbon?"

"I don't drink whiskey. Maybe occasionally, but I really never developed a taste for it."

He grinned as he removed the stopper, in the shape of a jockey on a race horse, held the bottle over the glass, and gingerly dribbled some of the whiskey into it.

"Beautiful bottle," she commented.

"What's in it is even more beautiful," he said. "The world's finest bourbon." He handed the bottle to her.

The name that was discreetly woven into the message on the label was Blanton's, the brand the waiter at the Hotel Inter-Continental said Pritchard had ordered.

"Take a sniff," Kneeley said.

"Very nice," she said, handing him back the bottle.

"Like fine cognac," he said. "It just occurred to me that your American Indian heritage would—well, probably cause you to avoid hard liquor."

"That's true, although I can drink it and not go on a drunken rampage."

He roared. "Another myth dashed. Good health!" He took a swig, smacked his lips, and swiveled in his chair so that his back was to her and he was facing the ocean. "One of the advantages of growing older, Miss Saksis, is the ability to truly ap-

170

preciate things." He suddenly completed his 360-degree swing and said, "And to not have to be afraid of anything."

"I suppose I'll find out for myself," she said.

"Yes, you will. Those magnificent features will wrinkle and fade, the breasts will droop, the belly will refuse to conform, and the thighs will become lumpy, like tiny berries beneath the skin."

She was startled by his sudden anger and hostility. She decided it was time to get to the point of her visit. "Are you a friend of George L. Pritchard?" she asked.

He stared at her for what seemed a very long time, smirked, and said, "The fallen FBI hero, slain in his own cave by his own species. Fascinating case. Are you in charge of bringing his slayer to bay?"

"Yes."

"I'm surprised."

"Why?"

"It's a weighty responsibility for a woman."

"No more so than for a man."

"Debatable. Why do you ask whether we were friends?"

"Because my information seems to point to that."

"What information?"

"Eyewitnesses."

"Who?"   .

"I don't think—"

"Don't come in here, Miss Saksis, and toss around terms like 'information' and 'eyewitnesses' unless you're prepared to back them up. I'm not some indigent unfortunate who cowers at being questioned by a member of Hoover's finest. Spell it out, Miss Saksis, or find your free lunch elsewhere."

His arrogance inspired her. She sat up on the couch and said, "Your offer of lunch doesn't impress me, Mr. Kneeley."

He cocked his head and smiled. "The feisty Native American special agent. That is the accepted term these days, isn't it, 'Native American'? I can never keep track—Negro, black, Chinaman, Oriental, Asian, Hispanic, Indian, Native American—it's all too much for me."

"It isn't difficult, Mr. Kneeley. Call me whatever comes to mind. It's easier that way."

He fluttered his fingers in the air and rolled his eyes. "Don't invite *that*, Miss Saksis. If I used the words on the tip of my tongue at this moment I would be faced with a very irate female."

"Try me," she said.

There was a knock at the door. "Come in," Kneeley yelled, never taking his eyes from her. Jubel entered carrying a tray. He arranged things on one end of the desk, sneezed, and asked whether Kneeley wanted him for the rest of the afternoon.

"Where are you going?" Kneeley asked.

"Out," Jubel said.

Kneeley sighed. "The child in all of us. Going out, doing nothing, I presume. Go. Be back for dinner. We have guests."

Jubel left without saying anything.

"Imposing specimen, isn't he?" Kneeley said to Saksis. "Eat. It won't get cold, but there must be an FBI regulation against accepting special agents as ravishing as you."

She couldn't help but smile. "Please, Mr. Kneeley, I appreciate the lunch and the compliments, but I would like to get on with my questions. You were good enough to invite me here and—"

"And that's the whole point, Miss Saksis. I invited you here. That should say something."

"Did you know George L. Pritchard?"

"Who?" His small smile was annoying.

"George L. Pritchard, the special agent who was murdered in the Hoover Building."

"Oh, *that* George L. Pritchard. No."

"You weren't friends?"

"That's right."

"Acquaintances?"

"No."

"Had you ever met him?"

"No."

"Ever heard of him?"

172

"Newspaper accounts of his unfortunate and untimely demise. Who done it?"

"Who—we don't know."

"You suspect me?"

"No."

"Then why ask me about him?"

"Because I know you knew him."

"Do you now? I think I'd better have another drink to brace myself against the flood of evidence the beautiful special agent is about to drown me with. Sure you won't join me? It's *very* smooth."

"Positive."

As nonchalant and unconcerned as he wanted to appear, Saksis noticed a change in his face. His mouth seemed to sag ever so slightly, and his eyes had lost their devil-may-care twinkle. He filled his glass and took a healthy swig.

She asked, "Did you sign in to the Hoover Building the night Pritchard was killed, using the name Raymond Kane?"

"Kane? Raymond Kane. That's fascinating. Years ago, when I was eking out a living to support my wife and child, I wrote a series of western paperback originals under the name Kane. Not Raymond—Richard. But, of course, you knew that, which is why you are here trying to link me up with some person who signed in to the Hoover Building under the same name— Kane, Raymond, you said? I was Richard. I don't know Raymond."

His attempts at cleverness were wearing thin on her. She decided to drop the questions for a few minutes and to eat. The sandwich was tuna salad on whole wheat. It was good. She ate half and finished the coffee that was in her cup. A silver pot held more, but she didn't bother refilling. He watched her as she ate, ignoring the plate of caviar and salmon in front of him.

"Very tasty," she said.

"Good." He turned his head and looked toward the ocean. "Ah, they're back." He got up and went to the telescope, aimed it toward the sea, and adjusted the eyepiece. He looked over his shoulder and waved for her to join him.

She came to his side. He backed away from the telescope and said, "Here, look, the jet set at play."

She peered through the eyepiece at a large luxury yacht barely moving through the water. On deck were three young women, two blond, the other with black hair. They were naked. Two men sat in deck chairs. Each held a glass and were laughing as they watched their female companions cavort about the yacht au naturel.

"They've been providing me with vicarious pleasure all summer," Kneeley said. Saksis allowed him to take his place at the telescope. He watched the scene for a few moments, then straightened up, stepped close to her, and reached his arms around her back. He pressed his body against her and tried to force his mouth on her lips.

"Get lost," she said as she pushed him away.

"You'll love it," he said.

She brought her knee up into his groin. He gasped, doubled over, and staggered back, knocking over the telescope. She watched as he fought to regain his composure. Finally he straightened and tried to keep the tears of pain from erupting from his eyes. "You bitch," he said.

She stood with her hands on her hips. "Tell me about Pritchard," she said.

"What the hell do you—?"

"He's been here. I have pictures. You knew each other pretty well, and I want to know under what circumstances."

He walked to his desk and sat heavily in his chair. "You have a hell of a nerve."

"So do you, and if you ever try that again you'll feel a lot worse than you do now."

"And if you ever do that to me again, with Jubel here, you'll—"

"Don't threaten a special agent of the FBI. It brings a long term."

"Get out."

"Pritchard."

"Never heard of him."

"You'd better reconsider."

"Threatening an American citizen doesn't sit too well with the courts, either."

"Last chance," she said as she went to the couch and gathered her belongings.

"This Pritchard character is your problem, not mine. You left half your sandwich. Want a doggie bag?"

"Feed it to Jubel."

"I will, along with red meat."

"See you again, Mr. Kneeley."

"You sure as hell will, Miss Saksis, and you won't be happy when you do."

She started across the room, stopped, returned to where he sat. She shoved the picture of Rosemary Cale beneath his nose. "Ring a bell?" she asked.

"Looks like just another—"

"You're right, she is. I'm not. Take it easy."

21

BILL TSE-AY WAS out when Saksis returned to the hotel. She showered and took a nap, awoke at five, fished Beth Pritchard's phone number from her purse and dialed. A man answered.

"Is Beth there?" Saksis asked.

"Yes, she is. Who's calling."

"This is Chris, a friend."

"I'll get her."

Beth came on the line.

"Beth, this is Christine Saksis from the FBI. You gave me this number."

"Oh, sure. How are you?"

"Just fine. Enjoying your visit?"

"Very much. Would you like to talk to me?"

"Privately? Yes. I'm in New York City. I was planning to leave late tonight but I can stay over. Tomorrow morning?"

"I can hop on the train and meet you for breakfast."

"Sure?"

"Yup. I take the train a lot."

"Okay, I'm at the Hotel Inter-Continental on Forty-eighth Street, just off Lexington Avenue."

"I'll be there at ten."

"Perfect. Beth, are you sure this is all right, that you won't get in some kind of trouble?"

"You know something, Miss Saksis?"

"What?"

"I don't care."

Bill returned shortly after five. After giving Chris a big hug and kiss, he took off his clothes and hopped in the shower. He returned a few minutes later wearing one of the terry cloth robes the hotel provided, sat on the bed, and said, "So, tell me about Fire Island and the great American author."

Chris joined him on the couch and replayed her visit with Richard Kneeley.

"A real creep," Bill said. "You're sure you thwarted his advances?"

"Stop it. I made a ten o'clock breakfast date tomorrow with Beth Pritchard. Mind staying over an extra night?"

"No, of course not. Who's Beth Pritchard?"

"The deceased's daughter."

"Oh, yeah, I forgot."

"I think she's bursting to talk to me about her father, and I'm curious about what she has to say."

"Want company?"

"No. I don't want to scare her off. What about your friend Billie Wharton? Did you see her?"

"No, but we will tonight. She was busy all day. We're having dinner at seven. What time is it now?" he asked.

She shrugged. "About five-thirty."

"Plenty of time." He took her face in his hands and kissed her gently on the lips.

"No more celibacy?" she asked.

"Maybe tomorrow. Right now it's the last thing on my mind."

The strolled hand-in-hand along Forty-ninth Street until they reached a red canopy that said *Antolotti's*. Billie Wharton was already there at a table next to a front window. She gave Bill a warm embrace and shook Chris's hand. Billie was short and heavy. She was dressed in a plain beige shirtwaist and her black hair was held off her face by a red bandana. A large turquoise Zuni pendant hung from a heavy gold chain around her neck.

"It's good to see you again," Bill said as he picked up a piece of celery.

"It's been a while." Billie looked at Chris. "This delightful, crazy man got me my job."

"So I heard. Sutherland House is a good one, I understand."

"Better than most, I guess. We do some pretty good books, at least we try to."

"I'd love to hear about them. Publishing is a foreign country to me."

Billie laughed. "What do you do, Chris?"

Chris gave a fast glance at Bill, then said, "I'm an investigator with a federal agency."

"Which one?"

"The Interior Department, Indian affairs." She hoped Bill wouldn't be annoyed at such a blatant lie.

A waiter appeared and asked for their drink order. Chris and Bill had white wine, Billie a perfect Manhattan. She laughed when she ordered it. "Publishing types are supposed to drink wine or Perrier. It's a pleasure to have a real drink. I've been corrupted by the industry all week long."

"Nice corruption," Bill said.

"I can think of some others I prefer," Billie said with an exaggerated wink.

"Here's to corruption," said Bill when their drinks were served. He held his glass in a toast.

"I'll drink to *that* kind of corruption," Chris said, "but working in Washington conjures up too many visions of the other kind."

After small slices of pizza bread were served they were handed menus. When they'd decided—spinach salads and chicken casalinga for Bill and Chris, veal Antolotti and pasta for Billie—Chris turned the conversation back to Billie's job at Sutherland House.

"Busy, busy, busy," Billie said. "They claim the industry is publishing fewer books these days, but you can't prove it by me."

"Do you work with big-name authors? Chris asked.

Billie nodded and finished the last piece of pizza bread. "I've been dealing with authors more and more, and I love it. They're a pretty nice bunch, with a few exceptions—those who think their book is another *War and Peace*."

"Who have you worked with lately?" Chris asked.

Billie named a few novelists, but added, "I'm pretty much doing nonfiction. Most of our list is nonfiction."

Bill talked about the book on American Indians he'd helped launch. Billie said another book on the subject was under editorial consideration and wondered whether he'd be willing to get involved again. He said he would, provided the message was palatable.

The table took on an increasingly festive air. Billie was good company, bright and funny, and Chris found herself relating to her as though they'd been friends for years. They joked about their Indian heritage, as only members of a clan can make fun of themselves. Chris was dying to mention Richard Kneeley but was afraid that Billie would sense an interest beyond simple curiosity. Too, she was feeling increasingly guilty, and wondered at times during the meal whether it wouldn't have been better for her to be up-front, to admit her professional interest in Kneeley, and to ask for Billie's help. But, somehow, she had the feeling that it wouldn't work to be that honest. She'd be asking Billie to betray a trust of her job with Sutherland House, and she doubted whether Billie would go that far.

There was also the question of Bill Tse-ay. Although he seemed willing to go along with Chris's charade, she wondered how he really felt about it. If she started playing the game, would he interrupt it, change the subject, and think less of her?

She decided that none of it mattered. She was under the gun, and unless she found a way to resolve the murder of George L. Pritchard, her reputation at the bureau was in jeopardy.

A large fruit basket was delivered to the table. They ordered coffee and decided to share a piece of rum cake. It looked large enough to be shared by six. While they were digging into dessert, Chris said, "I've been reading a book by Richard Kneeley."

Billie's eyes lit up. "He's one of our authors."

Chris laughed. "Is he? I never connect authors with specific publishing houses. He's terrific."

"What are you reading, *The Deceit Factory?*"

"Yes," said Chris.

"It was a big success. The paperback will be out in a few months. Of all the writers we have under contract, he has to be the strangest."

"Really?" Chris said. "Why?" She looked at Bill, who didn't seem in the least concerned at what she was doing.

Billie laughed and tasted a pineapple wedge. "Delicious. Why? I've met him a couple of times. He's nice personally. It's the way he works that tickles everyone in the office. Kneeley has to be the most paranoid writer we have on the list. He only transmits at night, and my boss told me he has state-of-the-art security devices on his computer."

"Transmits at night?" Bill asked.

"Yeah. He's one of the few authors we publish who uses a computer to directly feed into our own system. He's hooked in through modems, and he sends us what he's written over telephone lines. Kneeley has his own equipment, but we've started leasing computers to important writers who are working on big books for us. It's terrific."

"I don't understand," Chris said. "He just sends his material over the phone?"

Billie nodded and tried a forkful of cake. She savored it, then said, "That's right. I really don't understand all the technical aspects of it, but it's obviously the wave of the future."

"Amazing," Chris said, "especially when you consider the kind of books he does."

"I know," said Billie, "that's why he has security devices and only transmits at odd hours."

"Can you really protect against somebody tapping in to a transmission?" Bill asked.

Billie squinted and looked at him strangely. "You should know that, Bill, with all your computers."

He shrugged and tasted the cake. "I just know about using them to get out the newspaper. The whole business of security and late-night transmissions is beyond me."

Billie earnestly dug into what was left of dessert, and Chris decided to hold back any further questions. It was Bill who brought up Kneeley again. "What does Kneeley have to do to send his written material to you?"

"All I know is that every Tuesday night—actually Wednesday morning, between two and five A.M.—we have to have somebody on duty to receive what he sends. We have a system called the Gutenberg. It's some kind of software. Kneeley sends his material over the phone. Our computer receives it and prints it out. It's perfect."

"Fascinating," said Chris. "You say he only sends his stuff early Wednesday morning?"

"Usually. Sometimes, he'll call and arrange for a transmission at another time if there's something especially important, but most of it comes through on Wednesday morning." She frowned, then said, "You seem very interested, Chris. Frankly, I never pay much attention to it. I love books, not bits and bytes."

Chris smiled. "So do I, but as you said, this is the wave of the future. I suppose anybody who *doesn't* get interested in it is going to be left behind."

Billie nodded. "I know. The publisher wants all of us to take a computer course at NYU. They'll even pay for it if we agree to go. I guess I'd better before I find myself replaced by a robot."

Bill suggested they all return to the hotel for coffee, but Billie declined. "I'm leaving at six for Cape Cod," she said. "Things finally calmed down enough for me to grab some vacation time."

"I really enjoyed meeting you," said Chris.

"Same for me," Billie said as they parted on the sidewalk in front of Antolotti's. Bill and Billie hugged, and Chris wondered how close they had been.

Bill and Chris walked quickly back to the Hotel Inter-Continental. They found a table on the terrace overlooking the expansive lobby, ordered coffee, and looked at each other. "What are you thinking?" he asked.

"Lots of things, mostly that I'd give a million to see what Kneeley's working on."

"What if I could do that for you? I'd settle for dinner every night for the next hundred years."

She smiled and took his hand across the table. "Don't talk that way," she said. "It—"

"It what, Chris, makes you nervous? Good. I decided tonight that I'm all through playing sibling to the woman I love. I want you, and I'll do anything I have to to make it work."

She sighed and sat back heavily in her chair. "Bill, please try to understand that right now, I can't think clearly about anything except—"

"Except Richard Kneeley. Fine, let's get it over with."

"Get it over with?"

"Yeah, let's see what he's all about, and where he fits in with this case that has you spinning."

"Go on."

"If you want, I'll get a hold of Joey Zoe and set it up."

"Who?"

"Joey Zoe. He's a Shinnecock, lives out in Patchogue, on Long Island. Joey's not what you'd call the best public image for the American Indian, but he does have his value. He's probably the best redskin wire man in the country."

Chris sat up, waved her hand, and said with the threat of a giggle in her throat, "Hold on, Bill, wait a minute. Are you telling me that this Joey Zoe can find out what Kneeley is transmitting by tapping his phone?"

"Exactly. Joey owes me a few favors—"

"Along with every other Native American, it seems."

"You know how it is in journalism, Chris, you build up the due bills pretty fast. Joey's spent time in jail and I went to bat

182

for him. He's really not a bad guy, and I'll tell you this—he's a bonafide electronics genius who never took a shot at using it legitimately. If there's anybody can make it work, it's Joey."

Chris sat back again and slowly shook her head. "An illegal wiretap. That's insanity. I'm with the FBI."

"Yeah, and if you don't get this thing resolved, you might not be very much longer, which, I'm willing to admit, would make me a very happy man. However, I know it would devastate you, which prompts me to help. You're concerned about it being illegal? Could you get a legal order?"

"No. I'd never be able to show cause to a judge."

"Next question. Are you telling me that every tap the FBI puts on people is legal, comes through the right channels?"

She thought of the material in Kneeley's fie at the bureau, much of it obtained with illegal wiretaps of his hotel rooms. She didn't want to admit Bill was right, but she had to.

"See?" he said. "Well, what do you say? If Joey's in town, he'll do it for me."

Chris slowly took in the men and women at adjacent tables, all of whom seemed in high spirits and totally unconcerned with anything being said at their table. She asked Bill, "Why a wiretap? Why not just try to invade his computer?"

"That's more legal?"

"I know it's not right, but it's not as bad as a phone tap."

"Maybe so, Chris, but you heard Billie. Kneeley's a paranoid who knows damn well it's easy to intercept whatever he's working on. I'm not sure of all the details, but I do know that if he's added security devices, it'll be almost impossible to crash his system. The phone lines are another matter."

She sipped her coffee, put the cup down in the saucer with determination, and said, "No."

He shrugged. "Suit yourself, but I think you're wrong. You've been jerked around by a lot of people lately, not one of whom cares this much about Christine Saksis." He created a tiny space between his thumb and index finger. "Chris, please listen to me. I can set this up with Joey so that we'll know exactly what Kneeley's currently working on. Maybe it has nothing to do with Pritchard or the bureau or anything else, but it would be—well, it would be dumb to not rule it out. Joey can put in the tap, we get what Kneeley's sending to his publisher, the tap is pulled, and nobody knows the difference. Besides, what's the big deal about reading his pages? You're not stealing state secrets, just the writings of an author. You're not stealing his stuff for some rival publishing house, you're trying to solve a murder, and that's a hell of a lot more important than standing on protocol."

"Bill, I—"

"Trust me." He laughed. "I sound like a Hollywood agent."

"Can I ask you a question?"

"Sure."

"Don't take this wrong, but I'm seeing a side of you that I didn't know existed. You were always so against the FBI because of the way it intruded into people's personal lives, its secrecy, the—what did you call it, 'America's private police force.' But here you are suggesting that we use the same tactics."

"It's called pragmatism, my dear," he said. "The difference is that the personal life of the woman I'm madly in love with has been violated, and you know what happens when an Indian is dishonored by the palefaces."

She shook her head and waved for the waiter. "I'd love more coffee," she said to Bill.

"Good. So would I. Now, tell me about Kneeley's computer set-up."

"I didn't learn much about it. He's got an Apple Plus, modems . . ."

"Apple Plus?"

"Yes."

"That's an old model."

"I guess he's had it a while."

"Hmmmm. I assume he has the Gutenberg software Billie mentioned. He'd have to in order to link up with the publisher's equipment."

"I suppose so."

"Any idea of the specs?"

"Huh?"

"The specs, specifically the baud rate."

"Bill, I—"

"Forget it, Joey will figure it out. It's probably three hundred."

"If you say so."

The waiter delivered more coffee. Bill wiped his mouth and stood. "Let me try to reach Joey now."

"Bill, are you sure this is—"

"Trust me. Remember?"

While he was gone, Chris's thoughts turned to Ross Lizenby. He'd undoubtedly return and expect her to be waiting. She dreaded seeing him, knew she'd have to tell him about the weekend in New York and the rekindling of her affair with Bill. Under any circumstances, that would have been difficult, but there was that side of Ross that instilled in her an added fear, especially after what she'd been told about his ex-wife. She forced herself to dismiss that kind of thinking. It is ridiculous, and she felt mildly embarrassed at creating scenarios that were more appropriate to a dreamy high school girl with an overactive imagination.

Bill bounced back to the table. "I got him. It's all set."

"It is?"

"Yup. I'm meeting him tomorrow. He was a little shy about talking on the phone."

"I don't wonder."

"The only question is where you want to be when Kneeley starts transmitting. I could rent equipment here and set up in the room. No, that's no good. The hotel operator will break in on a line that's open too long. We can do it in Washington, right at your apartment."

"Really?"

"Sure. All Joey has to know is what number to hook up to the tap on Kneeley's phone."

She thought of Lizenby again. "Maybe my apartment isn't such a good idea, Bill. It's too close to home."

"Whatever you say. Just decide before I meet him tomorrow."

"If it is my apartment, do I have what we need?"

"No, but I'll pick it up in Washington. It doesn't take much. You have an Apple IIe, and a printer."

"Yes."

"And a phone."

"Of course."

"Got plenty of roll-feed paper?"

"None."

"I'll get that, too. Your printer takes roll-feed, doesn't it?"

"Sure."

"That's it. I'll pick up the Gutenberg program, too. Just leave it to me. We'll do it in your place?"

"All right." She'd decided she didn't want to extend the time in New York and could make whatever plans were necessary to be alone—alone with Bill—during the hours of between two and five on Wednesday morning.

As they waited for a check, Chris asked more about Joey Zoe.

"A remarkable type," said Bill. "Dropped out of junior high, bummed around, ended up in the Air Force, where he picked up a ton of electronics experience. He was booted out with a dishonorable discharge for playing with the computer at the PX. He had listed himself as a vendor and received payment for goods delivered. There weren't any goods."

Her eyebrows went up.

"He was lucky he didn't do time for it. He came out of the service and hooked up with some mobsters who used his electronics skills by tapping into a bank's computer and siphoning off a couple of hundred thousand dollars before it was discovered. Joey did time for it, his bosses walked free. It's funny what happened to him in jail. He ended up being assigned a work detail with the prison's computer set-up, which was hooked up to a statewide network. He swears if they'd kept him on that job for another couple of weeks he could have released half the prisoners in New York." They both laughed. "It turned out somebody reviewed his file and that was the end of his computer assignment. He spent the next two years in the kitchen."

"I'm having second thoughts," Chris said.

"Don't," he said. "Besides having a streak of larceny in his heart, Joey's an absolute charmer and has a strong sense of duty to our people. He did a tap for me on the New York State Bureau of Indian Affairs. I got a hell of a story out of it."

"You're impossible," she said as they walked to the elevators."

"Impossible . . . and adorable. Oh, and let's not forget sexually irresistible." Which he proceeded to prove.

22

BETH PRITCHARD WAS almost a half an hour late, which set Saksis on edge. She'd started to wonder whether the teenager had developed second thoughts about getting together. She was relieved when the room phone rang.

Beth was dressed in baggy jeans, a sweatshirt with a picture of Boy George on it, and sneakers—hardly the outfit for an elegant breakfast at the Hotel Inter-Continental. But no one looked askance as they went through the buffet line, found a table on the terrace, and started eating.

Saksis was filled with conflicting thoughts as she sat across from the young girl. There was something very vital and alive about her, the sort of spirit only the young seemed to possess. Beth played out all the quirks of her age, trying very hard to be sophisticated, yet betraying herself by using the jargon of her peers, overreacting at the wrong times, missing the point at others. Saksis felt very much the big sister. But that could get in the way, she knew. She *wasn't* her big sister, and was with her only because she wanted her to talk about her mother and father, to give information, to help Saksis resolve her own problems. There were those fleeting moments when Saksis wondered to what extent she could use Beth, play on her teenage naivete to reach her own goals, get inside her for her own selfish reasons. But Beth took her off the hook, in a sense, by saying after she'd cleaned her plate, "I want to talk to you about what happened to my father."

No need to con this kid, Saksis thought. She'd come to breakfast ready to talk. Saksis said, "I'd like that very much, Beth, because, frankly, I'm in the middle of a mess and don't have the answers to help me out of it."

"Are you in trouble?" the girl asked, her face serious and concerned.

"No, I don't want you to think that, but your father's death has caused a lot of problems for me, and for other people."

"Why?"

"Well, because he was who he was, a respected member of the Federal Bureau of Investigation. There's intense pressure to find who killed him, and any of us who are working on it naturally feel that pressure."

"My mother killed him."

Saksis stared across the table. Beth's lips were pressed tightly together, and Saksis saw that she'd clenched her fists into tight balls. She started to say something, but Beth said, "You don't believe me, do you?"

Saksis shook her head and looked around the terrace, leaned over the table, and said in a stage whisper, "Beth, you do realize what you've just said?"

"Of course I do."

"You—you have no doubts about it?"

"No."

"Do you have proof?"

"Yes."

Saksis sat back and twisted a strand of hair at her temple as she desperately tried to formulate a sensible comment, question, anything. Finally, she said, "Tell me about the proof."

"My mother was there the night he was killed."

"I know that, although she denies it. But you told me the first time I met you that your mother had been home that evening."

"Of course I did. If I hadn't, she would have killed me, too."

"Beth, do you—Beth, I don't want to sound as though I doubt what you say, but you're accusing your own mother of not only killing your father, but of being capable of killing you."

"That's right."

"That's—"

"I don't care what you think." Her eyes filled up and she was obviously fighting against making a scene. She pushed the edge of her napkin against her eyes and held it there for a long time. Saksis wanted to come around the table and wrap her arms around her, tell her that everything was all right and to make her forget about her father's murder. Had Beth continued much longer in the battle against her tears, that's exactly what might have happened. But she lowered the napkin, stuck out her chin, and said, "I just told you the truth, Miss Saksis."

"And I believe you, Beth. It's just that such a serious accusation has to be backed up with some pretty hefty proof."

"I told you I could prove it."

"Go ahead, I'm listening."

"I don't want to talk here."

Saksis nodded. "We'll go to my room."

Beth shook her head. "I don't trust anyplace, or anybody, not after what happened to my father."

Instead they walked east on Forty-ninth Street to First Avenue, then took a right until they stood in front of the United Nations. Flags of member nations rippled against a gun metal gray sky that threatened rain. Two small Hispanic boys wrestled with each other despite their mother's admonitions to stop. A young couple necked on a bench, the music from a large portable cassette player blaring what Saksis considered the antithesis of erotic music.

"Let's sit over there," she said, indicating a bench far removed from the others. When they were seated, she said, "Okay, Beth, let's get it over with. What you told me at the restaurant is shocking, but I believe you. Ever since your mother lied about that night, I've had to consider her a prime suspect in your father's murder. Can you tell me why she might have killed him?"

Beth looked at Saksis and screwed up her face. "See, you don't believe me."

"Beth, you have to understand that I can't simply accept what you say without asking questions."

"You just said, 'might have killed him.' *She did!*"

"Okay, she did. Why?"

"She hated him."

"Well, frankly, I gathered that your mother and father didn't have much of a marriage, but lots of wives hate husbands, and vice versa. That doesn't mean they act it out by killing."

"I know that."

"So?"

"So what?"

"So why are we here, Beth? Why did you slip me your phone number and encourage me to call you? I didn't suggest it, you did."

"Because I want the truth about my father told."

"And so do I. You say your mom killed him because she hated him. She wouldn't have had to come into the FBI building late at night to do that. That's taking a big risk. Why didn't she just kill him at home, or in a hotel, or—"

"She didn't kill him just because they didn't get along."

"She didn't?"

Beth leaned forward, her elbows on her knees, and slowly shook her head.

"Then why?"

"Because—because of Mr. Kneeley."

Saksis started to say something, swallowed it, and looked around the broad plaza. The lovers were still embracing, the little Hispanic kids were being hauled off by their mother, and a pair of New York City cops strolled idly along First Avenue, their attention riveted on the swaying shapely derriere of an attractive young woman wearing a sheer cotton dress.

"Miss Saksis," Beth said.

"Oh. I'm sorry. I was daydreaming."

Beth looked quizzically at her, and for good reason. To daydream in the midst of such a serious discussion was—.

Saksis smiled. "I was thinking about what you just said."

"About Mr. Kneeley?"

"Yes. He's the author, isn't he?"

Beth nodded. "He's writing a book about the FBI."

"Is he? Is it a serious book?"

"I guess so. That's what he writes, isn't it?"

"So I understand. Was your father working with him on the book?"

"No. My mother was."

"Your mother?" It was becoming a morning of one surprise after another. She asked Beth to elaborate.

Beth hesitated, then said, "Can I trust you?"

"I hope so. We're here because you wanted to be, and you've already told me a lot. Yes, Beth, you can trust me, but you also know I have to do my job."

"Arrest who killed my father."

"That's right."

"Even if it's my mother."

Saksis felt intensely awkward as she said, "Yes, even then."

They sat in silence for a few minutes until Beth again brought up the subject of her father's murder. "My father kept secret notes on everything he worked on, every case, every person he knew. He told me once that maybe he'd write a book when he was retired, but I don't know if he ever would have. I guess I'll never know."

"Where did he keep the notes?" Chris asked.

"I don't know, but sometimes, when he was home, he'd have them with him to work on. I read some of them once."

"You did? What were they like?"

"My dad was a good writer. I wish he did write a book. It would have been good."

"I'm sure it would have."

"He had notebooks filled up. He printed very small. It almost looked like it was typed. Do you know what I mean? It was so neat, just like him."

Saksis could sense emotion building inside the girl and felt bad for her. Still, she wasn't about to interrupt, break the spell, lose whatever revelations might come next.

"He had other stuff, too."

"Like what?"

"Papers, copies of hundreds of papers, letters to different people in the FBI, memos, notes from meetings."

"They sound important," Saksis said.

"I guess they were. A lot of them had *Secret* stamped on them."

"I'm surprised he left them around for you to see."

"Oh, he didn't. It was an accident. When he was home— that wasn't often—he and mom didn't sleep together. He had his own room, and he had a big safe in there. Sometimes he'd lock the door and just sit in there for a whole weekend working on things. Then, he'd pack it up and leave on Sunday night."

"How did you get to read his notes?"

"I didn't read many of them, just a couple of folders that he left in his room one Saturday. Mom was out, and he got a phone call from somebody. He told me he had to meet somebody in a big hurry and left. I went into his room. I guess he thought he'd put everything into the safe, but there were these two folders that he must have forgot. Anyway, I read them. I didn't understand a lot of it, but I knew they were important. I was afraid he'd know I read them so I made sure they were just where I found them when he came home. He asked me about them, but I said I wasn't in his room."

"Beth, I have to ask you this. You said that your mother killed your father, and it was because of Richard Kneeley. Why do you say that?"

"My mother knew all about my father's diaries and papers, and she got a hold of them one day."

"How?"

"I don't know. I just heard them fighting about it one night. That was when he was home more and had everything there. I don't think she stole them or anything, only maybe she did. She would."

Beth's voice was cold and bitter. "My dad used to talk to her

193

more, at least back then, and I know he told her some of the stories. He was so secret about everything he did, but he would talk to her, I guess because she was his wife."

"That's very common."

"Sure it is, only she wasn't the one he should have trusted." She looked up at Saksis and said, "I hate my mother, Miss Saksis. I really hate her."

"I'm sorry. That must be a horrible feeling."

"It used to be until—well, until she did to him what she did."

"Killed him?"

"Even more than that, things she did before, like stealing all his notes and papers and selling them to Mr. Kneeley."

"Are you sure she did that?"

"Yes. I heard all the fights about it. Mom wanted more money, always wanted more than dad had, and she forced him to do things to get it."

"What kind of things?"

"I don't know, tell people what he knew for money. It made him so sad all the time, and mad."

"And you say your mother sold his secret notes and papers to Richard Kneeley so he could write a book about them?"

"That's right."

"Do you know how much Kneeley paid?"

Beth shook her head.

"And your father was against it?"

"Yes, only he was afraid. My mother told him that if he did anything to get in the way she'd tell the FBI all about his notes and papers, and the FBI would think *he* sold them to Mr. Kneeley."

Saksis thought for a moment, then said, "I don't doubt this is all true, Beth, but it doesn't mean that your mother killed him."

The girl became animated. "Yes, it does," she said. "Why would she go there that night and then lie to you?"

"I don't know, maybe—"

"She had a gun."

"She told me it was stolen a long time ago."

"Another lie. She lies all the time."

Saksis leaned closer to her and said, "Tell me why she killed him, Beth."

"Because—I think because he was going to go to the FBI and tell them what she'd done."

"You *think.*"

"I don't know for certain, but I know she was there that night, and had the gun, and—"

"And—"

"And threatened him with it."

"At home?"

"Yes."

"When?"

"About a week before she did it."

"You heard the threat?"

"Yes. They thought I was asleep."

"What did she say?"

"She said that if he did anything to stop her deal—or arrangement, or whatever she called it—with Richard Kneeley, she'd kill him first before ever allowing that to happen."

"Let's go," Saksis said. They slowly walked back in the direction of the hotel. "Beth, tell me exactly what happened the night your father died."

"She went to his office to kill him."

"She said that?"

"No, of course not, but—you don't believe me, do you?"

"Of course I do, but you have to understand that I can't accuse your mother unless I have something tangible to go on, some proof, some definite testimony. Did you ever hear your mother say she killed your father?"

"Why would she do that?" The girl was becoming increasingly angry, and confused. She started to walk faster, as though she were suddenly anxious to get away.

"Beth," Saksis said.

The girl took a few more steps, realized Saksis was no longer with her, and stopped. She turned and glared, her cheeks stained from tears, her mouth set against an outpouring of them.

"I believe you," Saksis said, closing the gap between them. "I really do, Beth, but please try to understand the position I'm in."

"You don't care, do you?"

"Care?"

"About my father."

"Of course I do. I didn't know him very well, but I was shocked at what happened and—"

"I loved my father very much." She started to shake, and her voice became higher and louder. "I loved him and she took him away. I hate her, hate her, hate her." She slapped her hand against a wall, then leaned against it and wept openly.

Saksis wrapped her arms around Beth. "Take it easy," she said, "everything's going to be all right."

"I want you to believe me. She killed him."

"I know, and we'll make it right. Believe me, I'll do what's best."

Beth eventually gained control. Saksis handed her a Kleenex from her pocket and the girl wiped her eyes and blew her nose. "Thanks," she said.

They reached the hotel. "Want a cold drink?" Saksis asked as they stood in the lobby peering into the bird cage.

"No, thanks. I'm really sorry I acted like such a jerk."

"You didn't do anything of the kind. I'm glad you had enough faith to confide in me."

"What will you do now?"

"I'm not quite sure, but there are some other aspects of the investigation that can be combined with what you've told me. I suggest you not mention getting together with me to anyone. No one, Beth."

"I won't."

"Where's your mother?"

"I don't know, probably with some guy."

Chris Saksis thought her heart would break. She put an arm around the teenager and said, "Sometimes, we have to go through hard times before we enjoy the easy ones."

A slight smile came to Beth's face. "That's what my father used to say."

They walked to the lobby door. "What will you do for the rest of the day?" Saksis asked.

Beth shrugged. "Hang around, go to the Village."

"Be careful."

"I will. How about you?"

"Well, I have to meet someone in about an hour. He's working on the case, too, and maybe between us we'll find some evidence to support what you've told me."

"I hope so."

Saksis wanted very much to show Beth the photograph of Rosemary Cale, but she decided there really wasn't much to be gained from it. She kissed her on the cheek and said, "Keep that pretty chin up, Beth. You're a good person."

"So are you, Miss Saksis. Thanks for breakfast." Her eyes filled up again. "God, I feel like I have a big sister."

Saksis grinned. "I like being one. Take care. I'll call you as soon as I know more."

Bill Tse-ay concluded his meeting with Joey Zoe in a Chinese restaurant that Joey claimed was "safe." Bill gave him all the information he had, and Joey instructed him on what was needed at Bill's end. According to Joey, it was simple. Once the tap was in, whenever Kneeley dialed his publisher's number in Manhattan to transmit material between computers, the phone would ring in Chris's apartment. All she had to do was pick it up and place it in the cradle on the modem. Whatever Kneeley transmitted would come up on her screen, and would print out on her printer. "I don't think it'll format, though," Joey said, "but you'll get the words."

"That's all we need," Bill said.

"It'll cost," Joey said. "I need special equipment for the tap."

"Whatever."

"What about a fee?"

"Whatever you say, Joey, only remember you owe me a few."

Joey smiled and finished his coffee. Everything about him was square—body, face, hands. His cheeks were deeply pockmarked, and years of neglect of his teeth had left them yellow and uneven. He wore a faded, wrinkled brown corduroy sports jacket, a red-and-black plaid shirt, blue knit tie, and tan work pants. "I thought I paid that off a long time ago," he said.

"Yeah, you did, only I think we should keep it going as friends. We'll probably need each other again—more than once."

Joey chewed on his cheek. "Sure, you're right, only I have to get something."

"Two hundred?"

"Make it four. It's risky. And that's way below my usual price."

"You've got it. Just make sure the tap is pulled by six the next morning."

"Sure. You know, Billy, if this guy on Fire Island is as savvy as you say about computers and security, he might have hooked up a phone-tap meter. Once the tap is on, the impedance goes down. You know that. He could read it."

"I'm hoping he doesn't."

"You're sure we can't do it at the other end?"

"At the publisher? No way."

"It's easy in the junction box."

"Forget it. It's got to be on his phone on Fire Island."

"All right, but if it don't work, I still get paid."

"Of course."

"Could I have some now?"

"I'm a little short of cash. Here." He pulled a little over a hundred dollars from his wallet. "I'll get you the rest by Thursday."

They parted in front of the restaurant. "Good to see you again," Bill said.

"Yeah, me, too. You sure you don't want to tell me what this is all about?"

"I can't, Joey, you know that."

Joey started to laugh.

"What's so funny?"

"Remember when you were going with that broad from Maine, the one who ended up with the FBI?"

Bill nodded.

"You still see her?"

"Nah."

"That's good. All I need is you telling a spook about this."

23

THEY LEFT NEW York at three and arrived at Chris's apartment in Washington a little before ten, having stopped for a leisurely dinner along the way. As they approached Washington she found herself becoming increasingly uneasy. She couldn't get Ross Lizenby out of her mind, and was fearful that he'd be waiting there, angry, and would make a scene with Bill.

It seemed that her fears were unjustified. There was no sign of Lizenby as they parked in her garage, carried their bags to the elevator and up to her floor. A tiny red light on her answering machine indicated there had been five calls that had been recorded. She would have preferred to listen to them in private, but turned the switches anyway and heard the voices of a couple of female friends suggesting dinner or tennis dates, a salesman for a magazine distributorship offering her the "chance of a lifetime," the landlord informing her that all water would be shut off for twelve hours because of boiler repairs starting at noon on Wednesday, and Ross Lizenby, who simply said, "Call me."

"That's him?" Bill asked when he heard Lizenby's voice.

"Yes."

"He sounded mad."

"I suppose he has a right to be. I told you he wanted to meet me here this afternoon."

"Did you promise you'd be here?"

"No."

"Then he has no reason to be mad."

"He's—"

"Unreasonable. He sounds it from what you've told me. I think you ought to break if off clean and complete, Chris."

"I know. I intend to."

"That's all you need is to have word of *that* affair float around headquarters."

Chris had just gone into the kitchen to make a pot of coffee. She returned to the living room and said, "Did I hear what I thought I heard you say?"

Bill had sprawled out on the couch. He lifted his head and said, "What do you mean?"

"Something about—come on, Bill, you make it sound as though I have seven affairs going at once in the bureau."

"I didn't mean that."

"It sure sounded it. 'Rumors of *that* affair . . .' I resent it."

He went to her, put his hands on her shoulders. "Hey, don't go reading things into it. All I was trying to say was—"

"Just try to say it with a little more sensitivity." She started to cry and went into the kitchen. He came up behind, wrapped his arms around her, and gently rocked her back and forth, his lips to her neck. "I love you," he said.

"And I love you, too, damn it."

He turned her so that their eyes met. "Don't damn it, Chris. It's right."

"I don't know what's right anymore. I'm tired."

"You should be. It was a busy weekend."

"I'm going to bed," she said.

"Good idea. I'll stay with you."

"I'd rather you didn't."

"Why?"

"I need to be alone, sort things out, get ready for what's coming."

"You make it sound like the apocalypse."

"Maybe it is."

He kissed her wet eyes. "Okay, I'll go. Call me at the hotel if you need anything. I'll be out tomorrow buying what we need to crash Kneeley's system. What time do you want to meet up?"

"Tomorrow?"

"Yes."

"I don't know. Let me call you in the afternoon."

His face became serious. "You know, Chris, I haven't pushed this Kneeley thing for any reasons of my own. I just want to help, and maybe it'll uncover something useful."

"I know that," she said as she walked him to the door. "Bill, I'm sorry I snapped at you."

"You're tense, Chris, that's all. It'll all be over soon. Like I said—"

"Trust me." She broke into laughter.

"Yeah, trust me. Good night. Get a good night's sleep."

"I'll try. You, too."

The moment she closed the door behind him she went to the phone, picked it up, and dialed Lizenby's number. It was either do it then or not at all, and she wanted to get it over with. She was relieved when there was no answer.

Bill Tse-ay looked up and down the street in front of her building in search of a cab. He started walking to the corner, which was at the intersection of another small, quiet street, didn't find a cab there, and headed toward what looked like a busy avenue. Chris's street was dark and lonely. A heavy fog had drifted into Washington, which turned the few street lamps into shrouded balls of soft light. He paused because he thought he heard—sensed, actually—that there was someone sharing the street with him, behind him, footsteps barely audible, no real sound, just a presence. He glanced over his right shoulder, saw nothing, and took a few more steps.

Now, the footsteps were loud and deliberate, feet closing ground. Bill swung around just in time to catch the full force of a fist wrapped around a roll of dimes. His world became brilliant pinpoints of searing white light, a deafening roar, and a rush of pain. He slumped to the ground, one hand instinctively pressing his shattered left cheekbone. Blood oozed from his left eye and through his fingers as his head hit the red brick sidewalk.

His assailant quickly grabbed him by the shirt and dragged him into a clump of bushes surrounding a sedate Georgetown town house. He held Bill's battered face off the ground with his left hand, brought back his right—the one holding the rolled dimes—and hit him again, this time smashing his nose flat against his face. He let go; Bill's head thumped to the soft dirt.

Chris tried Ross Lizenby two more times without success. She called Bill at the Gralyn. He hadn't returned yet. "Message?" the operator asked. "No," said Chris. "I'll try him again tomorrow."

She climbed into bed wishing she hadn't asked him to leave.

Bill managed to crawl just far enough to be visible from the street. A late-night dog walker discovered him at three A.M. and called the police.

An ambulance rushed him to Doctor's Hospital, where, after a quick evaluation in the emergency room, he was wheeled into surgery to relieve a blood clot on the right side of his brain.

"He'll make it," one of the surgeons said to a police officer after Bill had been taken to Intensive Care. "Could be impairment, though. Did you notify family?"

"We're trying. He publishes *Native American Times*, the Indian newspaper. According to what was in his wallet, he lives on a reservation in Arizona."

"It'll be a while before he publishes anything," the surgeon said. "Whoever did it sure as hell didn't like him. Couldn't have hit him more perfectly to have done that kind of damage."

"It was robbery," the officer said. "Credit cards and cash gone. At least they left the identifying papers."

"What was he doing in Washington?"

"Beats me, doc."

24

SAKSIS WENT WITH trepidation to her office in the Hoover Building the next morning. She couldn't decide what she feared most—the certain confrontation with Ross Lizenby, facing the ramifications of the rumor about her affair with George Pritchard, or putting into reality the plans to crash Richard Kneeley's transmission of material to Sutherland House. Probably all three, she thought as she hung up her coat, poured coffee from the Ranger pot, and settled behind her desk.

There was a neat pile of memos that hadn't been there when she'd left on Saturday. One of the secretaries was obsessively organized. Pencils were always sharpened and lined up in strict formation, note pads had a clean sheet on top, and telephone message slips were arranged in order of the time they were received, the most recent on the bottom.

There was something else on the desk that hadn't been there Friday, a greeting card–size envelope with the name *Christine* written on it. She picked it up and recognized Lizenby's handwriting. Her hands trembled as she carefully opened the sealed envelope and removed a piece of yellow paper that was folded in half. She read the terse, typewritten message:

> You disgust me. You played games with me, and I hate women who play games. I heard about Pritchard and you, and know where you were this weekend and who you were with. You're a goddamn slut, and I'm sorry I ever wasted two minutes with you.

It wasn't signed.

She went through myriad emotions within seconds—burning tears, panic, wonderment, then anger. She went to the secretary's desk and asked in a voice barely controlled, "Where is Mr. Lizenby?"

"He's gone, Miss Saksis. Didn't you hear?"

"No. Gone where?"

"Special assignment. That's all I know."

She looked in on Jake Stein, who was having coffee with Joe Perone. "I just heard Ross is gone on special assignment."

Perone looked up from his newspaper. "Yeah, I heard that, too. Where'd they send him?"

"You don't know?" Saksis said.

Stein and Perone shook their heads. "Why do you think we would?" Stein asked.

"I don't know, I just thought that—"

Perone laughed and tossed the paper on his desk. "Come on, Chris, you know how it works around here. Nobody ever talks about where the Unkempts go."

"Did you see him before he left?" she asked.

"No," they said in unison.

"What about Ranger?"

The two men looked at each other before Perone said, "Jake's been put in charge."

"You have, Jake? I didn't hear about it."

Stein sighed and crossed his legs. "I just heard about it over the weekend. But don't view it as a big deal. I'm in charge of folding it up."

Saksis wanted to turn and run. It was obvious that they'd

heard about the accusation that she'd slept with Pritchard, and equally obvious that she'd been relieved of her temporary job overseeing Ranger because of it. Stein and Perone were openly uncomfortable talking to her. She resented that most. She slammed the door and said, "What's going on here? Ross leaves on 'special assignment,' I'm pulled off Ranger without being told, and you say it's being folded. Why?"

"Why what?" Stein asked.

"Why everything?"

"Look Chris," Stein said, getting up and leaning against a ledge that housed the air conditioning, "nobody wants to hurt you. Get that straight."

Saksis directed a stream of air at a strand of hair that had fallen over her face. She looked up at the ceiling and said, "Somebody's doing a damn fine job of it."

"What did you expect?" Stein asked.

She glared at him. "What do you mean?"

"Chris, I'm a great believer in people living their own lives, getting it off any way they want behind closed doors, but when you start playing around here in the bureau, you—well, god-damn it, you ask for trouble."

She took a few steps toward him, stopped, and pointed a finger in his direction. "You mean the lie about me and George Pritchard."

Stein shook his head and looked away.

She looked at Perone. "It's a lie, Joe, a vicious lie intended to hurt me."

"Yeah, I know, Chris."

"It *is.*"

Stein said, "It doesn't matter, Chris. It's all over the building."

"But—"

"And hooking up with Ross didn't help matters."

"I never—"

"That's a lie, too?"

She looked at the floor. "No." She asked, "Did Ross talk to you about it?"

"Not really," said Perone.

"What the hell does 'not really' mean?"

"He— forget it, Chris. Ranger's going out of business, Ross is assigned somewhere else, and we can all get back to the routine."

Her anger gave way to sadness again as she said, "And what's *my* routine—the bureau slut?"

"Nobody ever said that, Chris," Perone said.

"No? What do you think about it?"

"About what, a little office romance?" Stein laughed to show how insignificant it was.

"How about conflict of interest, Jake? That's what I was really accused of by Gormley, investigating the Pritchard murder without being unbiased."

Stein said, "It's water over the dam, Chris. It'll all blow away and be forgotten."

"Tell me that when you read my evaluation reports," she said.

"You can always protest. There's a system for it."

She went to the door, drew in a deep breath, turned, and said, "So, officially, who did it?"

"Who did what?" Perone asked.

"Who killed George L. Pritchard?"

Stein turned his back on her and said flatly, "It'll be announced this afternoon, at five."

"Oh, really? A press conference?"

"Yes."

"Who's announcing it?"

"Director Shelton."

"Right from the top, huh? Do *you* know, Jake?"

He looked at her. "Yes."

"And I can't be told?"

"That's right, only don't take it personally. No one is to be told until Shelton's announcement."

"Except you."

"There were reasons."

"Give me two. I was in charge of Ranger right up until today."

"Until Saturday," said Stein in a voice that indicated he was losing patience with the conversation.

"Until the 'revelation' that I'd been sleeping with the deceased. Who came up with that? Rosemary Cale at someone's behest?"

"Whatever you say, Chris," said Stein. "I have to go. I'm late for a meeting."

She looked at Perone. "Joe, this is all wrong."

He nodded and fell into step behind Stein. Perone's final words to her over his shoulder were, "Cool it, Chris. Don't make it worse."

She sat in her office for twenty minutes with the door closed. Someone knocked. It was one of the secretaries. "Miss Saksis, the building maintenance crew is going to start packing things up here. I've been told to inform everyone to have their personal effects in order before three."

"Thank you."

Ten minutes later she was summoned to Assistant Director Wayne Gormley's office. He was pleasant and warm as he said, "Now that Ranger is dissolved, the question of reassignment for its staff has to be settled. I've decided to assign you to a resident agency office in Montana."

"Montana?"

"Yes. We have a definite need there for someone of your background and experience in Indian and reservation affairs. It will give you a chance to get right back into an important area of bureau jurisdiction."

"I see."

"Frankly, I think I owe you an apology."

Her heart beat faster and she said, "About—about the accusation that I—"

He smiled broadly. "Yes, Miss Saksis. I think I overreacted. I can claim many things, primarily the pressure of the past few weeks because of the Pritchard matter, but I won't fall back on excuses. I realize that I'd come on rather strong to you on Saturday, and that was wrong. As concerned as we are—as everyone in the bureau is about maintaining strict discipline over special agent conduct—the capacity to understand and to accept human frailty isn't unknown. Up until this unfortunate incident, your record has been exemplary and we respect that sort of performance."

Her excited anticipation of a moment ago was replaced with the sardonic anger she'd felt all morning. She said, "But you don't want to deal with the question of whether what I was accused of is false."

Another smile. "I don't think it's germane to the larger issue, Miss Saksis."

She didn't know what to do, to argue it further with him or to accept graciously his offer of leniency. *Leniency!* I haven't done anything, she thought. But then Ross Lizenby came to mind. She'd broken bureau regulations with him. Did Gormley know about their affair? Did it matter? *Montana?* It represented banishment in bureau terms. Resident agency offices were filled with special agents who'd broken a rule, stepped on big toes, fouled up in some way, major or minor.

"I'd enjoy talking further with you, Miss Saksis, but I have other appointments. Thanks for coming by. I spoke with the agent in charge of the Montana office and he's anxious for you to arrive and lend a hand. I told him I'd see that you were there no later than Friday."

"Friday? Sir, that's impossible."

His eyebrows went up as he escorted her to the door. "It is short notice, Miss Saksis, but that's often the way it is with the bureau. Good luck on your new assignment. I'll be taking a personal interest in your development out there. And give my best to Bill Thompson. You'll be reporting to him. We go back a long way together."

The maintenance crew was busy emptying out Ranger when she returned. She entered her office and absently began putting some personal effects in a box she'd found outside. Her phone rang. "Christine Saksis?" a voice asked.

"Yes."

"This is Sergeant Flynn at MPD. We had an assault and robbery last night and are trying to trace people who might know the victim."

"Who is it?"

"His name's—I'm not sure how to pronounce it. It's spelled Tse-ay."

"Bill?"

"Yes, ma'am, William Tse-ay. Your name and number was on a slip of paper we found in his wallet."

"What happened? Is he hurt?"

"I'm afraid so. He's critical at Doctor's Hospital."

"Oh, my God."

"They performed surgery last night. The doctor's name is Goldberg, Leslie Goldberg."

"Thank you, I—you say he's critical."

"Yes. Miss Saksis, because you're with the FBI, I was wondering whether the victim had any dealings with you and the bureau."

"Dealings. Yes, he was—no, nothing official. We're very close friends."

"I see. Well, thank you. If you think of anything that might help us trace his movements leading up to the assault, or that might help identify his assailant, I'm here at headquarters, detective division."

"I'll call if I think of anything."

"Thank you, ma'am. Have a good day."

She didn't bother with her car, grabbed a cab in front of the Hoover Building and went to the hospital, where she was referred to Dr. Goldberg's office. He was there, and when she explained who she was, he told his receptionist to send her in. He explained quickly and simply what damage had been done to Bill's brain.

"Will it be permanent damage?" she asked.

"Hard to say. I'm optimistic about him. I can see signs of improvement already, but they're small."

"Can I see him?" she asked.

"He's still in Intensive Care, but I think it would be all right for you to spend a few minutes with him."

"Is he conscious?"

"In and out. I talked with him this morning and he"—the doctor grinned—made sense, but he slipped back into what's

211

basically a comatose state pretty quickly. Go on up. I'll cal
ahead and tell them to admit you, but only for a few minutes.'

Saksis was ushered into one of the rooms in Intensive Care
where Bill was hooked up to a variety of tubes and machines
His head was completely bandaged. Only his face was visible
It was purple, but relaxed, serene, as though he'd entered an
other dimension. "Just a few minutes," a nurse said.

Saksis stood at the side of the bed and tentatively touched
Bill's hand. She'd expected it to be cold; it was warm and soft
She twined her fingers into his and said, "Bill." He didn'
move, and his eyes remained closed. "Bill, it's Chris."

There was a flutter in his eyelids, and his chest heaved. He
opened his eyes and looked directly into her's. "Hi," he said, a
small smile forming on his parched lips.

"Hi," she said.

"Boy," he said, "I—"

"Don't talk, I just wanted you to know I was here. Dr
Goldberg said you're going to be fine."

"Who's he?"

"He's—he operated on you."

"My head hurts."

"I'll tell the nurse."

"Okay." He squeezed her fingers and said, "You have to ge
the stuff I was supposed to get."

"What stuff?"

"For Joey Zoe."

"Bill, forget about that. What's important is that you—'

"You have to. Please."

She didn't want to upset him. "Sure," she said. "What do
need?"

He pointed to a sheet of paper on his nightstand, on which
he'd listed everything before being attacked.

"Fine. You rest. They told me I could only stay a few min
utes. Go to sleep." She kissed his forehead.

"Get the stuff and hook in. It's important."

"I will. I promise."

"Get a print-out. I want to see it."

"Okay."

"Chris."

"What?"

"If I don't make it, be sure to pay Joey Zoe what I promised. I don't want to leave any bad debts behind. It's $300."

"I love you, Bill," she said, quickly turning and leaving so that he wouldn't see the wetness in her eyes.

25

CHRIS SAKSIS SPENT the afternoon racing around Washington in search of the items Bill said she'd need to crash Kneeley's computer transmission. She didn't bother returning to the Hoover Building, nor did she call in. It all seemed irrelevant, her responsibilities to the FBI. It left her with an emptiness in her stomach. She loved being a part of her country's most prestigious law enforcement organization. It was her family, gave her a sense of worth and motivation in her life. But the organization that fostered so many positive feelings had turned its back on her, like a mother or father who misunderstood and who refused to forgive, to listen, to give the benefit of the doubt.

She read the instructions that came with the telephone modem and the Gutenberg software, hoping that she understood and hadn't incorrectly hooked the components together—for Bill's sake. It had become a cause of sorts for him, and she wanted to have a clean print-out of whatever Kneeley transmitted to his publisher. It didn't matter how it affected the Pritchard case. What *did* matter was Bill Tse-ay. Her mind had been filled all afternoon with visions of him being rendered mentally incapacitated for the rest of his life—of their life. It couldn't happen, she told herself when those fears struck. He'd talked to her, had, as Dr. Goldberg said, "made sense." That caused her to smile, just as it had for the doctor. Bill would be fine and, with any luck, so would she. Montana! It wasn't fair, but she forced herself to view it positively. If it did involve working with crimes on reservations, she'd attack it with spirit and dedication. That would please Bill. She could stay with the FBI and help her people at the same time.

It was all so confusing—getting her computer ready, the mess at the bureau, George Pritchard, Beth, Helen Pritchard, Rosemary Cale, the dirty rumors, the truth about her and Ross Lizenby . . . What sense did it make?.

She turned on her television at six to the Cable News channel, where a longer report on the Pritchard press conference was likely to be carried. The conference was the third story. Director Shelton stood at a podium alongside a spokesman from the State Department. Shelton spoke first.

"It is with relief, and sorrow, that I announce today the resolution of the unfortunate death of one of the Federal Bureau of Investigation's finest special agents, George L. Pritchard. A thorough investigation of the circumstances surrounding his death has resulted in an understanding of what occurred, which I know each of you in the media, and in the American public, has been anxious for.

"Special agent Pritchard's death has led to one of the most exhaustive investigations in the bureau's history. It did, after all, involve one of our own, and everyone in law enforcement knows that when a *brother* is killed in the line of duty, there is no let-up until the case is solved.

"Before I proceed, I wish to extend my heartfelt thanks to the dedicated and professional men and women who worked night and day to identify the persons responsible for this loss, which we all feel very deeply at the FBI. Special agent Pritchard was a credit to this bureau and was an inspiration to every special agent, man and woman, black and white, and to every person who strives to make the bureau the exemplary organization it is, both here at home and in the world community."

Saksis shifted in her chair and silently wished he'd get on with it.

"Unfortunately," Shelton continued, "the facts as they've emerged do not close this case with finality. It involves not the simple act of murder, but an international conspiracy that special agent Pritchard spent much of his career with the FBI pursuing in the interest of wiping out world terrorism. His efforts were fruitful and rewarding to all Americans. Unfortunately, those same efforts also led to his death.

"Special agent George L. Pritchard was murdered in cold blood by the remnants of an international band of terrorists dedicated to the overthrow of democratic governments. In this particular case, the people responsible for his death are the same people special agent Pritchard had infiltrated a few years ago. The group is tied to South America, particularly Paraguay. In a few moments I will introduce to you Mr. Sergio Nariz who, fortunately, has been with us in Washington over the past few months establishing closer links between his native country, Paraguay, and the United States. Mr. Nariz is a respected and ranking member of Paraguay's law enforcement community, and we have agreed upon a joint effort to bring to justice those responsible for the murder of special agent Pritchard, and those responsible for terrorism in our hemisphere.

"The murder of George L. Pritchard has, ironically, its positive aspects. Because of it, not only has an international bond of law enforcement been forged with Paraguay, but a similar one has been established with other nations equally as committed to stamping out terrorist acts. It is of little comfort, I realize, to the loving wife and daughter left behind by special agent Pritchard, but his death has not been in vain."

Cable News cut away just as Director Shelton was about to introduce an undersecretary for Latin Affairs from the State Department. Saksis shut off the TV set and slumped in her chair. "What garbage," she said. "What a crock."

She called Doctor's Hospital and inquired about Bill. "Criti-

216

cal but stable," was the report. She spent a few minutes wondering who'd attacked him. They said it was robbery because his cash and credit cards were missing. It must have been. Why else would anyone have so brutally beaten him? But, she wondered, why such a severe beating if money were the motivation? The doctor told her he'd been struck twice, once to the side of the face, a second time to the nose. It was what always frightened her about being mugged. Today's breed of mugger didn't seem to be content with money. Once they had it, the anger had to be played out by beating, by killing. At least he was alive.

She sat in the darkening living room and halfheartedly ate and sipped coffee. She had to stay awake to be ready for Kneeley's transmission. Would it work? She could set the alarm and take a nap. She was very tired, emotionally drained.

The phone rang. It was the wrong number. She hoped no one would call close to the time she was to put into action Bill's plan to eavesdrop on Kneeley. She wouldn't answer. But then she realized that the phone ringing near that time could be Kneeley transmitting early.

She set the alarm and slept until midnight, got up and checked the equipment over and over, rereading the instructions, jiggling cable connections to insure they were tight, lining up the large paper supply with the friction feed on her Epson dot matrix printer, making sure a dozen times that the phone was securely in its cradle. "Let it work," she told herself. "Please, let it work and end this bad dream."

She sat and stared at the computer. All the proper lights were on, red and green, perpetual signals that the system was ready to function—provided it was given the proper input.

She wasn't watching the time. It dawned on her that she should get her watch from the bedroom. As she started to cross the living room the phone rang, causing her to freeze. She could feel her heart racing, and her throat was parchment dry.

Another ring. She went to the phone and picked it up. There was nothing but the sound of an open line. "The modem," she said. She placed the phone in its cradle on the modem and waited. A succession of green symbols flashed across her screen, and the printer made a series of "beeps."

Then, words began to appear on the screen, and the dot matrix printhead began its steady buzz across the first sheet of fanfold paper.

Before transmission of new chapters, it's imperative that the change in the identification of sources be accomplished throughout the manuscript. As I've indicated in recent conversations, the death of the FBI agent George Pritchard has, ironically, strengthened the book. Until his death, and as was agreed upon between us, this primary source of information was to remain nameless, our own "Deep Throat," as it were. But now, we can use his name. I will be making editorial changes and additions in material already written and transmitted to you, but be on your toes for places where it's been overlooked. In addition, I will be writing a lengthy end-paper explaining Pritchard's contribution to the book and the circumstances surrounding it.

CHAPTER ELEVEN

It was once said by some sage, "Life is what happens while you're making other plans." That certainly is the case with this book. My primary source of information was a veteran special agent of the Federal Bureau of Investigation, whose cooperation came with an agreed-upon restriction——that his name never be used. Those of us in the field of investigatory journalism——at least those of us who function with a sense of honor——have learned never to compromise sources such as this one. When I first entered into my arrangement with this special agent, I did so knowing full well that I would spend the rest of my productive days in jail rather than reveal his identity.

But now, in the midst of the painful process of bringing to the American people the *true* story of the FBI's internal workings, my source——my "Deep Throat"——was murdered, gunned down in cold blood in the FBI's own hallowed halls, on its firing range, in front of 200 curious American tourists who were there to celebrate the weapons expertise of bureau sharp-shooters.

What does that mean to you or, more particularly, to this author and to this book?

It means that the material contained herein may now be attributed to a real person. There are times when the cynics chuckle at a journalist's use of "respected sources" and point to the technique as yet another example of media irresponsibility. I was prepared to take those criticisms in the interest of alerting the American people to the abuses perpetrated upon it by America's federal police force, the Federal Bureau of Investigation, the house that Hoover built, esteemed in the eyes of children and their parents who witness impressive statistics and colorful anecdotes of "most wanted" brought to justice and, yes, and exhibitions of skill with rifles and handguns on the firing range.

But it is *not all it seems.*

And because of the courage of one man—George L. Pritchard—the real story can now be told. That's his name—George L. Pritchard—seventeen years with the bureau, a loyal special agent who, finally, came to grips with the abuses of his beloved FBI and who sought out this reporter to make amends, as it were, to cleanse his soul and to contribute to his fellow man in a way far greater than his work at the FBI could ever accomplish.

I mourn his death, yet I must view it positively. If that shocks you, so be it, but now, there can be no sniping at unidentified sources, no precious raising of eyebrows over expensive lunches in Washington, D.C.'s favorite watering holes because this observer was honor-bound to protect the man, George L. Pritchard. The man has died, and he leaves me—and you—the legacy of openness, of duty beyond and above his oath to the bureau.

The source material used in previous chapters to help understand the chain of events that led to the formation of a police force *within* the FBI was provided, in part, by George Pritchard, and by other sources this writer has cultivated over the years. The climate in which this was allowed to occur was established by J. Edgar Hoover himself, whose personality shaped every aspect of the bureau during his forty-eight-year reign. That is not to say that it is necessarily bad for one man to dictate an agency or company's direction and tone—not if that man is basically a sound individual. Was that the case with Mr. Hoover? It is the opinion of many who have closely monitored the FBI's seventy-six years of existence, and of this observer, that his personality and psyche was sufficiently deficient to allow all manner of abuses to fester and grow. The "Unkempts" are a fine example.

According to the meticulous diary kept by special agent Pritchard, he was present early in his career at a meeting in the spring of 1970 that included six young special agents and Robert Banks, a retired military officer who'd joined the bureau two years earlier as a "special consultant to J. Edgar Hoover." It was never clearly established what Banks's true role was, but it became evident to Pritchard following that meeting that his sole purpose was to put into motion the director's plan to have at his disposal a small and elite group of special agents whose moral and ethical views would not, as Pritchard put in his notes, "be at odds with eliminating individuals in society whose views were especially dangerous to America's survival."

What especially intrigued Pritchard early in that meeting was Banks's comment: "Each of you have been specially selected for a top-secret role in the FBI. Many things have been taken into consideration, including your record to date with the bureau, your background prior to joining us, your evaluation reports and *psychological profiles*" (emphasis mine).

Banks went on to explain that because of increasing domestic tensions caused by dissidents and those who would rejoice in the overthrow of the United States of America, it had been determined *by the director himself* that sterner measures, performed in total secrecy, might now be necessary if the Republic were to survive.

Bear in mind that this was a period of intense strain on Hoover. The activists of the 1960s had brought unrelenting pressure to bear on him to bring the Federal Bureau of Investigation more in line with the precept of a federal police force accountable to higher authorities. Those who knew Hoover can testify that, from his perspective, there was no higher authority than himself.

220

Too, the now famous Hoover files were becoming publicly nown. It was the practice within the Washington Metropolitan Police Department to carbon Hoover himself each time anyone with any government job was arrested, even for the most minor of infractions. Those files grew to such proportions that there virtually wasn't an office in the federal—and state governments, too—where there wasn't someone vulnerable to Hoover's private files. This list was added to by the bureau's policy of bugging hotel rooms and private homes in order to gather "dirt" on leading figures who'd spoken out against Hoover and his FBI. Martin Luther King, Jr., was a good example. So was this author, who knows through George Pritchard that his activities in hotels around the country had been wired, and his conversations recorded—"for the files."

According to Pritchard, the meeting with Robert Banks and the other special agents lasted two hours. The terms "killing," "murder," "assassination," and "execution" were never used. Instead, such words as "elimination," "neutralization of the enemy," and "ultimate steps to silence traitors" were bandied about by Banks as he explained the need for a special force within the bureau to take those "ultimate steps."

Pritchard's notes also refer to other meetings of this elite task force, during which the concept of a growing threat to America and to the FBI was constantly reinforced. Pritchard remembers a comment made by Hoover being discussed—that if it weren't for Hoover's willingness to put his ass on the line, the country would be overrun with dope fiends, anarchists, petty criminals, and the other elements of society who would bring America to ruin, just as happened with the Roman Empire.

Pritchard said to me, "What was amazing was that there wasn't one dissenting or questioning comment."

I asked Pritchard what acts he had specifically done in line with the movement to get rid of those critical of the FBI, those viewed as a threat to Hoover and to the country. He answered my question with a voice heavy with sorrow and remorse. This was a man who was not, by nature, violent. He leaves a wife and daughter, both of whom I have met and neither of whom had ever seen signs of a violent character in their husband and father. Yet, he did kill, not because it was in his blood (although his psychological profile must have triggered some recognition

221

in his leaders), but because he was told to do it by his employ ers. Bear in mind that his employer was the Federal Bureau of Investigation. He'd taken an oath. He loved his country, believed in it, and wanted it intact and prospering for his own child to inherit. Did he question those orders? Yes, of course at night when he tried to sleep and couldn't. But he would do these acts, as would others in his squad, because he was told it was for his country, for his president, for the future of a nation he loved.

As I progress with this book, I realize that I might be guilty of much the same thing, of justifying unsavory actions under the guise of a so-called greater good. I excuse George Pritchard for his actions because I understand, after years of research the milieu in which he functioned for his seventeen years with the bureau. I suppose there's also a personal and selfish reason for my admiring and defending George Pritchard. Without him, I would not be able to write this book and alert the American public to the dangers of a federal police force that accounts only to itself. Yes, with the death of Hoover in 1972, while still in office, there have been changes most for the better. The despot is gone, and the men who have succeeded him have brought to their sensitive job a more balanced and rational approach. These men who stepped into Mr. Hoover's shoes performed with a certain honor and respect for this democracy. But that does not mean that the abuses have been totally cut out of the bureau's operations. Far from it.

When George L. Pritchard died, the band of Unkempt charged with "eliminating" or "neutralizing" or taking "ultimate steps" remained in place, its ranks larger, its mission the same.

I spoke in previous chapters of papers Pritchard had kept during his seventeen years with the Federal Bureau of Investigation. One of them, obtained only six months ago from the office of Assistant Director Wayne E. Gormley, one of three assistant directors (Gormley's area is investigation; the others handle law enforcement and administration) points with alarming urgency to #.$%.$.$((%*%&%..$&$. ERROR ERROR

```
RROR .... 754654 *&&. *& DDDDDDDDDDDDDDDDDDDD
DDDDDDDDDDDDDDDDDDDDDDDDDDDDDDDDDDDDDDDDDD
DDDDDDDDDDDDDDDDDDDDDDDDDDDDDDDDDDDDDDDDDD
DDDDDDDDDDDDDDDDDDDDDDDDDDDDDDDDDDDDDDDDDD
DDDDDDDDDDDDDDDDDDDDD
```

The printer's constant buzz stopped. The tiny red and green
ghts were still on, but there would be no further printing of
ichard Kneeley's manuscript. It had ended for Chris Saksis
ith the string of deadly D's, a common computer print quirk.

The screen was blank except for the green outline of a fresh
age waiting to be filled with words.

"What happened?" Saksis asked herself as she flipped
witches and checked connections.

It didn't matter, she decided.

She'd try to get that answer—and a lot of others when she
isited Richard Kneeley on Fire Island tomorrow.

26

THE WEATHER IN Washington, D.C., at seven A.M. wa
bright, sunny, and crisp, but by the time the Pan Am je
reached New York's LaGuardia Airport at 8:05, rain poure
from the skies.

The first rental car wouldn't start; the second one did, an
Chris Saksis drove east toward Bay Shore and the ferry to Fir
Island. She'd used a coin-operated copying machine at Na
tional Airport to make a duplicate of the print-out of Kneeley'
transmission to Sutherland House, and slid the original be
neath the driver's seat. She also had with her the photo o
Kneeley and Pritchard together, as well as a series of notes an
questions she'd drafted after the transmission had been inter
rupted.

As she pulled into the parking lot and was handed a receip
by the attendant, she realized how tired she was. She found a
empty parking space, turned off the engine, leaned her hea
back, and closed her eyes. One thought kept crossing he
mind: why did she care? Assistant Director Gormley had got
ten her off the hook, in a sense. She could go to Montana, do
good job, and allow the past few months to fade into a fuzz
memory.

Obviously, the bureau was content with its story of foreign terrorists having murdered George Pritchard. That was its business. Why should she care?

She thought of the philosophy her father had passed on to her before he died, the concept that each person was a mere speck in the universe, sharing it with a leaf, a toad, each grain of sand, and drop of water. She wasn't that important. No, that wasn't it. *She* was important; her travails were not. Life was not to be trusted, and it was given as a loan, temporary, the days of one's life simply installments against that loan until, when it was time to be paid, the regularity of payment was considered in some grand ledger that determined one's eternal credit rating.

The thought of her father, and of her mother, was at once comforting and painful. What would they think of her now? She often wished that they were alive to see that she'd *succeeded*, at least in terms of the society around her. They were such proud people—that was it. That was why she was here, in a parking lot about to confront a writer named Richard Kneeley about what she thought had happened to George Pritchard. It wasn't Pritchard that mattered, and she knew it. It was Christine Saksis who counted. She'd been smeared and manipulated as though she were a toy to be abused and discarded by noon on Christmas Day. That feeling opened her eyes, propelled her from the car and toward the ferry.

Saksis's third ride to Cherry Grove was as rough as the first one had been, the vessel's windows splattered with water, the lower passenger cabin filled with the wind's whistle, the bow constantly elevated and slammed down by the water's swells, loose gear in the cabin threatening to go its own way at any moment. There weren't many people on board. An old man wearing a yellow rubber slicker and carrying a white miniature poodle pressed his nose against the glass and peered out into the gray, wet weather that engulfed the ferry. The dog panted and licked the old man's face.

"Hi."

Saksis turned at the sound of the man's voice. It was the bartender to whom she'd spoken her first time in Cherry Grove

"Paul, remember? I bought you a club soda."

"Sure, I remember. How are you?"

"Pretty good. Coming over to pack up the apartment an head for Florida. . . . Ever find him?"

"What?"

"Your brother—stepbrother. Any luck?"

She had to go back in time and resurrect her lie. "No, n luck. Still trying, though."

"That's the way, hang tough. Ever catch up with Dic Kneeley?"

"In a manner of speaking."

"I haven't seen him at all. I guess he's holed up working o his latest book."

Saksis thought of the photo in her purse. "Oh," she saic "let me show you something." She handed him the picture c Kneeley and Pritchard she'd purchased from the young Fir Island journalists.

He held it up, nodded, and handed it back. "That's Dick, he said.

"What about the other man?"

"Sure. He came in once with Dick, and I think he came i alone a couple of times. Why? That your stepbrother?"

"No," she said, "just an old family friend."

They stood beneath an overhang on the Cherry Grove sid The rain continued to pour down. "Got an umbrella?" h asked.

"No, but that's okay." She said good-bye and took off fc Kneeley's house. When she was on the other side of the dur from his property, she stopped and gathered her thoughts. was as though she'd arrived at that precise place and momer in time by rote, every system on automatic pilot since receivir the partial print-out of Kneeley's chapter.

She rounded the dune and walked to the locked gate. Tr rain obscured a clear view of the house, although she could se that all the drapes were closed. What if he weren't there, c wouldn't see her, both distinct possibilities. She'd considere

lling first but decided against it. All he had to do was say
, and then what could she do, go to someone in authority
thin the bureau and lay it out on the table for them? They'd
smiss it.
There's nothing to lose, she told herself as she pushed the
te's doorbell. When it didn't bring any movement at the
ont door, she pushed it again, holding it a lot longer this
ne. Again, no response. She now attacked it with a series of
rusts. A drape parted; she couldn't see who'd done it. She
ited. Nothing. Again, she pushed the button. Now, the door
ened. She'd expected Jubel, but it was Kneeley himself.
"It's Christine Saksis," she yelled.
He stood on the porch and looked at her as though he en-
yed seeing her standing in a deep puddle and being rained on.
"I want to talk to you," she shouted.
He continued to stare.
"You'd better talk to me!"
He went inside the house, and a minute later Jubel appeared
th a large striped golf umbrella, waddled to the gate, un-
cked it and glared at her as she stepped through and headed
r the open door.
Kneeley was waiting in the foyer. He wore white jeans that
ere too tight for his expanding middle, a maroon V-neck ve-
ur sweater, and deck shoes. His silver hair was as carefully
ifed as ever. He'd added additional chains and charms since
e was last at his house, and he wore glasses tinted a delicate
nk.
"Miss Saksis," he said with a phoney sweep of his hand and
slight bow from the waist. "Mr. Hoover's finest."
"Mr. Kneeley."
"You're wet," he said, a hint of mirth in his voice.
"Yes, I am."
"You must change before you catch your death."
"I'll be all right."
"I insist. I keep various wardrobes in the house and I'm sure
u'll find something to your liking."
"Mr. Kneeley, I—"

227

"Get dry. *Then* we'll talk. I can't stand women with wate dripping from their noses. It's gross."

She realized he was being deliberately fey, and wondere why, considering his awkward attempt to seduce her the la time. She followed him to a small bedroom, where he remove a yellow terrycloth robe and a pair of women's slippers from closet. "Come to the study when you're done," he said.

She was reluctant to undress, considering the circumstance and opted for replacing her shoes with the slippers and puttin the robe over her dress. Warmer now, she walked into th study, where Kneeley was looking out the window over th wind-swept Atlantic. He turned, smiled, and said, "So, Mi Saksis, you're back. Is this an official visit? Should I call my a torney?"

"No to both questions, Mr. Kneeley, although I didn't e actly drop in for tea."

He laughed. "Would you like some? I have an excellent var ety."

The thought of something warm to drink was appealin "Yes, that would be nice."

He called downstairs to Jubel and ordered two cups of te "Give Miss Saksis the rose petal. I'll have black currant."

"Fancy," she said.

"It's called gaining revenge by living well. Now, why don you tell me exactly why you're here."

She sat in an orange director's chair to the side of his des and he leaned against the credenza behind the desk, arn folded, a challenging smile on his face.

She took a moment to organize her thoughts, then sai "The last time I was here you told me you didn't know Georg L. Pritchard, the special agent who was murdered."

"I did?"

"Yes."

"I don't recall saying that. I think I told you I might hav met him socially."

"I'm talking about knowing him better than that."

"Oh, my," he said, sitting in his chair and swiveling. "Yo

come here and I graciously invite you inside because—frankly, Miss Saksis, I don't *know* why I'm this accommodating unless—well, I am known as a gracious host *and* as a patriotic American.

"The fact is, Miss Saksis, I'm thoroughly charmed by your company, but I have nothing to offer your investigation, absolutely nothing."

She picked up her purse from the floor, removed the photo of Kneeley and Pritchard together on Fire Island and slid it across the desk. Kneeley didn't move. "Would you look at this, Mr. Kneeley?"

"Must I?"

"I think it would be easier here in the comfort and privacy of your own home than in a courtroom."

His face reflected mock terror. "Not only is the lady beautiful, she's tough as nails." He laughed, took the photo, leaned back, and looked at it for a long time. Finally, he tossed it on the desk.

"Well?" Chris said.

"Well what?"

"That's you and George Pritchard. I also have witnesses on Fire Island who've seen you with him on more than one occasion."

"Witnesses. Many?"

"More than one."

"Two. Not very intimidating."

"One's enough."

"You say that man with me is this deceased agent, Pritchard. I think the man with me is my lawyer."

"I don't think he's your lawyer, Mr. Kneeley. I *know* that man is George L. Pritchard."

"Oh, you know George."

"Pardon?"

"George Pritchard, my attorney."

Saksis was suddenly filled with anger at herself for allowing a game to be played between them. She was a special agent of the Federal Bureau of Investigation; she should be dealing from the strength that her position afforded her. I should have shared what I know with the bureau, she thought. It was too late for that.

She looked across the desk and said, "Mr. Kneeley, you were involved with George Pritchard because of the book you're writing about the FBI."

He again adopted the expression of exaggerated shock, but he didn't sustain it. The corners of his mouth slacked, and he ran his fingers absently through his hair.

"Don't deny it, Mr. Kneeley. I *know* what I'm talking about."

"*You* tapped me?"

"I—yes."

"A legal tap?"

"How did you know about the tap?"

"Was it legal?"

"That's my business."

"Not when my civil rights have been violated. You might find yourself up on charges, Miss Saksis."

"We'll see."

"How did I know I was being 'crashed,' as the computer world terms it? I got sloppy, Miss Saksis. I always check for line drops in impedance before transmitting, but last night started sending without taking precautions. After a few minutes I remembered what happens to people who get sloppy. checked the meter. Sure enough, it had dropped, so I terminated the feed."

She smiled. "I thought it was my equipment."

He smiled, too. "Your equipment is fine. So, you have an inkling of the project I'm currently working on. The pages you did manage to see—they mentioned Pritchard."

"A great deal."

"And?"

"And I think your presence in the Hoover Building the night he was murdered, and the link between you and Pritchard makes you—well, Mr. Kneeley, I certainly wouldn't rule you out as a suspect."

He frowned as Jubel opened the door. "You're interrupting."

"The tea."

"Just put it down and get out."

Jubel placed the tray on the desk, looked at Saksis, and left the room.

"He's cute, but the elevator doesn't reach the top floor," Kneeley said of his manservant.

"I wouldn't know."

"Tell me, Miss Saksis, about the announcement made by Director Shelton. Unless my ears are failing—which is possible—I heard that Pritchard was killed by a member of the terrorist group he'd infiltrated a few years ago."

"Your ears aren't failing. That's what was said."

"And?"

"And I don't buy it."

"Oh, my goodness, you *are* in trouble, questioning the word of the director himself."

"I'm in trouble no matter what," she said, wishing she could retrieve the words.

"Are you? I'm so sorry. Add to it the illegal tap you put on my phones and—"

"I'll take my chances with that. Frankly, if it turns out that you murdered Pritchard, I don't think anyone will be too critical of me."

"Don't count on it. If I *did* murder Pritchard, and I walk free because of your sloppy police work, you'll be lucky to find a secretarial job on the reservation."

She knew he might be right. "How well do you know Helen Pritchard?" she asked.

"Never met the lady."

"Not true, Mr. Kneeley. She sold the Hoover files and her husband's notes to you. Was Pritchard about to blow the whistle? Is that what got him killed?"

"You know a lot, don't you?"

"I know what I hear."

"Good sources?"

231

"The best."

"Tell me about them."

"I'd rather not."

"You look ravishing in that robe. The color compliment your copper skin."

"Mr. Kneeley, this pleasant game is wearing thin. The file you possess, the ones about Mr. Hoover, were secret. Your pos session of them is illegal."

He shrugged. "Have your tea, Miss Saksis, before it get cold."

She ignored him. "No matter how you cut it, Mr. Kneeley you're in trouble."

His laugh bubbled up from deep inside. He made a grea deal out of trying to stop so that he could talk. "Miss Saksis, hate to say this, but you are a beautiful Native American pai in my butt." He stood and walked to the window.

She wasn't sure how to proceed. He obviously had the uppe hand and was playing it for all it was worth. She didn't hav proof that he'd killed Pritchard, which ruled out arresting hin for it. She could take him in for possession of stolen classifie documents, but that presented two problems: he'd make a bi deal out of having his First Amendment rights violated *anc* more important, no one in the bureau had instructed her t barge in on Richard Kneeley and arrest him for anything.

"Come here, Miss Saksis," he said without turning.

She joined him at the window.

"Lovely view, isn't it, even in a storm, particularly in storm."

He sighed and touched the window pane with the five fir gers of his right hand. "Are you happy with the Federal Burea of Investigation?"

"Happy?"

"Content with your job and the way you're treated."

"Yes."

He glanced at her. His face reflected cynicism. "It isn't th nicest organization in the world, Miss Saksis. With all its higl power PR, it's really quite tough underneath."

"I wouldn't know about that."

"Of course you would."

"Mr. Kneeley, if you think that by damning the FBI you'll manage to get me on your side, you're operating under a big misconception."

He thought for a moment, then crossed the room to his desk, sat in front of his computer, and clicked it on. He looked back at Saksis and motioned with his hand. "Come, come, let me present lesson number two in the *real* FBI."

She stood behind him as the screen came to life—a vertical green line on the right side, a horizontal one along the bottom. He looked up at her and said, "Ready?"

"For what?"

"An eye-opener."

He took a floppy disk from a locked case next to the computer, inserted it in one of the disk drives, and pushed a key on the keyboard. A long list of files stored on that disk filled the screen. He moved a cursor to one labeled *G.P. Notes; SPO-VAC—"Irony,"* pressed a key, and waited. A moment later the screen was filled with text.

Kneeley got up and offered Saksis the chair. "Sit, Miss Saksis, read and enjoy. You scroll through it using these keys."

"I'm familiar with it."

"Oh, of course, you must be. Take your time and digest it, my dear. When you're done with this, there are dozens more disks that spell out in exquisite detail that dark and rotten underbelly I spoke of."

"Mr. Kneeley, why are you showing this to me?"

"Because I almost consider you a collaborator by now, a partner. You've already managed to see some of it through your illegal tapping of my phone. You might as well see the rest. Besides, I have a feeling that once you do, you might view me in a slightly more positive light."

"But even if I do," said Saksis, "it doesn't change things. If you murdered George Pritchard, all the dirt in the world about the bureau won't—"

"Scroll and read, Miss Saksis. Then we'll talk. This particular disk contains the verbatim transcripts of long, introspective notes George Pritchard had made about his career. He was a remarkably fastidious man, describing everything in his daily diaries, neatly printed and quite literate for a cop. Enjoy. I'll be back."

He went to the door and flipped a switch that killed all lights in the room. It was very dark outside because of the storm; he face was illuminated by the green phosphorescent light from the screen.

Chris stared at the screen. The text displayed on it was the beginning of a new diary entry, according to Pritchard's note as to the time and place it was entered, the subject—"The Irony of SPOVAC"—and some general comments about hi state of mind at that moment. He'd written:

"So much over the years to disillusion me. It takes such faith to continue with enthusiasm when things like this occur. But should it impact on me to the extent that I give up what I love and believe in? I think not. Still, it makes it difficult, especially when you must work side-by-side each day with the source of it. Then, too, I must question whether this is unique enough to send me fleeing the bureau in search of something less volatile and crushing. Again, the answer is always a resounding NO. The bureau is my life, and despite its occasional (I'm being kind, I suppose) "slips," it is still an organization to be looked at with pride by every man and woman. It is, after all, nothing more than a gathering of human beings who happen to work in law enforcement, rather than in banks or advertising agencies the post office or a computer giant. People; the problem in people, but a towering organization that has done so much good should not be brought down by a person or persons Enough of my rationalization—one last note to myself. Should I ever decide to write the book based upon this inflammatory material I've ended up with, this sort of incident must not be part of it. It is, after all, just a person who has created this irony within SPOVAC.

Chris Saksis scrolled the lines of text on the screen and read Pritchard's recollection of the genesis of SPOVAC, at least

234

rom the perspective of his involvement. He discussed the need or an organization to tackle the increasing number of serial nd recreational murders across the country, to codify what information could be gathered on patterns and geographical inks, psychological profiles of those who killed serially and for pleasure and programs to combat the increasing phenomenon of such killings.

He went on page after page, and Saksis began to get bored. Until—

. . . at first, when Ross told me of what he'd done, I was incapable of believing it, or him. It was too monumentally horrible to accept, too bizarre, too close to home because of my own daughter for whom I would kill—all too ironic. But then I realized that he was telling the truth, and that his reaction to it was not the horror I felt but one of almost amused IRONY. Which it was, of course, but . . .

Chris Saksis's heart beat fast as she continued reading. According to Pritchard, "Ross" had admitted to having killed a young Indian girl near the reservation in Arizona. It was a mistake, he claimed. He'd met her, taken her for a drive, and an argument had developed. He'd been in Arizona at another SPOVAC conference (Saksis remembered Bill Tse-ay trying to interview him there), had an evening "*to kill*" (Pritchard's emphasis), met the girl, drove to a place where he intended to have sex with her, ended up in a fight and . . .

She turned away from the screen as the grim details were spelled out paragraph after paragraph, then forced herself to continue reading. At the end, Pritchard made comments about the incident, about his dilemma; report Ross or forget about it? He chose the latter course of action. He went on to say that he'd known of certain sexual proclivities on Ross's part but ignored them. What a man did in the privacy of his own home was no one's business, not even the FBI's. But, said Pritchard, the doubts persisted and would until the day he died.

The irony of a SPOVAC team member killing a teenage girl and having it appear that the murder was just another in a series of killings in Arizona—I decided it was good that I knew about it because, at least, I wouldn't be searching for clues to link her death with the others. I believed him. It WAS an accident, but it's ironic, that's all. What else can I say?

Saksis hadn't been aware that Kneeley had entered the room again and was standing a few feet behind her. The sudden realization made her start.

"Shocking, isn't it?" he said. "And ironic, as Pritchard recognized. I think about it a lot, Miss Saksis, that this man Ross whoever he is, is still functioning as a special agent of the FBI carrying his weapons and his shield and protecting America.' He laughed. "Actually, I think Pritchard did the right thing by forgetting about it. What was to be gained by sullying the bureau's reputation? 'Don't embarrass the bureau.' You've heard that more times than once, I'm sure."

Saksis silently nodded and closed her eyes against tears that were forming.

"George told me more about the incident. He said one of the reasons he hadn't reported the confession, if you can call it that—it happened when both of them were quite drunk one night in a bar in California—was that this agent named Ross was good, a real credit to SPOVAC and the bureau. Pragmatism at work. Sometimes it makes my skin crawl but—well, it has its moments, I'm sure."

Saksis composed herself before she asked, "Why, Mr. Kneeley? Why show me this thing?"

He sat on the edge of his desk and played with the chain around his neck. "Because I like you? Perhaps. Because I have this burning need to cleanse my soul of what I know of the house that Hoover built? Absolutely not. Because—because Miss Saksis, I want you out of here and off my back. I did not kill George Pritchard. We had a business arrangement—"

"You and his *wife* had the arrangement, as I understand it.

"Does it matter?"

"It certainly could where Pritchard's murder is concerned."

"Why? Are you suspecting his widow, poor thing, bereaved and despondent over the death of her beloved husband?"

"That's not the way it is."

"Of course it's not. She hated his guts."

"Did she kill him?"

"Ask her."

"I did."

"And she denied it."

"Yes, of course."

"Makes sense."

"What does?"

"Denying you murdered an FBI agent. That can get you in big trouble."

She had difficulty asking it, but managed. "This 'Ross' mentioned in what I read. Could he have—" It was impossible to finish.

"Killed Pritchard to keep him quiet? I doubt it."

"But it's possible."

"Anything's possible."

There was the faint sound of the doorbell. Kneeley went to the window and squinted as he tried to see who it was through the mist and rain. He turned quickly and said, "Well, Miss Saksis, I'm about to have another visitor."

She looked blankly at him.

"The bereaved widow is here."

"Helen Pritchard?"

"Yes."

"Did you expect her?"

"Today, no. One day, yes."

"I'm not sure I want to—"

"You won't have to confront her. Go rest in another room." He saw her dilemma and said, "Use that room over there and leave the door open a few inches. You won't miss a thing."

Saksis gathered up her purse and papers and went to a small room off the study. Once was was in it, the question of why he

237

was being so helpful hit her. There was only one answer, it seemed, and that was that he hadn't killed George Pritchard and wanted to put the question to rest. His involvement with the deceased naturally kept him in the spotlight as a suspect, and he knew it. But, it didn't matter what his motives were, she decided as she looked around the twelve-by-twelve, thickly carpeted room. There was a minimum of light through gaps in curtains over a small window that faced the ocean. There was a copper-colored love seat and two straight chairs. The overall effect was of a doctor's waiting room. She opened the curtains and looked out over the ocean, then went to the door. She could see Kneeley's desk and the immediate surrounding area, but not much more. The door to the study opened and Helen Pritchard stepped into the room. She wore an aquamarine raincoat and floppy rain hat, stylish ankle boots, and carried a large leather handbag. Saksis wondered whether she carried a gun in it. Silly. Saksis touched her own purse, in which was a bureau-issued .357 magnum. Cops and robbers. For the first time since her training days at Quantico she wondered what she was doing with her life.

"Tea?" Kneeley asked Helen Pritchard.

"No."

"Something stronger? It is after noon."

"I'd like a bourbon on the rocks. Do you have Blanton's?"

Kneeley laughed. "Yes, of course."

Helen Pritchard removed her wet coat and tossed it over the chair Saksis had been sitting in. She shook her hat over the rug and put it on top of the coat. She wore a tight jumpsuit the color of tangerines. Her wrists jangled with bracelets. Kneeley returned carrying her drink and one for him. She took it without saying anything and downed a healthy swig.

"So, Helen, to what do I owe this unexpected and thoroughly delightful visit on such a threatening day?"

"Money." She stood over the chair containing her coat and hat as though she didn't know where to sit.

"Ah hah," Kneeley said, picking up her clothing. "Let me hang this for you where it will dry."

"The chair's wet," Pritchard said.

"Terrible," he said, dragging over another director's chair. She sat and looked directly at Saksis. Saksis was certain she noticed her. It wasn't true.

Kneeley sat behind his desk and smiled broadly. "Money," he repeated. "For what?"

"For what I've been through."

"Poor Helen."

"Yes, damn it, poor Helen. You swine, Kneeley, you turned right around and tried to sell me out."

He didn't respond.

"Don't sit there like some smug clown without a worry in the world. You know what I'm talking about."

"I haven't a clue."

She guffawed and finished her drink.

"Another?"

"Yes."

"I put the bottle over there, on the table by the door."

"The gracious host."

"More gracious than some."

Pritchard went to fill her own glass, and Kneeley looked in Saksis's direction. Did he wink at her? Probably not, although it seemed that way.

Pritchard again took her seat and said, "You're trying to kill the book, aren't you?"

"Kill the—? That's absurd."

"No it's not. I've heard."

"From whom?"

"That's my business, and so is the book. I put my neck a mile out to see this book happen and I'll be damned if I'll see you bury it."

Her vehemence had an effect on Kneeley. Saksis could see his face twist into anger, and a hand that hung loose at his side knotted into a tight fist.

Helen Pritchard continued: "You don't fool me, Richard. I know you went to Shelton and offered to burn the book for a fee."

"Nonsense."

"No, Richard, the truth. You figured you could get more from blackmailing the bureau than from taking a chance on the book being published. What did Shelton offer you—a half million, a million?"

The anger in Kneeley's face slowly relaxed into a pleasant, contented, smug expression. "He didn't offer a penny. Mr. Shelton and his FBI are incorruptible." He laughed. "You know something, Helen," he said, rising and coming around the desk so that he loomed over her, "you give women a bad name. You drove your husband into an early grave with your greed."

"Oh, Christ—"

"What did it feel like to shoot the man you'd been married to for so many years?"

His question caused Saksis to suck in her breath. Pritchard's answer caused it to rush out of her mouth with such force that she was sure everyone had heard.

Helen Pritchard said calmly, "You should know, Richard, you were there."

He seemed to ignore what she'd said. "Come on, Helen, tell me what it's like to murder a loved one. I can use it in the novel I intend to write."

She started to reply, then pulled up short and quickly looked around the room. "What the hell are you doing," she asked, "getting me to talk for the camera?"

Kneeley's laugh was forced.

"You bastard," she said, getting up and walking from Saksis's view. When she returned, she stood toe-to-toe with Kneeley and said, "You'd better not ever think about selling me out, Richard. Remember, I—"

He held a finger up to her face. "Are you about to say something like, 'I killed for you'? Careful. Remember the camera."

She brought her half-filled glass up from her waist and tossed its contents into Kneeley's face. He sputtered, wiped it away with his hand, and pushed her out of Saksis's line of vision. Saksis was tempted to open the door further but was afraid of being seen. She listened as they argued about the book and Pritchard's contention that Kneeley had tried to extract a payment from the FBI in return for not writing it. Their voices became muffled, and lower, until Saksis could only hear the sound, not the words. She surmised they'd settled on a couch in a far corner of the study.

She backed away from the door until she reached the window twelve feet away. Until then she'd been totally absorbed with what was being said in the study. Now, all she could think of was Ross Lizenby and Pritchard's allegation that he'd killed the Indian girl. Allegation! Police talk. "The perpetrator was alleged to have . . ." She thought of his former wife who'd disappeared and had never been found. She thought of many things about Lizenby and their relationship.

A sound in the study brought her back to the present. She looked through the gap in the door. Kneeley had returned to his desk, where he slammed his glass down on its top, then stormed across the room, opened the door, and slammed it behind him.

Helen Pritchard came to the desk, looked back at the door through which Kneeley had departed, came around behind, and opened a bottom drawer. She pulled out a sheath of papers, placed them on the desk, and then opened her purse. Her hand went into it and came out holding a .22 caliber revolver.

Helen Pritchard placed the weapon in the drawer, covered it with the papers, and closed it. Seconds later Kneeley returned.

"I meant it," Pritchard said, pointing a finger at him.

"You don't frighten me, Mrs. Pritchard," he said, drawing out her name. "You entered into a business deal that's gone sour, no matter what steps you took to keep it alive. *Murder!* Drastic step to take for money. Passion is a much more attractive motive. *Money!* Shabby, Helen, tacky."

Pritchard seemed to be shifting gears as Saksis watched. She managed a smile and placed her hand on Kneeley's forearm. 'Richard, *we* killed George. That the gun happened to be in my hand is irrelevant. Let's sit and talk. I think that if we act

like reasonable people we can work this out for both our bene-
fits."

Kneeley cast a fast glance at the room in which Saksis hid.
"All right," he said, "sit down."

"Over there on the couch, where it's comfortable."

"I'd rather stay here."

Pritchard got up and walked away. Kneeley reluctantly followed her.

Saksis tried to hear what they were saying but could make
out only an occasional word. She thought she heard the doorbell, then the sound of a car door slamming. She went to the
window and pushed aside the curtains. A dark blue sedan had
stopped on the beach side of the house and two men wearing
raincoats and hats had gotten out. One of them carried an
M–16 rifle. Saksis watched as they stood next to the car, their
eyes trained on Kneeley's house.

She returned to the crack in the door and listened. Kneeley
and Helen Pritchard were still talking. Then, the door to the
study opened and Jubel came in, followed by four men. Saksis
stood frozen; she recognized two of them. One was Paul, the
bartender who'd befriended her. The other was Ross Lizenby.

Kneeley shouted, "What the hell is going on? How did—?
Jubel, why did you—?"

"Relax, Mr. Kneeley," Lizenby said. "We're FBI."

Kneeley spun around and yelled at Saksis, "You set this up!"

Everyone looked as Saksis pushed open the door and
stepped into the study. Lizenby smiled. "I figured you'd be
here," he said.

Saksis looked over to the couch where Helen Pritchard sat,
legs crossed, a sneer on her face. "Even Pocahontas is here,"
Pritchard said. "Should be some party."

Lizenby turned to the two men Saksis hadn't recognized and
said, "Go ahead." They went behind Kneeley's desk and
started opening drawers.

"Get out of there," Kneeley said, making a move toward
them.

Paul, the bartender, brought up a shotgun and pressed it
into Kneeley's belly.

Saksis said, "What's going on?"

"You tell me," he said.

"Do you have a warrant?" Kneeley asked Lizenby.

"Sure." He handed Kneeley a piece of paper.

"Son-of-a-bitch," Kneeley snarled. He said to Saksis in the same voice, "You're good, Miss Saksis, coming in here like a little lost lamb and getting me to talk."

"I didn't know anything about them," Saksis said.

They continued to empty Kneeley's desk, piling papers on one side, floppy disks on the other. One of the men tried to open a locked disk box on the credenza. "Key?" Lizenby asked Kneeley.

"Go to hell."

"Break it."

Each of the seven disk storage boxes was broken open and the disks tossed in a pile on the desk. Saksis looked at the computer screen. It was blank; the machine had automatically removed all text and lines in order to avoid burn-in. The disk containing Pritchard's story about Ross Lizenby was still in the disk drive. Please, don't touch *that* one, she thought.

"You'll hang for this," Kneeley said to Lizenby.

Lizenby laughed. "Not before you hang for George Pritchard's murder."

The bottom drawer containing the .22 was emptied, and one of the agents picked up the weapon with a handkerchief. "Look at that," Lizenby said.

"That's not mine," said Kneeley.

"We'll see," Lizenby said.

"It doesn't belong to him," Saksis said. "She put it there." She pointed to Helen Pritchard.

"Stay out of it," Lizenby said.

"No, I won't," Saksis said. "I was here and saw her take the gun from her purse and put it in that drawer."

"You're a liar," Pritchard said.

Kneeley, who was becoming increasingly agitated, said, "She's right, damn it. I never saw that gun before."

"Not even on the firing range the night Pritchard got it?" Lizenby asked.

"No, not even—"

Saksis turned to Kneeley. "You *were* there, weren't you?"

"No, I . . . Yeah, I was there, but I didn't shoot him. She did."

Helen Pritchard got off the couch, and joined the group near the desk. She said to Lizenby, "Is there any reason why I must stay here?"

He shook his head. "No, you're free to go."

"Wait a minute," Kneeley screamed. "She shot him, for Christ's sake. I was there and saw it."

"Why?" Saksis asked.

Pritchard fixed Saksis in an icy stare, then smiled and started for the door. Saksis reached into her purse and pulled out her .357 magnum. "You stay, Mrs. Pritchard," she said.

Paul, the bogus bartender, swiftly turned his shotgun on Saksis. "Take it easy," she said, "I'm a special agent, too."

"Without passport," Lizenby said. "Put it away. Go on, Mrs. Pritchard, get out."

Saksis kept her revolver on Helen Pritchard. She said to Lizenby, "I don't know what's behind all this, Ross, but it smells. I'm telling you as a special agent of the FBI that this woman placed that .22 in his desk no more than a half hour ago."

"Butt out, Chris. It doesn't matter."

Saksis looked at everyone in the room. Paul's shotgun was still leveled at her. She quickly went to the door, backed up against it and said, "I'm fed up with this charade, and I'm not moving until somebody starts acting responsibly."

Lizenby knew the others were looking to him for a resolution to the impasse. He said to Helen Pritchard, "Sit down."

"You said I was—"

"I said sit down!"

She muttered and went to the couch.

"Satisfied?" Lizenby asked Saksis.

"Not at all."

"Fine, I'll get to you in a minute." He said to the other agents, "Do it."

One of the men had carried into the study a large leather

catalogue case, the sort used by airline pilots to carry flight charts and manuals. He opened it and took out an electromagnet attached to a battery pack. There was a strap on the magnet that he slung over his shoulder.

"Hey, wait a minute," Kneeley said.

The agent carrying the magnet ignored him as he flipped a switch and held the magnet inches above the pile of computer floppy disks on the desk.

"Goddamn it, that'll—"

"Erase everything," Lizenby said, smiling. He told another agent to pack up every scrap of paper in the room and to remove it for immediate destruction.

The magnet was passed over every inch of the study—desk, credenza, cabinets, walls, and floor—while Paul and the other agent packed Kneeley's papers, including Pritchard's original notes and the Hoover files, into boxes. Saksis watched with a deepening sense of dismay, especially when the powerful electromagnet was held over and around the computer in which the disk containing George Pritchard's accusation about Lizenby was still in its drive.

But then she remembered what was in her purse. She'd brought the disk from her own machine that she'd used during Kneeley's transmission to his publisher. Although it didn't contain the material about Lizenby and Sue White Cloud, Lizenby didn't know that. Maybe, just maybe.

When Lizenby was satisfied that everything had been magnetized and erased, he instructed the others to cuff Kneeley and to take him to the car. Kneeley protested all the way out the door, especially to Saksis, whom he cursed out vehemently.

"Okay," Lizenby said to Helen Pritchard, "you're free to go." Saksis again started to protest, but Lizenby spun around and said, "This time I mean it. Butt out!"

Saksis slowly lowered her magnum and sat on the couch as the electromagnet was packed in its case and everyone prepared to leave. "The ferry captain knows you're bringing the cars back," Lizenby said to Paul. "Thank him for the cooperation."

Paul said to Saksis, "No cars on Fire Island. We had to work it out. Sorry for not playing straight with you, but that was the assignment."

She shook her head and looked down.

"I'll catch up with everyone later," Lizenby said. "Agent Saksis and I have some talking to do."

Saksis's head snapped up. "Talking?"

"Yes. Just sit still. I'll explain everything if you give me a chance."

When they were alone in Kneeley's study, Lizenby asked whether she wanted a drink. She declined, and he poured himself one from the bottle Kneeley had left. "Sure?" he asked.

"I don't want a drink. I want answers."

"Back off, Chris," he said as he sat beside her on the couch. He raised his glass: "To us."

"I don't believe this."

"Believe what, that I care about you even after my nasty note?"

"It has nothing to do with that note, Ross. It has nothing to do with us, with caring. That's out the window. I want to know what's going on here with Kneeley and Helen Pritchard—the whole mess."

He tasted his drink and positioned himself so that he was directly facing her. "Chris, you got in over your head. This turned out to be a lot bigger than Pritchard's murder."

"I gathered that. Please explain."

"Sure. Helen Pritchard was there that night with Kneeley. They intended to put the pressure on Pritchard about the files and notes he'd sold to Kneeley."

"She sold them."

"Yeah, and he went along for a while. He evidently had a pang of conscience about the whole thing and had told them he was about to spill to Gormley and Shelton what had happened. They argued. Frankly, I think *he* intended to kill *them*, but that's beside the point, too. The bottom line was that Helen used the .22 he'd bought her to shoot him. She and Kneeley shoved the target hook into his coat to keep him from falling and then they got out."

Saksis looked across the room at the pile of papers and disks on the floor and tried to think rationally about what he'd just said. He'd presented it so calmly and matter-of-factly, as though there wasn't a doubt in the world. But that didn't explain why he let Helen Pritchard walk free.

"If Pritchard killed her husband, why was Kneeley accused?" she asked.

Lizenby laughed and shook his head. "Gormley cut a deal with Helen Pritchard. If she'd help us lay it on Kneeley, she'd walk."

"Why? What was to be gained by that?"

"It neutralizes Kneeley. If he makes any further moves to write his goddamn book about the bureau, he's nailed with a murder conviction. He'll see the wisdom of sticking to poetry once it's explained to him. Do you know what the bastard tried to do? When he saw trouble brewing over the book because of Pritchard's murder, he went directly to Shelton and tried to cut his own deal. He'd drop the book in return for a half million. He's a swine, and when Helen Pritchard found out about it, she decided to protect her own interests by playing with us."

"What does she get out of it besides immunity for murdering her own husband?"

"I don't know the details, Chris. I don't want to know. My job was to put it together and bring it to this point."

"You instructed her to put the gun in his drawer?"

"Yeah. He's a dead man on the Pritchard murder unless he agrees to get his nose out of bureau business. You remember: 'Don't embarrass the bureau.' Those files and notes would have done just that."

"It's sick. They'll both walk free so that the bureau isn't tainted."

"Don't question it, Chris, it makes sense. There's more at stake than one agent's death. We're covered. Pritchard was murdered by a terrorist who's fled the country. Just another terrorist act." He smiled. "It took a lot of thinking to put this together. You think about it a little and you'll see the wisdom of it."

She got up and went to the window. The storm had abated;

247

a hint of sun to the west threatened to break through the fast-moving low gray clouds.

"I hear you're going to Montana," he said from the couch.

"Yes," she said, still looking out at the ocean.

"You don't have to."

"No?"

"I can square it with Gormley if you want. I wouldn't be doing it out of altruism." He came up behind her. "You know, Chris, now that this is over maybe we can pick up where it got nasty. There was too much pressure on the relationship for it to run smoothly. I miss you." He placed his hand on her shoulder. She violently shook it off, moved to the side, and looked at him incredulously. "You're sick," she said.

"I'm in love," he replied.

"You're—"

"Look, I made mistakes, Chris, but—"

"Like killing Sue White Cloud? Was that a mistake?"

"What?"

"Sue White Cloud, the Indian teenager in Arizona. Was that just 'a mistake'?"

He shook his head. "Is this what happens when you sleep with your Apache boyfriend, Bill what's-his-face? The Indian paranoia and fantasies come out to play?"

"I know you killed her, Ross."

"You know nothing. Where did you ever come up with such garbage?"

"George Pritchard."

"Really?"

"Yes, *really.*"

"Tell me more."

"Why? I'd rather tell the bureau and the Arizona authorities."

"They'd laugh at you."

"Not with what I have."

He said like a parent having fun with a small child, "And just what is it you have, my pretty little maiden?"

"Proof. Pritchard's own words."

"Show me."

"Some other time, Ross. Besides, I'm not the only one who knows. Helen Pritchard does, and so does Kneeley."

He slowly turned and went to Kneeley's desk, perched casually on its edge, and allowed one foot to dangle back and forth. He reached under his jacket and came out holding a .22 revolver. "The difference between you and them, Chris, is that they're pragmatists. They understand a deal and aren't filled with adolescent idealism." He laughed. "Helen Pritchard tried to put the arm on me once she saw her book deal going down the drain. They invented the word *greed* for her. We had a little talk and she very quickly saw that it was in her best interests to view it differently. That's the sign of maturity, Chris, the ability to shift gears. Being too rigid never works in the end."

"But why, Ross? What happened in Arizona?"

"A misunderstanding, that's all. What do you have, a set of notes from Pritchard? I doubt that. Helen says she gave Kneeley the originals. Well now, wait a minute. I know Kneeley put everything on disk. The material you intercepted last night when he was transmitting to his publisher didn't mention it."

"You know about that?"

"Sure. You tapped him, we tapped you. Everybody was hooked in, a nice little network."

"How long?"

"Were you tapped? A couple of weeks. The difference is your tap on Kneeley was illegal. Ours was legal."

"Ours?"

"The bureau. Jake Stein's unit."

He was dazzling her with confusion.

"The redundancy squad, Chris. Did you miss that lecture at Quantico? Happens on lots of big cases. You set up a unit like Ranger, then you staff it with somebody who's investigating the investigators. Stein was a torpedo in Ranger to keep tabs on it for Gormley. Your problem was you kept running in your own direction. That's not the FBI team spirit, Chris. Maybe you're lucky to have Montana to go to. If it were up to me, I'd—"

249

"Kill me?"

He frowned, then nodded. "Yeah, kill you. All things considered, I'd rather . . ." He grinned and started walking toward her. "Tell you what, Chris. This thing resolved itself pretty neatly except for you. Why not join Uncle Sam? He needs you. I need you. Everybody has some dark side, some shoebox in the closet that's all taped up and sealed. I have a skeleton in my closet, and I bet you do, too. Let's drop it, forget it, and get on with our lives. I really like you, Chris. You turn me on like few women have before. Let's play grown-up. Give me what you have and you can walk away, go to Montana and get your career back on track. Is it in your purse, back at the apartment, where?"

"It's . . ."

He slowly brought the revolver up so that it was aimed at her face. "I'm all through being nice, Chris. I don't have any trouble pulling a trigger."

She knew he was serious. He could shoot her and claim she was part of the Kneeley-Pritchard conspiracy to expose the bureau. And what did she really have? Nothing, a disk that didn't contain any reference to what happened in Arizona.

"It just dawned on me, Chris, that I'm wasting my time with you. It doesn't matter what you have. Hell, what does it amount to, the ramblings of a man who was selling out the bureau, and who was looking to make the story more sensational to sell more books." He defiantly stuck his chin out and smiled. "You're a loser like all the other Indians. You're dirt. And you're dead."

"I'll give it to you," she said. "You're right. No one would believe me anyway."

He visibly relaxed and lowered the gun. She opened her purse and went to reach inside.

"No games," he said. "Leave the magnum in there."

"I know." She handed him the disk. As he took it, she lunged for the hand holding the .22 and grabbed his wrist, the momentum of her move sending them across the study. She rammed his gun hand against the wall, and the revolver flew

250

into the air, landing in the center of the room. She twisted his arm up behind him and brought her knee sharply into his back. He grunted and fell to his knees.

She released her grip and tried to catch her breath. He suddenly propelled himself to where the gun had landed, sprawling on his belly a foot from it. She ran to the door, opened it, and stumbled outside. Directly in front of her was the spiral stairway. She grabbed the railing and started down but missed the first step. Her hand wrenched free of the railing and she tumbled down, head hitting metal, feet clawing for a foothold, one shoulder wrenched as she attempted to break her fall. She stopped falling halfway down by landing on her rear end, got up and continued.

She heard footsteps above her. Lizenby had reached the middle of the stairs and then stopped. He pointed the .22 at her and said, "I loved you!"

Then, from behind, the thick hulk of Jubel appeared. He raised both hands and brought them down on Lizenby's neck. The gun floated into the air and Lizenby came crashing down the stairs, landing at Saksis's feet. He was out cold.

Saksis looked up at Jubel.

"I heard," he said. "I'll tell them. They pay me."

"They? The FBI?"

He nodded and came down the stairs. "Kneeley was bad. They had to stop him. Paul's my friend."

Kneeley. They had to stop *him*. Neutralize him, she thought. Jubel was an informer—had been recruited by the bartender, Paul, who was undercover—an Unkempt.

She could manage only to say "Thank you" before the pain in her shoulder, arm, head caught up with her. She went to a chair and sat heavily in it.

"Can I get you something?" Jubel asked.

"No, nothing. How long?"

"What?"

"How long have you been an informant?"

"Not long. I'll take you to the ferry."

"All right, but first I have to make a call."

27

BILL TSE-AY SAT on a hard wooden bench in the first floor lobby of the Department of Justice Building. His hair had grown back sufficiently to almost cover the scar on his head that had been left by the surgery. A cane rested against the bench. His left leg still went its own way on occasion, but Dr. Goldberg was confident that he'd regain full use of it in time.

He checked his watch; Chris Saksis had been giving her formal statement for almost three hours. He'd brought some magazines to read, but found it impossible to concentrate. More than anything, he wished he could be with her. He knew the psychic pain she must be suffering.

Ten minutes later she came through a heavy set of doors. At her side was her attorney, Roland King, an Oglala Sioux who was active in many Native American causes. Their footsteps echoed from the marble floor as they crossed the broad lobby and joined Bill on the bench.

"How did it go?" Bill asked.

King shrugged and looked at Chris, who'd obviously been crying.

"Chris?" Bill took her hand.

"It went okay, I guess, everything considered. I'm sorry you had to wait so long."

"Come on, tell me, what's the verdict?"

King's smile was rueful. "I doubt if there'll be one," he said. "The FBI seems—how shall I say it?—seems reluctant to prosecute Mrs. Pritchard and Mr. Kneeley."

"Really?" Bill asked Chris.

She nodded. "It's pretty obvious that they'll stick to their deal with her—not prosecute for the murder of her husband in return for . . ." She choked up, swallowed, and finished. "For 'neutralizing' Kneeley."

"So much for justice," Bill said.

"*They* consider it justice," King said. "Making sure that Kneeley doesn't give the bureau a black eye with the public is justice enough. Besides, Kneeley didn't kill Pritchard, so letting him off the hook for the murder makes sense, I suppose."

Chris said, "Helen Pritchard's gone to California. She's getting married again." She managed a thin smile.

Bill spun the cane in front of him and stared at the movement of the handle, saying without taking his eyes from it, "What about Lizenby?"

Chris and Roland King looked at each other.

Bill glanced up. "What about him?"

Chris replied, "He tried to make a deal with Gormley. If the bureau would help get him off the hook for the Sue White Cloud murder, he wouldn't tell what he knew about Pritchard's notes and Hoover's files."

"And?" Bill asked.

"And they turned him down," King said. "In a sense, Helen Pritchard redeemed herself a little, with the help of some pretty heavy arm twisting. She'll testify against Lizenby in Arizona based upon her knowledge of her husband's notes and files. The Arizona authorities think there's enough of a case against Lizenby to prosecute successfully." He paused, gauged Chris's reaction before adding, "They want Chris to testify against him, too."

"Will you, Chris?" Bill asked.

"No."

Bill's eyes met King's. "Shouldn't she?" he asked.

"Not necessarily, although by not testifying, her own stock in the bureau doesn't go up. In fact—"

"I resigned," she said flatly.

"Resigned? Do you feel you have to?" Bill asked.

"No, not at all. If I testify against Ross, all sorts of good things await me. My assignment to Montana is canceled and I stay here in Washington as special agent in charge of national American Indian affairs for the FBI." She spat out the initials FBI as though trying to fling them as far away as possible. "If I don't testify, I go to Montana for a six-month probation period. My files will include a negative report from Director Shelton himself for failure to cooperate in 'matters vital to the bureau's reputation.'"

"That tough, huh?" Bill said.

"That tough."

"What do you say?" Bill asked King.

"As an attorney, I've counseled Chris that she should testify. I think she owes herself that, and if it helps convict Ross Lizenby, a wrong has been righted. But, as a friend, I can only suggest that Chris follow her own conscience. Obviously, there's more at stake here than seeing justice done. It might not be just for her."

King stood and tucked his briefcase under his arm. "I learned a long time ago, Bill, that justice has many definitions. You know that working as you have on Native American affairs. There hasn't been any justice with our people since the beginning, but we're not unique. I doubt if there's anyone alive today who hasn't been on the receiving end of injustice at least once in their lives. It isn't *just* for Sutherland House to have agreed to drop all plans to publish Kneeley's book. They have enough to proceed, assign another writer, bring at least *some* of the story to the public."

"They won't do that?" Bill asked.

"No. They've decided to cooperate in the spirit of—of patriotism and honor."

254

Chris and Bill watched King cross the lobby and exit to the street.

"I'm sorry," she said.

"About what?"

"About not testifying against Ross. I know you want me to because of Sue White Cloud and—"

"Chris."

"What?"

"I only care if your reason has to do with some lingering feeling for him."

She shook her head. "Believe me, it doesn't. If I thought he'd walk free, I would, but I think Helen Pritchard's testimony will do it. What I'd have to offer is third-hand. It'll rise and fall on her. Funny, but I think more about his ex-wife. I suppose we'll never know about that unless he decides to tell about it."

"You know what confuses me, Chris?"

"What?"

"I'd think the bureau would want it the other way around, have you *not* testify against him. Hell, it's embarrassing to have a special agent assigned to a unit investigating serial murders end up the killer of a teenager."

"There's been a leak. The press knows about Lizenby and Arizona. The bureau has no choice now but to cooperate. They're good, Bill, the best in the world. But I don't fit, at least not anymore. I'm off the team. I just hope those who stay do the job. I'll miss it. Aside from a few proverbial bad apples, it's okay."

They stood on the street in the sunshine. The air was cool; October would soon arrive.

"What will you do?" Bill asked.

"I don't know."

"Can I suggest something?"

"Sure."

"Give me a second." He pulled a slip of paper from his pocket, leaned on his cane, and read slowly: "*Kat cuwitpotu knoqtuhkayin.*"

"Huh?"

"It's the only Passamaquoddy I could come up with to fit the situation."

She started to laugh. "What does it mean?"

"Roughly, 'You shouldn't live by yourself.' Hey, don't laugh, it took me a long time to find even that."

"I'm not laughing," she said. She touched his cheek, closed her eyes, and laughed even harder.

"Thanks," he said.

"I love you," she said.

"And I love you—and you *shouldn't* live alone. Live with me. Marry me."

"*Aha?*"

"That means yes."